MW00613125

ALSO BY DAN SOFER

The Dry Bones Society Series

An Unexpected Afterlife
An Accidental Messiah
A Premature Apocalypse

Novels

A Love and Beyond

REVENGE

OF THE

ELDERS

OF

ZION

DAN SOFER

ISBN-13: 978-1-950139-04-0 (hardcover)
ISBN-13: 978-1-950139-00-2 (paperback)
ISBN-13: 978-1-950139-01-9 (ebook)
ISBN-13: 978-1-950139-02-6 (audiobook)

FIC060000 FICTION/Humorous/Black Humor
FIC052000 FICTION/Satire
FIC031010 FICTION/Thrillers/Crime
FIC031090 FICTION/Thrillers/Terrorism

Cover design by Milan Jovanovic

dansofer.com

To Sheila and Eric,
for always cheering me on

CHAPTER 1

TOP SECRET
FEDERAL BUREAU OF INVESTIGATION
OFFICE OF PROFESSIONAL RESPONSIBILITY
Transcript of interview with Mr. Hyman Schneider
Also present:
Special Agent A. Maynard
Special Agent in Charge M. Reed

HYMAN SCHNEIDER:

The fiasco began when Sol Zelig's kid stopped by my Manhattan penthouse late one evening with the worst idea I've ever heard. And what a fiasco that was! You don't need me to tell you that. The damage caused—the lives lost and property destroyed—boggles the mind. It simply boggles the mind. I think in your circles you'd call that a *cluster* fiasco. Am I right?

[LIGHT LAUGHTER]

My apologies. I'm an old man. I get carried away. You're busy people and so am I. I'll cut to the chase.

Back to that fateful evening. This was about two months ago. Sol Zelig's kid pitched me the worst idea I've ever heard. Trust me, I hear a lot of bad ideas. Young CEOs swarm to me like bees to a flower. Confident and dreamy-eyed to a man, they'll promise you the stars in heaven above to get their seed money. But you'd better be careful. If you can't tell the good investments from the bad, they'll sting you. They'll sting you bad.

I'd known David Zelig since his bar mitzvah. He'd filled out into a handsome young man with thick dark hair that needed a cut. He got his looks from his late father. If only he'd inherited his business sense, too.

It was his great-grandfather who started Zelig Pictures, you know. The Zelig progeny no longer ran the studios. David Zelig, the last of the family line, loved the industry but his heart wasn't in management. He wrote screenplays—spy stories and conspiracy thrillers. The executives never greenlit his scripts for production, but rejection didn't get him down. Zelig Pictures was still his family's private company; he should never want for money. He should've been lazing on a yacht somewhere, sipping margaritas and chatting up pretty young women. Or so I thought.

Instead, he'd turned up here. He sat right over there where you're sitting, his hands fidgeting with his whisky glass. After a minimum of small talk, he pitched me the mother of all bad ideas. The pitch was so bad I had trouble wrapping my head around it.

I said, "You mean like a secret society?"

"*The* secret society," David told me. "The Elders of Zion. The one the Gentiles have always accused us of running. They already believe we control the world. What's stopping us?"

Had this been anyone else, I would have kicked him out. But David's late father had been a close friend. Over the years, he'd gotten me out of many a tight spot. The least I could do was steer his kid away from a colossal mistake.

"David," I told him. "Why on God's green earth would you want to get mixed up with such nonsense?"

A fire burned in the kid's eyes. "You read the news, Hymie. There's been one synagogue shooting after another.

2

It's like open season for anti-Semites, and law enforcement is powerless to stop them. Maybe it's time we took matters into our own hands."

The kid had good intentions, but he needed to calm down. So I poured him another shot of Balvenie and told him a story.

Two yids are sitting in a Berlin coffee shop in the nineteen thirties. One is reading a neo-Nazi newspaper, *Der Stürmer.*

"How can you read that garbage?" the other yid says, outraged.

"Why not?" the first yid replies. "When I read the Jewish newspapers, I learn that the Jews are poor, persecuted, and at each other's throats. When I read this paper, however, I discover that the Jews are wealthy and united, they control banks and are taking over the world. Which story do you prefer to read?"

I hammered home my point to avoid any misunderstandings.

"It's a myth, David," I told him. "A delusion. Jews are too busy bickering among themselves and worrying about what their Gentile neighbors think of them to pull off anything like a global Jewish conspiracy."

He said, "I'll settle for a national one." This, you understand, was one very stubborn young man.

"There is no Elders of Zion society pulling the strings of history," I told him. "Never was. Never could be. The 'Jewish world domination' fantasy is riddled with contradictions. It's as irrational as anti-Semitism itself. People have hated Jews for promoting democracy and for promoting communism, for being rich and for being poor, for sticking to themselves and for trying to assimilate. In times of change and uncertainty, the haters look for scapegoats and they blame the Jews. But it's all in their pickled brains. They pick on us *because* we are powerless."

The kid still wasn't backing down. "But what if we weren't powerless? What if we worked together and fought back?"

"David, do you have any idea how difficult it would be to

run a secret organization? Think about how many people would need to keep their mouths shut. That's why all those conspiracy theories are wrong. Governments are barely competent enough to govern, never mind hide aliens or fake moon landings."

Your organization excluded. I have great respect for you and your fellow FBI officers.

M. REED:

That's "agents," Mr. Schneider. We call FBI employees agents.

HYMAN SCHNEIDER:

Thank you for pointing that out. Agent sounds much sexier, doesn't it?

[LAUGHTER]

Where were we? Right. Conspiracy theories.

"It's a fool's errand," I told him. "Forget about it. You don't need the money. And as for power—power is just a bull's-eye painted on your head. It's not worth it, David."

The kid deflated like an old party balloon. He seemed weighed down by all the world's problems. Only later did I learn the true reason behind his crackpot scheme. You see, David had just lost Zelig Pictures. The last remaining Zeligs had been cheated out of their family legacy and all that went with it. David knew this for a fact but he couldn't prove it. And so his mind had filled with conspiracies.

"I'm glad you turned to me for advice," I told him. "I'm flattered. And I'm sorry to be so blunt. But cheer up, for God's sake. Find something better to do with your time and energy. For example, you could find a nice young woman and settle down. Your father would have liked that."

David Zelig sighed. Then he shook my hand and left. But do you think he listened to me? Ha! If he had, we wouldn't be sitting here, would we?

CHAPTER 2

"David Zelig, to what do we owe this *rare* honor?"

David stiffened when he heard the familiar oily voice. A smiling middle-aged comb-over sashayed toward him from the other side of the Lincoln Center foyer.

Rare honor. The implied criticism was well-founded. All his grown life, David had avoided the showy fundraisers of the Jewish American Public Initiative, the non-profit known by the unfortunate acronym, JAPI.

All around him, gray-haired donors in Canali suits gorged themselves on finger food and snatched wine goblets from floating trays, while their Botoxed wives lectured trapped diplomats on politics. Through the tall French windows, the skyscrapers of Manhattan loomed over Central Park, their myriad yellow eyes leering at David as the evening sky faded to black.

The sudden urge to flee gripped David as Gerry Cantor, the JAPI chairperson, swooped down on him like a smiling vulture, but David held his ground. Tonight, Gerry Cantor was just the kind of man David had wanted to meet at the JAPI Northeast Gala—a man with connections to powerful Jews.

David suppressed his gag reflex at the fawning smile and

shook the outstretched hand.

"The honor is all mine, Gerry."

Cantor wrapped David's hand in both of his to prevent his quarry's escape. "I've been trying to get a Zelig to speak at our events for decades. Our foundation deeply appreciates your family's leadership." By "leadership" he meant money. Would the chairperson still swoon over him once he learned of the Zelig family's recent financial troubles?

The man's doublespeak triggered David's mean streak. He pointed at the poster depicting the evening's entertainment, a ventriloquist from Vegas. "Is that meant to be ironic?"

Confusion swept Cantor's face. "What do you mean?"

"You know. Ventriloquists—people who put words in their dummies' mouths." The chairperson maintained his look of blank noncomprehension, so David elaborated. "At a fundraiser for a partisan lobby group. I hope the show won't offend the politicians."

A hint of annoyance passed over Cantor's face like a speeding cloud, then his gracious-host persona bounced back. "We prefer the word 'education' to 'lobby.'"

"I'm sure you do."

Cantor launched right into a proposal. "What about the JAPI Convention?"

"What about it?"

"It's two weeks from now. We'd love for you to deliver the keynote speech. People are tired of seeing the same old fogeys every year. It's time they heard from the new generation."

"It's time," whispered the simultaneous translation in David's brain, *"for the new generation to renew their families' pledges to the JAPI coffers."*

David's brow prickled with sweat. The very thought of delivering a speech before the conclave of Jewish philanthropy triggered a panic attack.

Cantor had hit him with a large ask. David had attended the annual convention in Washington over a decade ago as a curious teenager tagging along with his father, and he had no intention of repeating that mistake. But he'd do well to ingratiate himself with the showrunner. Soon, David would hit back with his own even larger ask.

"What's the theme this year?"

Cantor framed an invisible banner with his hands. "Protect America's Minorities."

Now that was a cause David could rally behind. At last, a Jewish organization was facing the Hydra of anti-Semitism.

"I like it. It's about time we did something about those synagogue shootings."

"Synagogue shootings?" Cantor said, aghast. "No, David. We're talking about African and Latin Americans. We're talking persecuted minorities—those who suffer from systemic prejudice and racism. Not Jews! America has treated us very kindly."

Being gunned down in a house of worship wasn't David's idea of kind treatment, but he let the comment go. Was Cantor the wrong man for the job or had David approached him at the wrong time? During the fundraiser, the JAPI chairperson was on set and in character. But on a different soundstage would Cantor sing a different song?

"Gerry, I need a favor."

"Anything, Mr. Zelig. Name it."

"Can we speak in private?"

Cantor swallowed hard and nodded, unable to deny the request of an important donor, but probably sensing a dressing down by the young heir. He led David behind a curtain and into a side room jammed with stacks of padded conference chairs.

"Yes?"

"Isn't it time we used our clout for our own protection?"

"What do you mean?" Again, Cantor seemed genuinely confused. Was the source of his confusion David's talk of their clout or their need for protection?

"A group of Jewish leaders to get things done on the quiet. Behind the scenes. Like the Elders of—"

Cantor clamped a hand over David's mouth. "David," he

hissed. "Never say such a thing!"

David's heart thumped in his chest. The hairs on the back of his neck bristled. Did the Elders of Zion already exist? Was this toady his gateway to a hidden world of Jewish domination?

When the hand released his mouth, David whispered, "Does the Elders exist?"

"No, of course not! But the haters will use any excuse to fan the flames. Do you have any idea how precarious our situation is? Supremacists gun down Jews in synagogues. College kids beat up Jews on campus. A rolling pogrom is ravaging Brooklyn, but that doesn't even make the news!"

A hunted expression transformed Cantor. "You talk of power and clout. 'The all-powerful Jewish lobby.'" He rolled his eyes and groaned. "Don't mistake JAPI for power. These events of ours are glorified ransom payments. 'Here, enjoy this tasty dinner. Now, please, pretty please, treat us like everyone else!' We're begging for scraps at the table of human rights, David. A protection racket, that's what JAPI is up against. A protection racket that demands payment in caviar!"

The old man had stunned David into silence. There was no Elders of Zion. Jewish money was a fanciful illusion. But Cantor wasn't done.

"You know why your great-grandfather started Zelig Pictures?"

David shrugged. "He saw an opportunity."

"Opportunity, my hairy behind. Back in the day, nobody thought movies would amount to much. Moving pictures were glorified peep shows. They were beneath the dignity of the Gentile upper class. Nobody dreamed that films would have such an impact. And television was beyond imagining. Trust me, your great-grandfather would have preferred to become a hotshot lawyer or industry tycoon. Do you know why he didn't? Because the Gentile elites shut Jews out of the corridors of wealth and power. Ivy League colleges invented rules to exclude Jews. The country clubs barred entry to dogs and Jews. So the Jews made films the way the Indians opened motels, and the Chinese went into dry cleaning. That, my friend, is the real story behind Zelig Pictures and all the other big studios."

His chest heaved; his comb-over dangled at his ear. "And the bigotry didn't end with business. A hundred years ago, an angry mob lynched Leo Frank in the streets of Georgia while law enforcement looked on. Don't get me wrong. We've come a long way since then, David, and we've worked very hard to get here. Anti-Semitism is less socially acceptable, but it still lurks beneath the surface. We're sitting on a barrel of dynamite." He jabbed a finger at David's chest. "So don't you go striking sparks with talk of Jewish conspiracies. If you do, synagogue shootings will seem like the good old days."

Cantor straightened his tie, adjusted his comb-over, and returned to the buffet hall, the oily smile back on his face.

David composed himself with deep breaths. Cantor could not help him. He was a scared old man from a bygone generation. But he'd gotten one thing right. David was tired of listening to old fogeys. The time of the new generation had come.

CHAPTER 3

"You didn't say he'd be here," Jordan Brody said.

David's carrot-haired best friend had just stepped through the front door of David's loft apartment in the Upper West Side and spotted David's other best friend flopping on a coffee-colored leather couch.

Mitchell Joffe was the negative image of the straight-laced, techie newcomer. With his tanned arms folded behind his head and chest hair sprouting from his white silk shirt, Mitchell was the quintessential carefree playboy. He turned from the view of the Hudson River and shuttered his eyes at Jordan, a gesture of bored disdain he had stolen from Jack Nicholson.

"He didn't want you to chicken out," Mitchell said.

Jordan's shoulders rose. David knew that pose. The three friends had learned each other's every quirk and gesture well during the many ski vacations their families had shared in Aspen. Ten years later, their inner teenagers still surfaced whenever they got together. David had five seconds before the meeting devolved into a squabble.

"Guys, this is important—maybe the most important thing I'll ever ask of you. Can we put aside our differences for a few minutes?"

Jordan folded his arms over his chest. "I will if he will."

After a suitably melodramatic pause, Mitchell nodded. "Whatever."

"Good."

Jordan joined Mitchell on the couch, leaving a large demilitarized zone between them. David stood before his friends.

"You've heard about the synagogue shootings." The statement cleansed the air of teenage grudges. "But have you heard of the Elders of Zion?"

Jordan wrinkled his nose as though he'd tasted pee in his beer. "The secret Jewish organization that controls the world?"

Mitchell's eyes widened. "Awesome!"

"It's a myth, you moron," Jordan snapped. "A conspiracy theory anti-Semites use to blame Jews whenever things go wrong."

"But what if it wasn't just a myth?" David blurted before another fight ignited.

Mitchell said, "You mean like JAPI?"

"JAPI's a dead end. I spoke with Gerry Cantor. JAPI has no real power, and Cantor foamed at the mouth at the very mention of the Elders. But what if we created the Elders of Zion? People would think twice before they walk into a synagogue with an assault rifle."

"Ooh!" Mitchell said. "Like those Nazi hunters in that movie, what was it called?"

Jordan laced his sideways glance with loathing. "*Inglourious Basterds?*"

"Yeah, that's it! They shot up a theater full of Nazis. That was wild!"

Jordan shifted further away from Mitchell. "That was just a movie, and I am not about to step into a Tarantino film. *Or* become a vigilante. Violence isn't a Jewish value. And Jewish extremists tend to end up dead like Kahane. No thank you very much!"

"No," David said, his hands spread to calm his friend's concerns. "No violence. Nothing like that. Just *influence.*

Pulling the strings. Behind the scenes."

"Is that even legal?"

David hadn't considered the legality of running a secret organization.

Mitchell rolled his eyes. "Not if we do nothing illegal."

David shrugged. "It's not as though we're going to apply for non-profit status."

Mitchell slapped his leg. "Good enough for me, David. Count me in."

"Great!" David relaxed. That had gone easier than he had expected, and now that Mitchell had signed on, Jordan would not be outdone. The two secret society members glanced expectantly at Jordan, who buckled under peer pressure.

"Fine," he said, "I'll join your secret club."

"That's my man!" Mitchell raised his hand for a high five, and Jordan grudgingly played along. The mood in the living room warmed. The three friends had put aside their differences to pursue an important mission.

"What are we going to call ourselves?" Jordan said.

"What do you mean?"

"We can't use the Elders of Zion. That's a dead giveaway."

"Right," Mitchell said, and he brightened as an idea presented itself. "Well, there's three of us so—"

Jordan interrupted. "Don't you dare say *The Three Musketeers*."

"What's wrong with *The Three Musketeers*? That was a great movie."

"Book, you idiot. It was a book by Alexandre Dumas long before—"

"Guys," David said, diving in again to keep the peace. "What did the Romans call that group of three rulers?"

"A triumvirate?"

"That's it! The Triumvirate. What do you think?"

The two men wiggled their heads, trying the title out for size.

"I like it," Mitchell said. "The Trio."

"*Triumvirate*," Jordan said.

"Like you said. Trio."

Jordan glanced at David with frustration, but David gave in. "Trio works too."

"That settles it," Mitchell said. "Welcome to the Trio, the world's first *real* Jewish secret society."

They smiled at each other, savoring their first shared accomplishment.

Mitchell rode the waves of creative juices. "We'll need a secret handshake too."

"No secret handshakes, Mitch."

"You sure?"

"Positive."

"OK," Jordan said, and he inhaled a sharp, impatient breath. "What now?"

"What now?"

"How do we control the world?"

"Right." David scratched his chin. He hadn't thought this through. To be honest, he hadn't expected the idea to take off with so little resistance.

Mitchell raised his hand. "We'll need money."

"We have money," Jordan countered.

"Um, no. Jordan, you might have loads of spare cash with all your hot-shot hi-tech companies. I've just got the trust fund."

"Mitch," David said, "we all need to pitch in." How David would do so after losing Zelig Pictures was a good question. Once the Trio earned a few notches on its clandestine belt, he'd turn the society's attention to his own personal troubles.

"I will," Mitch said, defensive. "I'm just saying Jordy-boy should be the first to fork out."

Jordan sighed. "Whatever. For argument's sake, let's say we've put the cash together. What do we do with it?"

They shared an awkward silence. The silence begat more wordlessness, and soon a tribe of unspoken accusations surrounded the friends and poked them with their silent spears. The newborn Jewish conspiracy had no clue what it was doing.

In David's defense, he had hoped that Jordan would do the strategic heavy lifting. David was the founder, Jordan was the brains, and Mitchell... well, a two-man secret society had seemed a little lame.

"I've got it," Jordan said, and the other men exhaled with relief. "We don't need to figure anything out."

Relief became suspicion.

"We don't?"

"Why not?"

They eyed Jordan with foreboding, expecting a sarcastic punch line. None followed. Instead, Jordan beamed at them.

"It's all planned out for us already," he said. "We just need to read the handbook."

CHAPTER 4

"Holy crapola," Mitchell said. "This stuff is intense!"

The Trio had reconvened in David's apartment two days later after they'd reviewed the materials. Jordan had bought three copies of *The Protocols of the Learned Elders of Zion* from a secondhand bookstore in Harlem. He'd paid in cash to prevent their fledgling secret society from growing a paper trail. The thin paperbacks were dog-eared and coffee-stained, and David wondered how many anti-Semites the books' meandering, diabolical contents had spawned over the years.

"That's an understatement," Jordan said.

Mitchell said, "There's something I don't understand."

"That's as expected."

Mitchell ignored Jordan's gibe. "So there's this meeting of the Elders of Zion and they discuss their plans for world domination. That much I got. But what's with all the philosophy?"

"That," Jordan said, "is because *The Protocols* was plagiarized from another work of fiction." Jordy read from his copious notes on the MacBook Air he'd opened on David's coffee table. "*Dialogue in Hell*, by Maurice Joly. He staged a philosophical discussion between Machiavelli and Montesquieu as a veiled criticism of Napoleon III. Only in *The*

Protocols, the philosophers became the Elders of Zion."

Mitchell frowned. "That wasn't in the book."

"No, Mitch. That wasn't in the book. That's what we call research."

Mitchell scoffed. "Typical. We get one book for homework, and you read two. Overachiever."

David stepped in. "Guys, let's focus on our mission."

"There's something else I don't get," Mitchell said. "The elders of Zion are supposed to be these big, bad bogeymen. But all they seem to want is democracy and free markets. What's so evil about that?"

"Those *are* evil," Jordan said, "if you're Nicholas II."

"What's Father Christmas got to do with *The Protocols*?"

"Not Saint Nicholas, you moron! Nicholas II, the last tsar of the Russian Empire." Jordan sighed at the blank stares but deigned to explain. "Nicholas II was one of the wealthiest, most powerful men in history. He saw the democracy and freedoms spreading across Western Europe as a threat to his absolute monarchy. So the Okhrana, the Russian Secret Police, forged *The Protocols* in the late eighteen hundreds to discredit the anti-monarchy movements, depicting them as part of an evil Jewish conspiracy."

"Well, that's stupid."

"And deadly. Nicholas II encouraged pogroms against Jews in the Russian Empire, claiming the mob violence unified the people behind the government."

"Son of a bitch," Mitchell said. "I hope the Elders got him."

"Mitch, *The Protocols* is a fake, remember."

"Oh, right."

"Historians think they've tracked down *The Protocol*'s creator." Jordan looked at his notes again. "Golovinskii, an Okhrana operative in Paris, showed an early manuscript of *The Protocols* to a Russian princess, Katerina Radziwill. He boasted that the book he'd forged would frame the Jews for a global conspiracy. Pyotr Rachkovsky, the director of the Okhrana, had created similar forgeries to discredit other perceived enemies of Imperial Russia. Jews had little to do with the fall of the Russian Empire. Nicholas's refusal to adopt political reforms sparked revolutions, which ended his reign. But instead of free markets and democracy, the Russian people got communism, and in 1918, the communists executed the tsar along with his entire family and entourage."

Mitchell whistled. "That's what happens when you mess with the Jews, pal."

Jordan turned to David, exasperated. "Has he heard a word I've said?"

David changed the subject to get the meeting back on track. "I made a list of action items based on *The Protocols*, the points that are still relevant." He read from his notepad. "One. Propaganda."

Mitchell raised his hand. "Piece of cake—social media. I get all my news from Facebook. A few targeted ads should do the trick."

David turned to Jordan, who reddened. "Actually, I agree with Mitch on that."

"I don't believe it," Mitchell said. "The world must be ending."

"Great," David said. He jotted down the suggestion and pushed forward. "Two. Divert public attention from important to trivial matters."

Mitchell raised his hand. "What, like reality TV? Lolcats?"

"On second thought," David said, "that's already taken care of."

Jordan said, "What about Hollywood? David, maybe you can get Zelig Pictures to plant a few subliminal messages?"

David swallowed hard. He had hoped to avoid revealing how Zelig Pictures had been stolen from under his nose. "The thing is," he said, "I don't have any real influence. I've never been able to push any of my own scripts into production, so..." He trailed off.

"Sorry," Jordan said.

"Bummer," Mitchell said.

"Yeah, well it is what it is." Dave drew a line through item number two. "Three. Censorship of the press. Do we have any contacts at traditional media outlets?"

"We could buy a newspaper?" Jordan suggested.

"Screw that." Mitchell again. "Nobody believes the Fake News anymore. What's next?"

"Four. Encourage atheism and pornography."

"Ha!" Mitchell said. "Plenty of that going around, boys. Just ask Jordy-boy about the porn. He hasn't had a date in years."

Jordan kept his eyes on his laptop screen but raised a finger in warning. "Don't go there, Mitch."

David said, "Come to think of it, I don't see how either atheism or pornography helps us. Moving on. Five. Promote a Jewish king. Does anybody want a king? I didn't think so. Six. Control the stock markets."

Jordan waved his finger. "Insider trading. That's illegal."

David crossed it off the list. "So much for that. Seven. Nullification of education—"

"What education?" Mitch asked.

"—and organization of disorder."

Jordan waggled his finger again. "Inciting to riot. Illegal."

"OK, then. What does that leave us?" David counted the items on his fingers. "Propaganda, aka social media ads. Um, that's it."

Mitchell said, "How's that going to help us stop the next synagogue shooter?"

Jordan said, "We could monitor anti-Semitic accounts. Look for suspicious activity and tip off law enforcement."

"Good," David said, "I like that." He jotted it down. "What else?"

David's pen tapped against his notepad as the afternoon sun sank over the glittering waters of the Hudson. The horn of a barge honked, the sound muffled and far away.

"I don't know," Mitchell said. He sounded disappointed. "Snooping around social media and snitching to the cops—is that the best we can do? That's not exactly in the spirit of the Elders of Zion. We need to fight the bad guys head-on."

Jordan scoffed. "We could wear capes and beat up thugs in the streets."

Mitchell's eyes lit up. "Now you're talking!"

"For the record, I was being sarcastic. The Elders of Zion didn't have superpowers and neither do we."

"I thought you said they never existed." Mitchell flashed the whites of his eyes, convinced he'd caught Jordan out.

"And neither does Batman."

David said, "Mitchell has a point. A secret society should have real power. The Trio shouldn't be just another neighborhood watch."

Mitchell said, "Yeah. We should be like the Punisher."

Jordy snorted. "Why not Superman? At least he was created by Jews."

"He was?"

"Sure. Like the Golem of Prague—a hero with superhuman strength who protects the powerless. Only the Golem was made of clay. Come to think of it, Mitch, you have a lot in common with the Golem."

"Hey, watch it!"

"Guys!" David said. "We're trying to find a real way forward here. Comic books and superpowers aren't helping and neither is your constant fighting."

His friends holstered their sarcasm, and the Trio pondered the problem in silence.

"Information is power," Jordan said.

The beginnings of a smile curled David's lips. He liked this new direction.

Even Mitchell got on board. "Nice! We collect embarrassing information about powerful people and blackmail them to do what we want."

"Extortion is illegal, Mitch."

"Geez, Jordy, how are we supposed to run a secret society if we never break the law? That's why it's secret—so we don't get caught!"

"Don't be naïve, Mitch. We live in a digital age. The NSA knows everything about everyone. The only way to stay out of prison is not to break the law. Which reminds me—we must use secure communications from now on. To cover our digital tracks, we'll connect to the Internet through a VPN and browse the web with Tor."

"Whoa, easy on the mumbo jumbo, dude."

"Relax, Mitch. I'll set it up for you. Here, have a look." David and Mitchell shifted closer to their techie friend and his laptop. Jordan clicked on an icon and a browser window opened. "Tor is an anonymous browser, which encrypts and routes all traffic through multiple anonymous servers. It's our untraceable window to the Dark Net."

"The Dark Net," Mitchell repeated. "I like the sound of that. What is it?"

"Sites hidden from regular search engines like Google."

"What's Torch?" David said, reading the name of a search page that looked very last-millennia.

"Tor Search. A Google for the Dark Net. It allows you to search for hidden sites, forums, you name it. If it's out there, you'll find it."

"Search for something."

In the search box, Jordan typed the words "Elders of Zion" and hit enter. The long list of results surprised David.

"Where's Wikipedia?"

"This is the Dark Net, David."

"Oh, right. Try that one." He pointed, and Jordan clicked.

After five seconds of stunned silence, Mitchell said, "Holy crap. Are these guys for real?"

The page displayed an Elders of Zion forum. Jordan clicked through the discussion threads. The subject lines read "World Domination," "Creating Disorder," "Propaganda," and "Diversions," but the messages were short and cryptic. Only an adept would understand their true meaning. The usernames had a Biblical bent: azri3l, samael1, jacobjacob, delilah666.

The floor fell out from David's stomach. He'd just created a Jewish secret society, but all the while the Elders of Zion already existed, lurking in the dark underbelly of the Internet.

"Some members are online," Jordan said.

Mitchell said, "Chat with them."

"Which one?"

"Any of them!"

Jordan registered at the forum, using a weird-looking email address and "darkhorse" as his username, then opened a chat window with jewbabe29.

"Hi," he typed.

"*Hi?*" Mitchell said. "Is that all you've got? No wonder you never get any."

"This is the Dark Net, Mitch. Jewbabe29 could be a two-hundred-pound hairy guy or, more likely, an NSA agent."

The speakers emitted an electronic beep, and a reply appeared in the chat window. "Hi."

"Wow," Mitchell said, deadpan. "You sure know how to sweep a girl off her feet."

"What should we say?"

"What should *you* say," Mitchell corrected him. "You're the guy hooking up on the Dark Net. We're just looking over your shoulder."

"Thanks a bunch. I knew you'd have my back."

"Ask how we join them."

"They'll know we're outsiders," David said. "Ask what's new."

Jordan typed, and they waited for the buzz. The reply read, "same old."

"Does she know we're not one of them?"

"Hard to tell."

The buzz sounded again. The three men stared at the screen.

"'Darkhorse, wanna ride?' What is that—code?"

"She's flirting, Jordy-boy. Go on. Flirt back."

Jordan shrugged. He typed, "ride to Zion?" and hit enter.

"Ride to Zion? You call that flirting? What was that?"

"That's me signaling we're one of them."

"You're sad, man. So sad."

Another buzz sounded. "Gotta run," jewbabe29 wrote,

followed by a series of characters: "cu @ cs." And jewbabe29 left the chat session to the sound of a closing door.

"See you at CS?" David read, his heart pounding in his ears at their unexpected progress. "What's CS? Is that a person or a place?"

They voiced some suggestions: Coming Soon, Caught Stealing. Jordan searched the web for more: College Station, Computer Science. They were getting nowhere. Was CS even in English? David wished he'd taken Latin instead of French in college. She'd said, "see you." A meeting would take place soon. Somewhere in the world, the Elders of Zion were getting together and David would miss the event.

Then Jordan laughed à propos of nothing. David and Mitch stared at him. "What is so funny, Jordy?" David said.

"I know what CS is. It's obvious when you think of it. Where else would members of a Dark Net forum meet?"

"Spit it out, Jordy!"

Jordan shut down Tor, opened a regular Internet browser, and searched the legal web for two words. Wherever the Elders were convening, David would be there. He'd buy a plane ticket if he needed to.

The page loaded. "Oh," David said. The answer made sense. And he wouldn't need a plane ticket. The Elders of Zion were meeting tonight in Manhattan.

CHAPTER 5

"Are you sure we're at the right place?" Mitchell asked Jordan.

David was wondering the same thing. The posh interior of the Grand Hyatt Hotel did not seem like the stomping ground of hackers. Name-tagged executives in business suits chatted in the foyer. They did not look the type who broke into Pentagon servers for fun.

The words *Cyber Summit* appeared in large white letters on a roll-up poster. The conference was as good an interpretation of CS as any, but David's initial excitement for the evening ebbed. He seemed to have landed up at another JAPI Gala dinner, only the guests were younger and the women more attractive.

"Wait here while I sign in," Jordan said, and he made for the table of uniformed attendants with laptops.

What had David expected—flaming torches and dark robes? Digital vigilantes with leather jackets and tattoo-sleeves? He'd expected something more clandestine and exotic, that was sure; a portal into the dangerous world of covert Jewish power. At this computer conference, the only danger David would face was falling asleep. He'd try to escape before the lectures began.

Mitchell scoffed. "I think Jordy got this wrong."

David agreed. At least they had dressed appropriately for the occasion in their dark trousers and button-down shirts.

Jordy rejoined them and handed out name tags on straps of blue fabric. "Put these on." He seemed energized at the prospect of an evening of technology and computer jargon.

David's name tag read "Guest One, Consultant." Jordy had registered them for the conference without exposing their true identities.

"Where are the hackers?" David asked.

Jordy squinted at him in confusion.

"The geeks," Mitchell said. "All we've seen so far are suits and evening dresses."

"The Cyber Summit isn't for programmers, guys. It's where senior executives discuss the latest in digital security."

David and Mitchell exchanged irritated glances. Jordy had roped them into a snore-worthy lecture-fest, not a secret convocation of Jewish conspirators.

"Jordy," Mitchell said. "Aren't we barking up the wrong tree? I doubt any of these suits belongs to the Elders forum."

"Don't be so sure. Think about it. We're looking for power brokers, not script kiddies. Besides, it's the only lead we've got and there's free food. C'mon. The party started twenty minutes ago."

"Party?" Mitchell brightened. "Why didn't you say so?"

David and Mitchell donned their name tags and followed their techie friend down a hallway. Perhaps the evening would not be a total loss.

"This is the last day of the conference," Jordan explained as they walked. "The cocktail party is where all the networking happens."

They entered a banquet hall lit with soft light. Waiters weaved between pockets of chatting executives around small, tall tables where they rested their drinks and appetizer plates. A string quartet played acoustic covers of eighties songs.

"We should split up," David said. "See what we can find out."

"How do we spot an Elder?" Mitchell asked.

David shrugged. "Good question. I don't know. Mingle."

Mitchell rolled his shoulders, flashed his playboy smile, and charged toward a tall blonde in a red dress. Jordan rolled his eyes and moved off.

David circled the crowd. He cast furtive glances at the faces. What did an azri3l look like, or a samael1 for that matter? He studied the name tags. The suits represented IBM, Verizon, and a bunch of unfamiliar companies. A large delegation belonged to Google. The world's most popular search engine could disseminate propaganda and mold public opinion. And Google's founders, Sergey Brin and Larry Page, were Jewish. Had the Elders been hiding in plain sight all along? How had David not thought of that before?

As he drifted around the hall, eyes alighted on his name tag, then moved on. A nameless consultant was a nobody here. Maybe Jordan should have chosen a company name with more technological clout like Microsoft or Facebook? Then again, if Jordan had done so, even the shortest of conversations would have outed David, the technology ignoramus. Besides, there was something liberating about being a non-entity. For once, David wasn't the heir of Zelig Pictures. He could be anybody.

David circled the hall twice, passing Mitchell, who was still chatting with the blonde in the red dress. "That's why I always insist on a test penetration," he told her.

Her brow wrinkled. "You mean a penetration test?"

"Yeah." He flashed her a mischievous smile. "That too."

David picked a smoked-salmon pastry from a passing tray and floated on. He had two minutes to locate jewbabe29 before Mitchell either left with the blonde or got them all kicked out. He scanned the evening dresses. A woman with red curls giggled at an unheard joke. A brunette ran her tongue over her teeth for rogue flakes of food. None of them looked Jewish or inclined to clandestine societies.

He made for the bar. A drink would loosen him up. David ordered an Old Fashioned and tapped his fingers on the counter while the bartender mixed his drink. The young woman beside him ordered a screwdriver. Her voice, confident and pleasant, had the soothing, sultry tone of a late-night radio presenter. David sent a furtive look her way. Thick auburn curls fell to her backless dress and the patch of milky skin that made his core tingle.

Their drinks arrived together and, as the two strangers turned toward each other, their eyes met. Hers were large and intelligent. She had a delicate nose, and a playful, commiserating smile curled her full red lips. They turned their backs to the bar but lingered there, tasting their drinks and gazing at the crowd. Neither was in a rush to return to the melee. Whisky and bitters swirled over David's tongue and tickled his mind. He wanted to stay beside her a little longer. Bolstered by the whisky and anonymity, David cleared his throat.

"Do you come here often?" he said, hoping his ironic delivery had spiked the cliché with an endearing dash of meta-humor.

She gave a short, amused laugh. "Once a year, when I have to."

His gambit had worked. David snuck a glance at her name tag. "Amy Anderson, Security Vice President, Cyber Gate," he read aloud. "Pleased to meet you." He offered his hand.

She reciprocated. "Pleased to meet you too, Guest One, Consultant. I don't think I've ever met a One before."

Oh, crap. He'd forgotten about his suspicious name tag. How was he going to explain that away? The whisky answered for him.

"You're right," he said. "You haven't. I'm the only One. The one and only." David felt hot under his collared shirt. He was flirting now. What the hell had the bartender put in his drink?

Her dainty eyebrows peeked with exaggerated suspicion, as though she doubted his words but would play along. "And what consulting work do you do, Mr. One?"

"To be honest, I have no idea. I'm not really supposed to be here. I tagged along with a friend. We're only here for the girls."

Another laugh. "And how's that working out for you?" Her voice was addictive. Her smile lingered, anticipating his reply. He wanted to make her smile again, over and over, today and tomorrow and all the days that followed.

He said, "Better than expected."

They gazed into each other's eyes. A comfortable silence developed between them, and David forgot all about anti-Semites and secret societies. All that mattered was standing here and basking in her magnetic presence. *Amy Anderson, where have you been all my life?*

An elbow jabbed him in the ribs, making him jump as though rudely awakened from a very pleasant dream. Jordan stood beside him.

"Let's go."

David glared at his friend. "Jordy, I'm busy here, can't you see?"

"We know where they're meeting."

"Who?"

"The El—You Know Who."

"What? How?"

"Mitch got the time and place from an Indian guy."

"Mitch?" How had all this happened so fast? David had barely had time to chat with Amy Anderson.

"Come on, let's go. We need to make plans."

"OK, just give me a second."

David turned back to apologize for his hasty exit and get Amy's number, but the dazzling young security consultant had disappeared.

CHAPTER 6

"Are we there yet?" Mitchell whined from the back seat the next evening.

Jordan's Tesla Roadster gunned toward Upstate New York under the bright streetlights of I-87 North. The electric sports car combined the cutting edge controls of a fighter-jet cockpit with the creature comforts of a high-end luxury vehicle. But the designers had created the back seats for malnourished six-year-olds, not lanky adult playboys.

David shifted on the comfortable front passenger seat and inhaled the scent of new leather. His discomfort stemmed not from their travel conditions but their destination.

Jordan glanced at the navigation map on the car's large digital display. "Not much further," he said.

The address Mitchell had scribbled down at the Cyber Summit was a set of coordinates, which Jordan mapped to a vacant spot outside Newburgh. The riddle had added a note of mystique to the occasion but created a new problem. Google Earth provided only a blurred-out square in the satellite image for the location. Either they were heading for a US military installation or the tentacles of the Elders of Zion had penetrated even Google.

Amy Winehouse sang "Some Unholy War" on the surround speakers. David, who had become obsessed with the British jazz singer's music, had invaded the car's sound system by Bluetooth and selected her playlist on his phone. But not even her deep soulful voice could soothe his nerves.

As daylight faded, they'd traded Manhattan's skyscrapers for forested knolls, then silent fields. Long stalks of grain waved at them in the moon's silvery glow. The city slickers were entering a strange new world.

The online discovery of the Jewish secret society had enthralled David. But now that they hurtled toward an actual physical meeting with the Elders, his spider-sense tingled. If the Elders of Zion already existed, they had not foiled the synagogue shootings. Either the organization was toothless or its agenda differed from that of the Trio. Did David and his friends know what they were getting themselves into?

David opened his eyes. "Mitch, tell me about the Indian guy."

"Again?"

"What did he look like?"

Mitchell sighed as though he'd told the story a thousand times. The true count was eight.

"Like I said, there's not much to tell. He was Indian, and he knew what I was talking about right away."

"What exactly did you say to him?"

"I said I wanted to meet the Elders. He gave me this serious look and whispered the when and where."

"Did he ask for your username or tell you his?"

"Nope."

"Did he read the details from a note?"

"No, he knew them by heart."

David turned to Jordan. "What's the likelihood he was pulling Mitch's leg?"

"Hey," Mitchell objected, "he was not kidding around. It's all legit. What I can't figure out is why we had to take this car."

"What's wrong with my car?" said Jordan.

"Let's see, besides the sardine-sized back seats, it's a red sports car. It stands out. We're a *secret* society, remember? We need to blend in. If you were going undercover, would you drive a Roadster?"

"James Bond drove an Aston Martin."

"Oh, please, Jordy. You are no James Bond. Me—maybe, but you—no chance."

"Whatever. The Roadster is silent and fast. You'll appreciate that if we need to leave in a hurry."

They considered that possibility for three seconds while Winehouse sang of bitter battles.

"Why would we need to leave in a hurry?" Mitchell said, suddenly concerned.

Jordan scoffed. "Because we don't know who these people are or what we're getting ourselves into."

"Are you chickening out?"

"I'm not chickening—"

The sound of clucking chickens filled the air. David lurched forward as Jordan slammed the brakes and pulled over onto the bumpy side of the road. The highway had dwindled to two lanes, trading its cement barriers for wide grassy shoulders. They had ground to a dead halt in that creepy liminal space New Yorkers called The Country.

"Son of a bitch. Get out of the car!"

The chicken noises continued from the back seat.

"Guys," David said. "We need to calm down, OK? How are we going to get through tonight if we're always fighting?"

Jordan turned off the music. "We're not going anywhere until he apologizes."

"Mitch, please apologize to Jordy."

Mitchell shuddered with pent-up laughter. "I'm sorry for calling you a chickenshit scaredy pants."

"Oh, grow up!"

David glanced at his wristwatch, which read 10 PM. They were running late.

"Mitch, Jordy's right. This is serious. We don't know who these people are yet. If the three of us can't stop fighting, we could get into serious trouble. We might as well turn back now."

Mitchell sobered up. "OK, whatever. Jordy, I apologize. I won't call you chicken again."

Jordan ground his teeth. "Apology accepted."

"Thank you!" David said, his patience growing thin. "And, to be on the safe side, I suggest we hightail it out of there at the first sign of danger. Agreed?"

Jordan said, "Agreed."

"Fine," Mitchell said. "Next time, I'll bring a gun."

"A gun? Nobody said anything about guns!"

"Relax, Jordy. I'm just kidding. This is a *Jewish* secret society, remember? What's the worst they can do to us—send us to Hebrew school?"

Jordan chuckled nervously, and the tension diffused. David wasn't sure he agreed with Mitchell's forecast, but at least they were back on track.

"Good," he said. "Now, let's move on and change the subject."

Jordan sped up and rejoined the flow of traffic. Silence reigned again for another three seconds.

"So how's your new girlfriend, Dave?"

David's cheeks warmed. He could sense Mitchell smirking behind him. David had asked for a change of subject and Mitchell had delivered. "What girlfriend?"

"The babe at the bar. You seemed to hit it off."

"Yeah, I suppose." There was no use in denying his encounter with the attractive cybersecurity consultant. David had thought of little else all day.

"What's her name?"

"Amy Anderson." The name rolled off his tongue. She didn't know who he was. David liked that. He avoided using his full name in social settings. Girls responded differently once they knew he was the heir to Zelig Pictures. Dollar signs danced in their eyes. He hated that. And the girls he met knew who he was in advance. But Amy Anderson had seemed to like him despite not knowing anything about his family.

"Are you going to see her again?"

David had asked himself the same question. So long as he was engaged in covert activities, he should avoid distractions. "I don't know."

"So you don't mind if I call her?"

Jordan stepped in. "Yes, Mitch. He *does* mind. Geez, you have no boundaries."

"OK, OK. Take it easy, guys. I was just kidding. I prefer blondes anyway."

"There's our turnoff," Jordan said. "We're almost there."

"Oh, thank God."

A few turns later, the GPS guided them onto a gravel road with no street lights. Loose stones pinged against the underside of the car.

Jordan swore. "This road will scratch the paint."

"All for the greater good, Jordy," said Mitchell, who for once seemed to enjoy the ride.

A rusty metal cattle gate stood open, a heavy chain trailing in the tall grass. "This must be the place."

They cruised through the gate, only the crunch of gravel and headlight beams betraying their presence. As they rounded a clump of tall trees, a dark house lurked in the moonlight, a large, sprawling mansion.

"Wow," Jordan muttered.

Flaming torches lined the gravel driveway, which opened onto an ample parking lot lined with high-end sports cars.

"Now we're talking," Mitchell said.

Jordan reversed into an empty spot between a Ferrari and a Lamborghini. Judging by the other cars, their fast getaway would have to be very fast. They got out, gravel crunching under their feet. The brainy Roadster looked a little insecure among the lineup of vehicular brawn, a clean-cut upstart among the steroid-stuffed bodybuilders.

Groaning and moaning, Mitchell unfolded his body from the backseat and stretched his limbs. "Man, I need a massage."

"C'mon," David said. "Looks like they already started."

The flaming torches led to a tall entrance with double doors of old, dark wood. The Trio stepped onto the threshold. David cleared his throat. He had never expected to find the Elders of Zion, never mind attend their secret meetings. And so he hadn't prepared an elevator pitch to convince the Elders to let the Trio join the society. By now he should have learned to plan ahead.

"Should we knock?" Jordan whispered, noting David's hesitation. A large iron knocker lay on each of the double doors, the business end carved in the shape of a world globe.

"This place reminds me of a movie," Mitchell whispered. "Did you see *Eyes Wide Shut* with Tom Cruise and Nicole Kidman? The secret cult met in a big mansion just like this. Underneath the cloaks and masks, everybody was naked, and the meeting turned into a huge orgy." Mitchell sounded hopeful.

"Thanks, Mitch," David said, more to shut him up than to express gratitude for the unsolicited Hollywood trivia. "But I don't think the Elders is about wild sex."

"Yeah," Jordan said, jumping at the opportunity to criticize Mitchell. "But we'll use the same set when we turn this into a movie." They had bombarded Mitchell into silence.

As David reached for the knocker, he noticed that the door on the right wasn't closed. He pressed his fingers to the coarse wood, and the door inched inward.

"It's open," David said, an explorer recording his impressions on a Dictaphone in case the ground swallowed him up and he never made it back to civilization.

Another push and they stood before the scratched parquet of a large antechamber lit by flaming sconces. Pale squares on the elaborate wallpaper showed where large paintings had hung. Thick cobwebs looped from a dark and dusty chandelier that dangled from the high ceiling. Through the walls, an unintelligible sonorous voice droned.

Questions jostled each other in David's head. Did the Elders always meet here or did they select a new location for each occasion? Had the Trio missed the important bits?

Judging by the vacant antechamber, they had missed the pre-event buffet and mingling.

The Trio stepped inside, and David tried to locate the source of the voice.

"Look!" Mitchell said, pointing to a pile of black fabric bundles in a corner. He picked one up, and his eyes sparkled in the flame light. "See—I was right. Cloaks!" He kicked off his shoe.

"What are you doing?" David hissed.

Mitchell paused. "Getting undressed."

"Mitch, do you see piles of abandoned clothes?"

"No, but—"

"Do you see any gym lockers or changing rooms?"

"Dave, you—"

"Nobody's taking off their clothes, OK?"

Mitchell clenched his jaw, then relented. "OK, all right," he said, not wanting to risk being the only naked conspirator at the meeting.

He pulled the cloak over his clothes, and his face disappeared into the shadow of the deep cowl. For all they knew, he could be some other lanky, robed idiot.

"How do I look?"

David and Jordan exchanged impressed frowns. "Creepy."

They enrobed. The fabric, thick but soft, reminded David of a quality spa robe. With the cowl over his head, he could only see a few feet ahead, enough to avoid colliding with major obstacles. A large weight lifted from his shoulders. In this disguise, nobody could see his face, allowing him to dispense with introductions. That was, he realized, the entire point. None of the Elders of Zion knew the others, but they worked in harmony, like the many organs of a single articulated body.

David turned his head from side to side. The droning voice emanated from the tall wooden door on the left.

He pulled back his cowl. "Hoods off." His friends obeyed. "Let's stick together. The last thing we need is to get lost." They nodded. "One more thing. We're here to listen and observe. If they address us, let me do the talking, OK?" More nods.

"Hey, guys," Jordan said. For once, excitement sparkled in his eyes and bubbled in his voice. "We found them. This is really happening!"

"I know, it's freaky, right?" Mitchell said.

They grinned at each other, and David swallowed his misgivings. The two men might be the last friendly human faces he'd ever see again. They pulled their cowls back over their heads.

"OK," David said. "Let's do this."

CHAPTER 7

David placed his hand on the door handle. The trick was to slip inside unnoticed. He eased down the handle. The mechanism, probably unoiled for decades, creaked, and the sonorous voice fell silent. David cringed, but there was no turning back now. *Whatever you do, David, do not piss your pants!*

David paused on the threshold, his heart pounding in his chest. In the tunnel vision of his cowl, torchlight flickered over the floor of scratched wood. He lifted his head and glimpsed the hemlines of two dozen black cloaks. And feet. Some wore leather Oxfords, others Birkenstocks. None belonged to women. There would be no orgies tonight, at least not the kind Mitchell had in mind. But orgies were the least of David's concerns.

The robed conspirators turned around to face the noisy latecomers. David's legs trembled. Hearing neither cries of attack nor welcoming greetings, he stepped forward, held the door open for his companions, and shut the door behind them. The Trio huddled together. David kept his head down and hoped the others were doing the same.

A throat cleared on a loudspeaker. "Is that all of you?" The deep voice spoke with a familiar guttural accent.

David nodded his cowled head and conjured the deepest,

most un-David-like voice he could manage. "Yes."

"Yes, *Grandmaster*," the unseen speaker said, with irritation.

"Yes, Grandmaster," David repeated.

"Good. Now that we're all here, we can get back to business."

The feet turned around again, away from the Trio, and toward the speaker.

David breathed a sigh of relief. They were inside! They had joined a convocation of the Elders of Zion. Ha! Hymie Schneider was wrong! Ditto Gerry Cantor. The Elders of Zion were alive and well, and the Trio had joined the board of directors.

The resonant voice continued. "Our plan is progressing well. First the United States. Then the world."

David huddled closer to Jordan, at least he thought it was Jordan, and jabbed him with his elbow. "Jordy," he whispered. "What accent is that—French? Ouch!"

Their heads had collided. "Israeli, I think."

"Right!" That made sense.

Jordy whispered. "The Mossad?"

"I guess."

David straightened, eager not to get caught talking in class on his first day of school. *The Mossad*. Of course, the Elders worked with the Israeli CIA. Why wouldn't they? This was a *global* Jewish conspiracy, and the Israeli secret service specialized in covert operations.

"Our training camps," the Grandmaster continued, "now number two hundred across the country. American-born volunteers are learning the requisite skills for the battles ahead. All are eager to die for our cause."

Two hundred training camps! The Elders was larger than David had expected, but the talk of battles and death unsettled him. He hazarded a quick upward glance. On a raised dais in the torch-lit hall, the cloaked Grandmaster spoke into a microphone connected to a portable speaker.

David stole glances at the other cloaked figures. Who were these people? And how long had they belonged to the

Elders? Far longer than the Trio, that was clear.

A suspicion rattled him. Did David know some of them? Was Hymie Schneider hiding underneath one of the black cloaks? Gerry Cantor too? All those Jewish power brokers who insisted that the Elders did not exist and wanted nothing to do with such ridiculous ideas.

One disturbing thought led to another. Why the training camps? Were they nurturing Jewish secret agents to protect Jewish institutions? David liked the idea, although he'd be the last to volunteer for guard duty. Fortunately, this meeting seemed designed for upper management, not foot soldiers.

"The United States government still knows nothing of our activities," the Grandmaster continued. "Our roots have spread deep and wide. Soon we shall be unstoppable. We have sown fear into the hearts of our enemies. None of them dare act against our coreligionists."

What? Did he just say nobody dared to act against their co-religionists? That was too much. David's blood boiled, and his hand shot into the air before he could stop it.

The Grandmaster cleared his throat. "It seems we have a question."

David used his new deep voice. "What about the synagogue shootings in Pittsburgh and San Diego?"

A sinister silence filled the hall. *Oh, crap.* A shiver crawled up David's spine. He had blown it. He had questioned the Grandmaster, ignoring his own advice and turning the Trio into a pariah faction. What did secret societies do to mutineers? David's imagination did not have to work hard. The Trio had to leave—and fast. He hoped Jordan's Roadster could outpace the turbo-charged showroom parked outside.

"Yes," the Grandmaster said, eventually. "We can learn much from those incidents."

David put his flight plans on hold. He released the breath he'd been holding. The Elders of Zion was a forward-thinking secret society. Management welcomed questions and constructive criticism. Hell, they probably selected their Grandmasters by democratic vote. *Secret* ballot, of course.

"Which brings us to our final agenda item," the Grandmaster said, meaningfully. "Our next major operation. To finance the mission, we propose a small fundraiser, and who better to execute this task than our newest members."

A lump of terror lodged in David's throat. The Grandmaster was talking about them—the Trio! David kept his head down and his shoulders hunched. David hated fundraisers with a passion, and he had no desire to plan one! He played dead, hoping the Grandmaster would pick on someone else.

"Yes, you," the Grandmaster said. "You at the back with your heads down. The three latecomers led by the questioner."

The game was up. The Grandmaster had cornered the Trio like a sadistic stand-up comedian who picked on the cowering introverts in the back row.

"What do you call yourselves?"

Was the Grandmaster punishing them for David's question? The thought injected him with defiance. David straightened. He'd take his medicine like a big boy. Finding his un-David-like baritone, he said, "The Trio, Grandmaster."

The Grandmaster scoffed. "How innovative." He was enjoying this. "The Metropolitan Museum in Manhattan is hosting a special collection this week—all nine imperial Fabergé eggs. Their sale on the black market should cover the costs of our operation. Your mission is to steal the eggs within two weeks. Your Grandmaster commands it."

Jordan elbowed David. "Did he say 'steal'?" he whispered.

David ignored his friend. "Yes, Grandmaster." David felt another jab in the ribs. What the hell was he supposed to say?

"Good," the Grandmaster said. "Are there any other matters for discussion?"

The leader's attention had moved on, and David loosened up. The Trio had survived the meeting. He'd deal with their mission later. They had joined the Elders of Zion, and the Grandmaster had assigned them their first task. This was an initiation ritual, not punishment. After completing the mission, the Trio would become card-carrying members of the most secretive society in modern history.

"Seeing that there are no other matters," the Grandmaster continued, "we will conclude with our traditional salute."

David perked up. The Trio had dispensed with secret handshakes, but the Elders had a traditional salute. Would they sing the Israeli national anthem, "Hatikva"? Perhaps the folk song "David, King of Israel" or a simple "To life, l'chaim"?

The assembly chanted the salute thrice, and the two words echoed through the surrounding hall. Although he had guessed wrong, David was very familiar with the phrase. Too familiar. David's legs shook, and the blood ran cold in his veins. The Elders had shouted *"Allahu akbar!"*

CHAPTER 8

ONE WEEK EARLIER...

David lurked in the lobby of The Ritz-Carlton, nursing the ulcer of anxiety in his gut. He perched on the edge of a Victorian-style embroidered armchair and sent furtive glances at the well-dressed guests who entered the hotel from Central Park Street. So far, Preston Clancy was not among them.

I know you're staying here, Preston. Show yourself.

David had manned his post since the afternoon. Every few minutes, a middle-aged man walked through the glass doors, launching David from his seat only to let him down.

The desk clerk with the upturned nose had refused to confirm whether Preston was staying at the hotel. Hours into David's vigil, the snooty clerk still sent annoyed glances at the lobby's new squatter. David ignored him.

Daylight faded over Manhattan. As the lights brightened, the street-facing windows turned opaque and mirrored David's pensive reflection. Doubts gnawed like rats on the frayed edges of his mind. *What if Preston didn't show?*

He would. He *had* to. If he didn't, David would be out on the street. "Within a month," according to the eviction notice folded into the pocket of his jacket. Both the envelope and the typed letter within bore the logo of Zelig Pictures, adding insult to injury.

Preston Clancy was David's only hope of holding onto the life he knew. David had never pulled strings to get by, but that evening he would pull every string in sight.

And Preston would help him. He owed everything to the Zelig family. David's father had taken Preston under his wing ten years ago after the small production studio Preston founded had folded. Sol Zelig had seen a potential protégé in the aspiring executive with the smooth voice, suave manner, and gray hair at his temples. Preston had not disappointed, climbing the executive ladder until he made vice president. David's father had trusted him implicitly, inviting him over for meals at the Zelig home when David was in high school. After David's father passed away five years ago, his mother had entrusted Preston with the presidency of Zelig Pictures. But the Zeligs' troubles were not over.

Two months ago, Preston had called an urgent meeting at the offices of Zelig Pictures in the San Fernando Valley. He invited David's mother and David, who by then had moved to Manhattan to write a small pile of spec scripts.

Preston, his voice cracking with concern and his great fingers clasped over his desk, delivered the devastating news. Zelig Pictures was neck-deep in debt and hemorrhaging money. Preston blamed rising production costs and competition from online streaming services. The film industry had evolved, and Zelig Pictures was the oversized dinosaur that lumbered far behind the crowd of quick-footed mammals.

David and his mom had stared at the company's balance sheet in shock. David's dad had always presented a rosy facade of business as usual. There had been no hint of their family company's financial problems. Not only was this the end of David's great-grandfather's legacy, but hundreds of employees would lose their jobs.

Preston had found one last-ditch hope for saving the company. A Swiss hedge fund was expanding its portfolio into the entertainment industry. The fund was prepared to swallow the company's debt in exchange for full ownership, but would pay the Zeligs close to nothing. Preston urged David's mother to accept the offer. She and David would never see another cent from Zelig Pictures, but at least the company—and the family name—would live on.

His mom had signed on the dotted line, and David returned to New York, dazed and depressed at the family's unexpected misfortune. He tightened his belt, whittling his expenses to the bare minimum, and polished his pile of screenplays. He needed a new source of income. Luckily, he had connections in the film industry. Or so he had thought.

He mailed his best script to Preston and bided his time. A follow-up email went unanswered. Preston's secretary promised that her boss would return David's calls. He never did. An ulcer of anxiety formed in David's gut. When the eviction letter arrived, the ulcer ballooned. His apartment apparently belonged to Zelig Pictures, which now belonged to a Swiss hedge fund, and their bean counters wanted David out.

Only Preston could right that wrong, and David's need for face time with the president of Zelig Pictures became urgent. After a few more desperate calls, Preston's secretary had let slip that her boss was in Manhattan and would leave early the next morning. And so began David's stakeout at The Ritz.

Another gray-haired man entered the hotel, prompting another false-start from David. Sighing, he settled back on the padded chair.

A malignant lump of paranoia joined the ulcer. Had Preston been avoiding David? And what did his Swiss overlords think of their executive's splurge on fancy hotels?

"Can I help you?"

The snooty clerk had materialized beside David.

"No, thank you. I'm waiting for someone."

"Wouldn't you be more comfortable waiting in a room of your own?"

The disapproving tone implied that someone with David's clothes could afford a night at The Ritz and should not camp out in the lobby like a vagrant.

"That won't be necessary."

The clerk raised a pair of scandalized eyebrows and returned to the front desk. At eight o'clock, the desk attendants changed shifts. At ten o'clock, David was ready to give up and head home for the night. As he rose from the armchair, a tall, suited man with graying temples marched into the hotel. David sprinted into his path.

"David," Preston said, his eyes widening along with his smile. "What a pleasant surprise! I was just thinking of you."

"You were?"

"Of course. I about to look you up."

David whacked his suspicions on the head. Preston's secretary had reached him, after all. This was all a big misunderstanding. Preston would fix everything, and once again David would sleep peacefully, knowing that the Swiss would not steal his apartment from under him.

"You got my messages?"

"Messages? What messages?"

David gasped, frustration and angst escaping like steam from a pressure cooker. "About the apartment... and my script..."

Preston raised a hand to calm his ruffled friend. "Let's talk upstairs."

Preston's hotel room did nothing to calm David's suspicions. The enormous top-floor suite commanded magnificent views of the city and probably cost half of the Zelig Pictures debt.

"Business must be booming," David said, a nervous chuckle in his voice.

Preston removed his suit jacket. "Yes. It is. Please sit down." He pointed to an armchair in the lounge.

David obeyed. His fate rested in the hands of this man. David had never felt so vulnerable before. The sooner this was over the better.

"Would you like a drink?" Preston indicated the well-stocked bar.

"No, thank you."

Preston sat down opposite his visitor. "Now, tell me everything."

David started with the apartment, expressing his shock at the eviction notice and stressing his urgent need for a home. He tried not to beg. Then he pitched Preston his script, a spy thriller, and presented a synopsis of the plot.

Preston listened in silence, his brow furrowed with concentration as he drank in every word. David had the president's full attention. His hopes and fears had found a sympathetic ear.

"Well, what do you think?" David asked when Preston made no response.

Preston leaned back in his chair and smiled to himself. What was so funny? Then he chuckled and David's confusion grew. The chuckle became a laugh, then exploded into a hearty fit of hysterical giggling that infected David with a bout of nervous tremors.

Preston recovered his composure, wiped a tear from his eye, and looked David squarely in the eye. "I could help you, David," he said, matter-of-fact. "I could transfer the apartment into your name and green-light your script."

"Thank you, Preston," David began, but a raised hand cut his thanks short.

"I said I *could* help you, David. But I won't."

"Why not?"

Preston shrugged, as though the answer was as obvious as it was simple.

"I don't want to."

David stared back at him, numb with disbelief. The man his father had rescued, the man who'd eaten at his childhood dinner table, the man who owed everything to the Zelig family, simply didn't want to help.

Preston leaned forward. "Let me tell you a little secret, David. Zelig Pictures is rolling in money. In fact, the company has never done better."

David found his tongue again. "But the company was

running at a loss. You showed us the numbers."

Preston ignored David's words. "Do you know why I came to Hollywood?"

David didn't, so Preston continued. His grand revelation flowed like a speech he had rehearsed in his mind for years.

"Because I hate Jews! I hate the Jews in the media. I hate the Jews in the banks. Above all, I hate the Jews in Hollywood. I went to Hollywood to get the Jews out!"

His face twisted with undiluted loathing, and he seemed ready to froth at the mouth.

"How I despised your father. Sol Zelig made me sick to my stomach. His pity. His charity. But I stuck it out. When he threw a stick, I ran. I sat, I begged, I rolled over. But every night I dreamed of biting that hand to the bone. And now I have. Everything he once had is mine now. So don't thank me, David Zelig. And don't expect any favors. I should thank you. I've been waiting for this day for a very long time. And your pitiful misery has been the cherry on the top."

He laughed again, his voice maniacal. This wasn't just an ingrate. Preston Clancy was a rabid anti-Semite.

"What do you mean *yours*? Zelig Pictures belongs to the Swiss now." If Preston wouldn't help David, at least David could cut him down to size.

Preston shook his head at David, his laughter subsiding. "You have no clue, do you? Who do you think owns the Swiss?" A sudden need to boast seemed to grip him. "I spent a long time planning this maneuver, David. And I executed my plan to perfection."

David's face felt hot and cold at the same time. Preston had robbed his family blind.

"We'll get Zelig Pictures back! We'll sue you."

Preston chuckled. "For what—saving Zelig Pictures from bankruptcy? Go ahead. That's what the books will show. You saw them yourself. I was very careful, David. You'll never prove a thing. By the time a judge throws your conspiracy theory out of court, you'll have drowned in legal fees."

He was right. David was clueless about the company's accounting and he had no money—let alone hard evidence— for a protracted lawsuit. Preston had cheated David's family out of everything and he would get away with it. But he had more to say.

"The tide is turning, David Zelig." His tone had turned menacing, losing all traces of humor. "Look around you. Those synagogue shooters aren't alone. Soon, this country won't be safe for Jews. You'd better crawl back to Europe while you can, you filthy Jew!'"

CHAPTER 9

"Jesus!" Jordan said as the Roadster ate up Interstate 87. "Jesus! Jesus! Jesus!"

In the back seat, Mitchell had selected a different word for repetition—the F-word. He no longer complained about the cramped legroom.

David said nothing. His hands trembled. His face felt cold from shock. After the final salute, the Trio had fled the meeting hall of the Elders of Zion. Make that the *Islamic* Elders of Zion. Dumping their black cloaks in the antechamber, David and his friends had converged on Jordan's car with one goal in mind—to get as far away from there as fast as possible.

Jordan's hands strangled the steering wheel, his knuckles white. David glanced at the speedometer. "Slow down, Jordy. You're doing over a hundred."

"Don't tell me to slow down! We were in the middle of effing Al Qaeda in there! They're still after us."

"Nobody's after us," David said, unsure of the facts but certain he didn't want to end his life as a smear on I-87. "They think we're one of them."

"One of them?" Mitchell yelled, losing all semblance of playboy unflappability. "If they find out we're Jews, they'll massacre us! They blow up kindergartens and fly planes into skyscrapers. Murdering us will be a cakewalk for them."

"Please," David said. "Everybody calm down. Nobody's chasing us, and nobody's getting killed."

"What about the eggs? They expect us to break into the Met and steal some friggin' eggs."

"Nobody will steal anything."

"They won't like that."

"Mitch, they don't know who we are or where we live. Who cares?"

"And," Jordan added, "we agreed we wouldn't do anything illegal, right?"

"That's right, Jordy. Nothing illegal."

Jordan eased off the accelerator, and the car slowed to within the legal speed limit. He exhaled a deep breath. "We have to disband the Trio."

"What? Why?" The meeting had also freaked David out, but he wasn't ready to throw in the towel.

"They know about the Trio now. They can use that name to identify us."

"Then we'll choose a new name."

"Dave, listen to me. They could have lynched us back there. Tonight cured me of secret societies. I've had all the covert excitement I can take for one lifetime. They can probably trace us using their Dark Net forum." He swore. "I'll wipe my laptop and reset your Internet router as soon as we get back. Crap! What if they saw my registration plate?"

David unclenched his jaw. Jordan was right. They had nearly lost their lives and all for what—a harebrained pipe dream? Ever since Preston Clancy had confessed to stealing Zelig Pictures, David had sworn he'd get back at the anti-Semite. If David had no powerful connections, he'd conjure them from thin air. He'd resurrect the Elders of Zion from the graveyard of myth and strike fear in the hearts of the haters. Nobody would dare victimize Jews again if the shadow of Jewish Power stretched far and dark. But what was he thinking? If he played with fire, he'd end up as a pile of ash. The Trio was a terrible mistake from the get-go.

"OK," he said, his voice small and defeated. "We'll disband the Trio."

"So we're giving up, just like that?" Mitchell said. He seemed to have forgotten his panic attack from seconds ago.

"Jordy's right. We're in over our heads. This could go belly up in a hundred different ways. Tonight we got lucky. Next time we could end up in a shallow grave. It just isn't worth it."

Mitchell huffed with frustration. "What's the deal with the eggs, anyway? Why are they so valuable?"

"Because they're made of gold and jewels," Jordan said. "The Russian tsars had them made as Easter presents about a hundred years ago. They must be worth millions."

"Millions? Not bad. What do you think their 'major operation' is?"

David said, "We can assume it's not to beef up synagogue security." His conscience twinged. "We should report this to the police."

"The police?" Jordan said. "Hello? And how will we explain our knowledge of the Elders of Zion? 'Oh yeah, we just started this secret society and hung out on the Dark Net?' Are you kidding me? We'll be on criminal watch lists for the rest of our lives!"

Jordan had a valid point. David needed to think this through. "We could make an anonymous tip-off."

"Anonymous tip-off about an unspecified attack," Jordan said, his voice dripping with sarcasm. "The police will take that very seriously."

Right again. They drove on in silence.

Mitchell said, "Who knew Muslims were into Easter eggs?" He laughed at his own joke and, after a tense pause, the others joined in.

"Yeah, that's bizarre," David admitted. The countryside whizzed by his window, the moon lending a silver lining to the trees and houses. "And I guess the Grandmaster isn't with the Mossad, either."

High on spent adrenaline and the joy of still breathing,

they giggled like schoolgirls.

"That's one great story for the grandkids, though," Jordan said.

"Yeah," David said, the mention of grandkids sobering him up. On his phone, he resumed his playlist, and Amy Winehouse sang about cheating herself and being no good.

His thoughts turned to another Amy and her glorious smile at the bar of the Grand Hyatt. *Amy Anderson.* At least one good thing had come from their short-lived secret society. He'd look her up. One day, decades from now, he'd tell her the real story behind how they met, and they'd laugh about it.

Jordan descended the ramp of the parking garage beneath David's apartment building and let Eddie, the valet, park the Roadster in a guest spot. "Nice wheels, Mr. Brody."

"Thanks, Eddie."

"Have a good night out?"

The three friends traded ironic smiles. Sweaty and disheveled, they must have looked like they'd hit the city's night clubs.

"A night to remember," David said.

They leaned against the walls of the elevator as it rose.

"How long will it take to reset the router?" David asked Jordan.

"A few minutes."

"I need a drink," Mitchell said.

David grinned. "We all do." The adrenaline had drained him but he wasn't ready to sleep. He needed to decompress.

The doors opened. David stepped into the corridor, fished his keys from his pocket, and stopped dead in his tracks.

Two men, clean-cut but unsmiling in their brown suits, stood by the door of his apartment.

"Mr. Zelig," said the Latino, who was shorter and stockier than his balding white associate. He spoke as though they'd been expecting him. He turned to David's friends. "Mr. Brody and Mr. Joffe, we're Special Agents Hernandez and Worth. You need to come with us."

CHAPTER 10

"You are in deep trouble," Special Agent Marco Hernandez said. "So I'll ask you one last time. Where did you and your friends go tonight?"

He sat opposite David at the table of an interrogation room. David hadn't seen his friends since they'd arrived in the back of an unmarked cruiser at the downtown FBI building on Federal Plaza over an hour ago. He imagined Jordan and Mitchell were enduring the same endless rounds of repetitive questioning.

David glanced at his wristwatch. "You mean last night? It's after twelve." He knew he shouldn't be a smart ass, but he was tired and he'd already answered the same question twenty times. Whatever they asked, he had only one answer.

His first impulse had been to make threats. His friends in government would be really pissed off to hear the FBI had accosted their dear friend, David Zelig. But David had no friends in government, no names to drop, and no strings to pull. If the Jewish Elders of Zion had existed, maybe the FBI would have let him go home.

Hernandez gave him an ironic grin. "Last night."

"Like I said, Officer, I'd like to speak with my attorney before answering questions." At least, David had remembered that handy tidbit from the many TV police shows of his wasted youth.

"Special Agent," Hernandez said. "The Bureau has agents, not officers."

"*Special Agent* Hernandez."

"And you still have no idea why you're here?"

"With all due respect, Special Agent Hernandez, I'd like to speak with—"

Hernandez waved his hand in the air. "I know, I know, your attorney. Here's the thing, David. It's early in the AM, and your attorney will not show up soon. We think you have time-sensitive information that might save American lives."

David fidgeted with his paper coffee cup, the second coffee the agent had made for him. Hernandez was right. Handing the FBI the location of the Elders' meeting could enable them to round up the Islamic extremists—or it might have a few hours ago. By now the abandoned mansion would be empty, and confessing to meeting with a terrorist organization would only incriminate him. David hoped Jordan and Mitchell had come to the same conclusion.

Hernandez yawned. "Listen, we all want to go home tonight—this morning. I know you're a good guy. You've got no priors or open warrants, only a parking ticket from a few years ago. Here's what I'll do. I'll level with you. Here's what we know. We know you and your friends formed a secret society called the Trio. You searched the Dark Net hoping to contact other secret groups."

David almost swallowed his tongue. How could they know that? Had they bugged his apartment or hacked his Internet connection?

Hernandez plowed on. "But you were just playing around. You didn't know what you were getting yourself into. Associating with a terrorist organization on US soil was the last thing you wanted."

There came a knock on the door, and Hernandez frowned. He did not welcome the interruption. But the timing was perfect for David, who, sweat trickling down his back, had been about to break down and come clean.

"What is it?"

The door opened, and Special Agent Edward Worth walked in, a broad smile on his lips. David liked Worth better than Hernandez. He had an easy, amicable manner that reminded David of Woody Harrelson. Special Agent Worth approached his colleague, a spring in his step. "You're gonna love this one, Marco."

Worth had a mild Southern accent that David found reassuring. He leaned down and whispered into the ear of his colleague, who nodded while he listened, then turned abruptly to the speaker. "Did you say 'orgy'?"

Worth placed his hand over his mouth but snickered despite himself. "But wait, there's more." He continued his whispered tale.

Whatever Hollywood-inspired insanity Mitchell had told the FBI, the lie would circle back to bite the Trio in the ass.

When Worth finished speaking, Hernandez shook his head in disbelief. "I have heard some crazy shit in my time at the Bureau, but this takes the cake. Bring 'em in."

Special Agent Worth left the room, returning with David's friends and two extra chairs. Jordan gave David a meek frown of commiseration. Mitchell gave David a broad smile and a double thumbs-up. David wanted to crawl into a hole and die of shame. They all sat down.

Hernandez stood. "OK, guys, here's the deal."

Mitchell leaned closer to whisper in David's ear. "I knew they'd crack."

"Mr. Joffe, do I have your full attention?"

"Yes, you do. Please proceed with your deal."

Hernandez hooked his thumbs in the pockets of his trousers. "I have never met such a sorry bunch of amateurs. Three suspects, three different stories about what went on tonight." He glared at David. "*Last* night. And as entertaining as those stories were," he eyed Mitchell with disgust, "here's your problem. Now we've got you on Obstruction of Justice. According to two of you, you contacted a terrorist organization, so Homeland will love to get their hands on you."

David had heard enough. Lawyer or no lawyer, he had gotten his friends into this mess and he would clean it up. "Special Agent Hernandez, you were right. We were just fooling around. We had no idea what we were getting into and we are truly deeply sorry for what we've done."

Hernandez raised his eyebrows. "No more lies?"

"No, sir. No more lies." David answered Mitchell's annoyed glance with a threatening stare, and Mitchell relented. "The truth and nothing but the truth."

"So now you're willing to cooperate?"

"Yes, sir. We'll disband the Trio right away and never engage in any secret activity again."

Hernandez chuckled. Why was he chuckling? "Disband the Trio—is that what you think this is about?"

David shrugged.

"We don't want you to disband the Trio."

"You don't?"

"Oh, no. We want the Trio to help us bring down the bad guys."

Mitchell punched the air. "Yeah!"

Jordan frowned. "Bring down the bad guys? Us? There's no way. No way!"

David agreed. "That's not fair."

"Or," Hernandez said, "we can arrest you right now. Obstruction of Justice is a felony, boys. Have you ever spent time inside a federal prison?" The friends shook their heads. "I didn't think so. You'll make a lot of new friends there. They'll expand your horizons... and other parts of your anatomy."

The friends engaged in a wordless discussion. The FBI was blackmailing them, but they had no choice. As Jordan had warned them, once you break the law you're at the government's mercy. His friends nodded their reluctant agreement.

"OK," David said. "We'll do it."

Hernandez beamed. "Thank you for your cooperation,

gentlemen. Now, I'll call in our team leader, Special Agent Smith, and we'll get started."

"Your team leader?" Jordan said, confused. "Where's he been all this time?"

The answer arrived when Worth opened the door and a woman walked into the room. David's jaw dropped to the floor of the interrogation room. The attractive lead agent had long auburn curls and a small, delicate nose. She gave David a quick, demure smile before addressing the three friends.

"Welcome to the FBI," Amy Anderson said.

CHAPTER 11

Dave scraped his jaw off the floor of the interrogation room and traded wide-eyed WTF glances with his friends. They had recognized the FBI team leader at once. But when David had met her at the bar of the Grand Hyatt a few days ago, her name had been Amy Anderson, not Special Agent Smith.

As his shock faded, a realization stung. David had thought they'd hit it off at the Cyber Summit, but she'd given him a false name. Her interest in David was part of the same deception. He felt wronged.

Special Agent Smith spoke with sure-footed confidence, as though they'd never interacted before.

"My name is Special Agent Amy Smith," she said. "Gentlemen, the group you encountered tonight is a highly dangerous extremist Islamic organization. They are responsible for a number of terrorist attacks on US soil. Known as the Elders of Zion, they model themselves on the fictional secret society described in the infamous forgery known as *The Protocols of the Learned Elders of Zion*. Their activities include anti-American propaganda, infiltration of US organizations, and the running of several terrorist training camps across the country."

"Two hundred," David blurted. The sting of the deception

had worn off. He'd attended the cyber conference under false pretenses too. She, at least, had used her real first name. He felt the irrational urge to pick up their first conversation where they'd left off. More than anything, he wanted to please her. "The Grandmaster said they had two hundred training camps."

The FBI agents sent each other meaningful glances, and Special Agent Hernandez jotted the detail down on his notepad. Their decision to co-opt the Trio had already paid off.

"To earn your immunity, you need to tell us everything you know."

Jordan and Mitchell turned to David, nominating him as their spokesman. "The Grandmaster gave us a mission. We're supposed to steal the nine imperial Fabergé eggs on display at the Met. Obviously, we would never do that."

"Why you?" Special Agent Hernandez asked.

David shrugged. "We were new to the Elders, and we'd arrived late. I think the Grandmaster was picking on us."

Amy said, "Or giving you a chance to prove your loyalty and earn your place in the group. Initiation rites are a typical characteristic of secret societies."

David nodded his head. He had thought the same thing.

"Did the Grandmaster say why he wanted the eggs?"

"He said the Elders need them to fund their next major operation."

Special Agent Smith harrumphed, as though not convinced of the explanation.

"How much are the eggs worth?" Hernandez asked.

"Millions," Amy said. She seemed to arrive at a decision. "You must complete the mission to win the Elders' trust and infiltrate the leadership's inner circle."

"Whoa," Jordan said. "We just told you all we know. Nobody said anything about infiltrating inner circles."

"The FBI and Homeland Security have been trying to embed an agent in the Elders for years. This might be our best chance at a penetration operation." At the word "penetration," she gave Mitchell a dirty look. Apparently, she had heard of his pickup line at the Cyber Summit.

"But," Jordan objected, "if they'd found out who we were tonight, they would have killed us."

"Probably," Special Agent Hernandez said.

Jordan gave a short, incredulous laugh. "We want to cooperate and all, but not if it means winding up dead!"

"It won't come to that," Amy said. "We'll be beside you every step of the way. We'll arrange things so you'll never be in any real danger."

Jordan shook his head. David knew how he felt—he was in no rush to attend another meeting of the Elders either—but they were in a bind.

"Special Agent Smith," he said, "may I consult with my friends for a minute?"

"Sure."

The Trio shifted their chairs closer and huddled.

"This is crazy," Jordan said.

"It's also pretty cool," Mitchell said. "Admit it. A real-life FBI operation—this is exactly the kind of action we were looking for!"

"I wasn't looking for any action," Jordan hissed.

"Neither was I," David said. "But think about it. These Elders are building serious power and they hate Jews. The synagogue shootings are nothing compared to the attacks these fanatics are planning. This is our chance to stop them—to do something good and meaningful."

Jordan mulled the words over, fear and conscience wrestling on his forehead, and David felt a prickle of guilt. Had his saintly intentions convinced him to stick out his neck or was he just eager to spend more time with Special Agent Amy Smith?

"OK," Jordan said. "We'll do this. But the moment the operation is over, we're done."

"Agreed." The huddle dispersed. "We'll help," David told Amy.

"Thank you," she said, and her grateful smile melted his heart.

Special Agent Worth said, "The eggs are on loan from the real owners. I don't think they or the Met will be happy handing them over to the FBI."

"It's a matter of national security," Special Agent Hernandez said. "They'll have no choice."

"That won't work," Amy said. "The Trio can't just hand over the eggs. The Elders will smell a rat and break off all contact."

"What do you suggest?"

"The Elders are expecting a heist," Amy said, and she smiled. "Let's give them a heist."

CHAPTER 12

"Beautiful, aren't they?" said the elderly man behind him.

David, who had been staring at the display case of thick glass deep within the Metropolitan Museum, turned to the speaker, Professor William Hendricks, the museum's director.

"Yes, they are."

David and his friends had trouble taking their eyes off the eggs. Tall marble arches bordered the expansive sanctuary on every side. Beneath the high central dome, the golden eggs sat on their glass thrones and glinted in the glow of spotlights. The footfalls of museum security officers and FBI agents echoed around them, their voices hushed in this cathedral to the opulence of Imperial Russia.

The eggs dazzled their beholders, their pure gold expertly worked with intricate patterns and encrusted with diamonds, sapphires, and rubies. Some of the Easter eggs opened on golden hinges to reveal an inner surprise: eggs within eggs, oversized jewels, miniature sculptures, and timepieces. Each egg outdid the next in grandeur and elaborate design. They whispered of the unfathomable wealth and prestige of a long-lost era.

Two days after the ordeal in black robes, the Trio had converged on the Fifth Avenue entrance of the Met, the largest museum in the United States, after closing time. They climbed the broad steps, passed between the towering pillars, and walked the long hallways to the Imperial Fabergé Egg Exhibit, where their FBI handlers performed their final review of Operation Humpty Dumpty.

Professor Hendricks gave a satisfied grin. "Tsar Alexander III commissioned the first of the eggs in the late eighteen hundreds as Easter gifts for his wife, the tsarina. Their son, Nicholas II, the last tsar of the Russian Empire, continued the tradition." He pointed to the roll-up poster with the portrait of a young man in ceremonial military uniform. Nicholas II made up for his paucity of medals with a well-trimmed beard and an impressive mustache.

"Each egg and its surprise is a unique work of art and each has a name." The director pointed to each egg in turn, enunciating the names with pride as though introducing heads of state at an imperial ball. "The Hen Egg; Hen with Sapphire Pendant; Cherub with Chariot; Diamond Trellis; Imperial Coronation; Lilies of the Valley; Mosaic; Tsarevitch; and the Order of St. George."

Professor Hendricks sighed at the vanished glory of forgotten eras.

"This is the first time in a hundred years that all nine imperial Fabergé eggs have gathered in one place. It took no small amount of cajoling and money to loan the eggs from museums and private collections around the world. The eggs were last united shortly before Communists deposed Tsar Nicholas II during the February Revolution of 1917. A year later, the revolutionaries executed the former tsar, his wife, their four daughters, and young son, along with their entourage. The firing squad had trouble killing them because of the many jewels sewn into the royal family's clothing. So the killers shot them in the head at close range and stabbed them with bayonets. Then they stripped the bodies, dumped them in a pit, and poured acid on the naked corpses."

The museum director seemed deeply saddened by the brutal fate of the last tsar of the Russian Empire. "There were ten imperial eggs in total. The last egg, known as Victory, disappeared before the revolution. Many have tried in vain to locate it, and this Easter egg hunt continues to this day."

"Professor," Special Agent Hernandez said. "Can we have a word? About the eggs' insurance policy."

"Of course."

The director stepped aside to discuss the details with the FBI agent.

"I like that one," Mitchell said, pointing to—if David was not mistaken—Imperial Coronation. The golden egg with the silver lattice pattern and immense diamond at its base contained a miniature golden carriage complete with a functioning door. "It reminds me of a model chariot my grandfather had in his study."

David grunted.

Jordan whispered, "I still can't believe they're going through with the heist."

"It's not a heist if they're letting us take them. It's just a show."

"Still. Together they must be worth over fifty million dollars. When did you last walk around with fifty million?"

"Relax," Mitchell said. "We'll be fine. The only thing you should worry about is falling off the roof."

The Trio had spent the past two days rappelling off a low, brick structure at an FBI training school outside Brooklyn. Their instructor, Agent Tucker, had taught them how to throw a Capewell grapple hook by swinging a length of Kernmantle rope, and how to shimmy down the side of a building using a figure-eight descender on a harness. Jordan's first try had left him spinning from his waist halfway down the practice wall. David had completed the task successfully. Special Agent Amy Smith had observed their training sessions with interest, and David had wanted to make a good impression.

Amy had kept her distance at first, but during a break, engaged David in a short chat.

"Why the Trio?" she had asked.

"Well, there's three of us, and—"

"I don't mean the name, dummy. Why start a secret society to begin with?"

"Oh." David had blushed at his fumbling of a simple question, then told her about the synagogue shootings and his desire to protect his Jewish brethren. Amy had nodded her head and glanced at her feet, and David had felt another pinch of guilt. The honest answer to that question was less heroic, but he could not bring himself to destroy the brave persona he'd created in her mind.

Later, when she'd helped him adjust his harness, their hands had touched for a split second, and David was sure a spark had passed between them. If Amy had noticed, she had made no sign of it.

Now that the fun and games were over, David was no longer sure he could pull off the break-in at night and under pressure.

"Listen up, everyone," Amy said. She looked very professional in her FBI plainclothes suit, and when she spoke, people listened. "We'll review our operational plan one last time. Special Agent Hernandez?"

"At one AM tonight," Hernandez said, then he glared at David. "That's one AM early tomorrow morning, the Trio will approach the Met building from the service entrance off East Drive in Central Park. Agent Tucker of Special Ops Training will accompany them to make sure they don't break a leg."

"Oh, thank God," Jordan muttered.

"Five FBI agents in civilian clothes will observe the area to make sure no bystanders interfere or call nine-one-one. We don't need any well-meaning civilians or officers interfering with the heist. At one oh five, the Met security crew will deactivate the perimeter sensors and intrusion alarms for twenty minutes. The nearest door on the roof will be unlocked, avoiding any need to break locks or otherwise damage the property."

He pointed to Jordan. "Jordan will remain with Agent

Tucker on the roof while David and Mitchell proceed inside the museum. The path from the service lift to the Fabergé exhibit will be clear. Do not diverge from the path we walked together earlier or you'll trigger motion detectors and the museum will go into lockdown. Understood?"

David and Mitchell nodded.

"Using the suction pad and the diamond-edged cutter, David will trace a circle in the display case and remove a circle of glass. Then he will reach through the hole and extract the eggs. Special Agent Worth, the carry case?"

Worth opened a metal briefcase in his arms and exposed the black foam interior with nine egg-shaped cutouts.

"One by one," Hernandez continued, "Mitchell will place the eggs, their surprises stored inside, into the custom holes in the carry case. Do not force the eggs into place, understood?"

Mitchell nodded. "No problem."

"Once the eggs are secure, David and Mitchell will return the way they entered, rejoin Agent Tucker and Jordan on the roof, and rappel down the building to their escape vehicle, a black GMC. We'll meet up at FBI headquarters and store the eggs securely. Questions?"

Mitchell raised his hand. "When do we get our guns?"

"You aren't getting any guns. Next question."

Jordan raised his hand. "If we're trying to minimize damage, why break the glass display?"

"Good question. An hour after the operation, museum security will perform a routine patrol of the museum and discover that the eggs are missing. Security will call NYPD to investigate the break-in."

"But—" Jordan objected, and Hernandez raised his hand to cut him short.

"We need the Elders to believe the Trio stole the eggs, so we're aiming for as much realism as possible. The museum will close for a few days. Professor Hendricks will release a statement to the media about the break-in but without specifying whether the thieves stole anything. Only Professor

Hendricks and a select few on the Met security staff will know that the heist is a hoax."

Mitchell turned to David, his eyes wide. "This is so cool," he whispered.

Hernandez wrapped things up. "With luck, we'll infiltrate the Elders quickly and return the eggs to their owners within a few weeks."

Jordan was still unsatisfied. "What if the Elders ask to see the eggs—are we just going to hand them over?"

Amy stepped forward, taking control of the discussion. "That won't be necessary. We've planned for a number of eventualities. If need be, we can fake a sale on the black market and provide the Elders with cash instead of the eggs. But by that stage, the Trio should be able to step away from the mission and return to their everyday lives."

"Good." The mention of everyday lives stopped Jordan's flow of questions.

Amy said, "If that's all, we'll meet up at our designated locations later tonight."

The museum director wished them good luck, and the FBI agents dispersed.

"Mr. Zelig, may I have a word?" Amy said.

David nodded for his friends to continue without him. "Please, call me David."

She nodded. "I guess I'll see you after the mission."

"Aren't you coming with us?"

"I'll monitor the operation from the surveillance van." She looked away and seemed wistful. Had she wanted to join the vanguard? Did she want to be with David? She looked him in the eye. "I just wanted to tell you I appreciate what you're doing. You're brave."

David shrugged off the compliment. "I don't really have a choice."

She wasn't letting him off the hook. "I don't mean the heist. Everybody heard about the synagogue shootings. Most civilians stood by and did nothing. You started the Trio. That makes you brave in my books. Or stupid." She smiled as she said the word, and an exhilarating thought raced his heart. Was she hitting on him? They were alone in the exhibit hall. She was standing very close to him. All he had to do was lean in and kiss her.

Go on, David. You're brave. She just said so. Do it. Kiss her!

Amy grinned at him. "Good luck tonight," she said. Then, she turned and walked away.

David watched her go. Maybe she was right about him. He was stupid.

CHAPTER 13

TOP SECRET
FEDERAL BUREAU OF INVESTIGATION
OFFICE OF PROFESSIONAL RESPONSIBILITY
Transcript of interview with Mr. Hyman Schneider
Also present:
Special Agent A. Maynard
Special Agent in Charge M. Reed

M. REED:
   Mr. Schneider, I'd like to backtrack a little, if you don't mind.

HYMAN SCHNEIDER:
   No, not at all. By all means.

M. REED:
   So we have these Islamic terrorists operating in the United States and they've modeled themselves on the fictional Elders of Zion. Am I right?

HYMAN SCHNEIDER:
   Correct.

M. REED:

And they just let David Zelig and his friends walk right into their secret meeting—wearing black robes they conveniently left at the entrance?

HYMAN SCHNEIDER:

Those are good questions. I've been thinking about the whole story for some time now. I figure if I had to set up a secret meeting I'd make the gathering as low-key as possible. No obvious security. No armies of thugs or what-have-you. Robes are a little tacky, I'll agree, but they serve a purpose. I expect the abandoned estate house was a one-off venue. They probably reveal the location of each meeting shortly ahead of time. Only those who belong there are in the know.

M. REED:

Which brings me to my next question. The Trio discovers the location of the meeting at the Cyber Summit with ease. But both the FBI and Homeland Security had failed to infiltrate this organization for years.

HYMAN SCHNEIDER:

The Trio got lucky, I guess. Over the years, I'm sure the Elders had developed a sixth sense for sniffing out law enforcement officers too. Otherwise, they wouldn't have lasted so long.

M. REED:

Hmm. What troubles me is the activity of law enforcement here. According to what you've told us, these FBI agents enlisted a group of civilians to embed themselves within a violent criminal organization under the threat of prosecution. That seriously violates the Bureau's SOP.

HYMAN SCHNEIDER:

Excuse me. SOP?

M. REED:

Sorry. SOP stands for standard operating procedures. Our job at the Office of Professional Responsibility is to investigate the misconduct of federal agents. This fake heist operation seems poorly thought out to me. They should have sent a tactical unit to break into the Met instead of the Trio. Special Agent Smith seems to be operating with very little supervision. That might explain what followed—the *cluster fiasco*, as you put it.

HYMAN SCHNEIDER:

Special Agent Reed, we're only getting started. Here, let me pour you gentlemen some whisky. You'll need it.

CHAPTER 14

"Nervous?" Special Agent Edward Worth asked David. They sat on a hard bench inside the black van, which sped from downtown toward the Metropolitan Museum. The floor of the van shifted as the engine growled. The contents of David's stomach shifted too. He should never have eaten that tuna sandwich from the vending machine in the FBI building.

"Yeah," David admitted. "A little."

Mitchell leaned over on the opposite bench and slapped David on the shoulder. "Nothing to be nervous about, buddy. The match is fixed; the stakes are as real as pro wrestling. Right, Special Agent Worth?"

Special Agent Worth flashed his Woody Harrelson grin. "That's right, Mitchell."

"Call me Mitch."

"OK, Mitch."

"Can I call you Eddie?"

"Sure, why not, Mitch? We are serving together, aren't we?"

"So, Eddie, now that we're on first-name terms, can I have a gun?"

The smile widened. "No, Mitch, you cannot have a gun."

"*He's* got a gun." Mitch pointed to Agent Tucker, who sat

on the other side of Jordan. Tucker was a muscular bulk with blond hair longer than regulation length. He listened to the interchange with an amused smile on his lips and a large black handgun strapped to his thigh.

"Agent Tucker is a sworn officer of the Federal Bureau of Investigation. You are a civilian. Have you ever fired a gun before?"

"No."

"Ever held one?"

"Nope."

"That settles it. Now don't ask me again," he said, still grinning, "or I'll have to shoot you."

Except for Special Agent Eddie Worth, they all wore black tactical gear with Velcro straps and black ski masks folded over the top of their heads. Jordan's skin looked green in the dull light of the ceiling bulb.

David said, "How are you holding up, Jordy?"

"I'll be glad when this is over."

David sympathized. The tactical gear restricted the flow of blood in his legs and made his crotch itch.

"Aw, c'mon, guys," Mitchell said. "This is the coolest thing we've ever done. How often do you get to break into the Met in the middle of the night, steal fifty million dollars' worth of golden eggs, and get away with it?"

Jordan said, "Once, I hope."

The van lurched to a halt.

"Looks like we're there, boys," Eddie said. "Earpieces in."

They shoved the single buds into their left ears and tested the miniature microphones strapped to their chins.

"King's Horses," Agent Tucker said. "This is Humpty, do you read us?"

"Humpty, this is King's Horses," came Amy's voice in the earbud. "Loud and clear. You have a green light."

"Masks on, boys," Eddie said. "Go get 'em."

The doors at the back of the van opened, and Special Agent Hernandez stood aside so they could pour into the night.

The midnight air carried a mild chill. David followed Agent Tucker along the sidewalk, his tactical black sneakers padding over the asphalt. They climbed a grassy mound and picked their way through a clump of trees and thickets. Crossing another stretch of grass, they crouched at the base of a twenty-foot wall of smooth stone.

Tucker wasted no time. He extracted the grapple hook from his black gear bag. Swinging it twice by the length of cord, he released the business end to launch over the wall and onto the roof. After hearing a satisfying clink, he pulled the cord to test the hook's traction.

"You two first," he whispered at David and Mitchell. "And stay low." Without waiting for a response, he threaded the BlueWater Assaultline through David's harness and shoved him forward.

David gripped the rope, leaned back, and walked up the wall. The line pulled downward as Mitchell followed. If David slipped, he'd take his friend down with him. David pushed the thought from his mind, putting one foot in front of the other. His muscles burned in his arms and legs, but soon he stepped over the upper ledge.

He'd done it! David had cleared the first obstacle. That wasn't so bad. When this was over, maybe he'd speak to Amy about joining the FBI. Or maybe he'd just ask her out. He stepped onto the roof and unhooked his harness from the rope. Sitting on his haunches, he stared through the roof and into the darkened hallways of the museum. David had known the roof was glass. Agent Tucker had warned them to walk only on the seams. But now, as he stared down into the void, a wave of vertigo overwhelmed him.

Mitchell bumped into him. "What's the matter?"

"The roof," David whispered back. "You can see right inside."

Mitchell peered downward in the moonlight. "Yeah, I know. Done sightseeing?"

"Right." Keeping his body as low as possible, David climbed the incline, stepping on the metal seams between the glass panes. The clump of trees had cloaked them as they'd scaled the wall, but the rooftop was in plain sight of the skyscrapers on Fifth Avenue. He hoped insomniac Peeping Toms wouldn't spot them and call the cops.

Reaching the top of the incline, he descended the downward slope and padded toward a door in the main building.

Mitchell joined him and they flattened their backs against the wall. "Oh, crap," Mitchell said, panting through the mouth hole of the ski mask.

"What?" Had someone spotted them?

"I forgot the case in the van."

"What?"

"The briefcase for the eggs. I left it in the van."

David swore. Now they had to go all the way back. Mitchell's screw-up might abort the entire mission.

"Just kidding. It's right here in the backpack."

David wanted to slap him. "You almost gave me a heart attack!"

"I got you, admit it."

David shook his head, then laughed despite himself. They were on track. Or were they?

"Where are the others?"

"I don't know. They were right behind us."

"They aren't anymore. What do we do?"

"We go ahead without them."

"You sure?"

"Yeah. Open the door."

David eased down the handle of the service door. "It's locked."

"Yeah, right."

"I'm serious, it's locked tight."

"Listen, David, I'm sorry I pulled your leg. I won't do it again. Now just open the door."

A voice crackled in David's ear. "Where the hell are you?" It was Agent Tucker. In all the excitement, David had forgotten all about their wireless communications equipment.

David pressed the talk button. "We're at the door."

"No, you're not. We're at the door."

Crap. David had led Mitchell to the wrong door. "We went straight ahead and we—"

"Never mind. Move due north and you'll find us."

"OK." To Mitchell, David said. "You heard him. We need to go due north."

"OK." Mitchell stayed put. "Which way is north?"

"I thought you knew!"

"No, I don't!"

This was ridiculous. David hoped Amy couldn't hear them. He wasn't cut out for this line of work. They were lost on the roof of the Met, dressed like cat burglars. They couldn't exactly ask a cop for directions. *Think, David, think!* "OK," he said. "The Met is on Fifth Avenue."

"So?"

"The avenues run north to south."

"Right!"

David pointed. "That's north."

Mitchell nodded. "Lead the way."

David moved along the side of the main building, then peeked around the corner. Agent Tucker and Jordan stood by a door and waved. "There they are!"

"Thank God!" On the rooftop of the Met, Mitchell had found religion.

"Welcome," Agent Tucker said as they met up. "Got your equipment?"

They nodded.

He glanced at his tactical, non-reflective wristwatch. "We have eighteen minutes before the sensors activate again. Make it quick."

Eighteen minutes. They had burned two minutes getting lost on the roof.

"Plenty of time," Mitchell said.

"It'll go faster than you think. Move!"

Tucker swung the door open, and David led the way inside. *Keep to the path*, Hernandez had said, and David did just that. He turned back every ten seconds to make sure Mitchell wasn't playing hide and seek. He found their marker, the service elevator, and followed the path he'd memorized and practiced only hours before.

Statues and displays cast ominous shadows in the glow of emergency light. David and Mitchell raced ahead and ignored everything else. David turned one final corner, and they glimpsed the Fabergé egg exhibit from a distance. The friends shared a celebratory smile. They were almost there.

A premonition loomed in David's heart as they approached the display case, and he almost expected the eggs to have vanished into thin air. But his fears were unwarranted. There they stood—all nine imperial eggs, fresh for the taking.

David removed his flattened backpack, extracted his equipment, and assembled the pieces. The suction pad stuck to the glass surface. As he'd practiced at the FBI training school, he drew a perfect circle around the center with the diamond-edged cutter. The glass circle gave way with little resistance.

Placing the equipment on the floor, he stuck his arm through the hole and grasped the first egg. Carefully, he extracted the egg and handed it to Mitchell, who pretended to drop it.

"Cut that out!" David hissed.

"Geez, you're jumpy tonight," Mitchell complained as he slipped the egg into the allotted foam hole in the open brief-case.

"Hmm. I don't know. Maybe it's because we just broke into the Metropolitan Museum!" David reached for the next egg. He was regretting inviting Mitchell to join the Trio.

"Chill out, dude. This'll be over in a minute. Then we'll all get back to our boring lives."

David moved the eggs, one by one. As the display case emptied, regret clouded his heart. Mitchell was right. This was a game, and soon the game would be over. When had he become such an uptight jerk?

"I'm sorry, Mitch," he said. "I guess I'm still wound up from the other night."

"No problemo, amigo."

David glanced down the hallway. When would he ever have the entire Metropolitan museum to himself again? He had half a mind to take the scenic route back to the roof, but he knew he wouldn't. They had minutes left before the sensors activated, and they were not home free yet.

Having extracted all the eggs, David released the suction pad from the glass and packed his equipment back into his bag while Mitchell zipped the briefcase into his backpack.

Amy's voice crackled in his ear. "King's Men, this is King's Horses, do you read me?"

David touched the microphone. King's Men was his call sign. "This is King's Men, reading you loud and clear."

"How are the hatchlings?" Despite the static interference, David thought he heard a playful lilt in her voice.

"Ready to come home."

"Roger that."

King's Men. King's Horses. Amy had assigned the call signs. She was the horse, David the rider. Was that a not-so-subtle innuendo?

"What are you smiling at?" Mitchell said.

David snapped back to reality. He hadn't thought the smile would show through the ski mask. "Nothing. Are we done?"

"Yep. Locked and loaded. Ready to roll."

"Good. Let's go."

He led the way back to the roof, his thoughts drifting back to Amy. He was looking forward to handing her the eggs, their mission completed. Then they could explore the metaphor of their call signs at leisure.

"This way," Agent Tucker said, seconds later. At the outer edge of the building, he hooked their harnesses to the cord. One by one, they rappelled down the wall of the museum and onto the soft patch of well-trimmed grass.

"What about the grapple hook?" Jordan asked when they'd all assembled on solid ground.

"It stays. A clue for the NYPD."

Startling noises tore the night, the roar of engines. A breeze hit David, and an off-road motorbike sped toward him, launching into a wheelie. The front wheel collided with Agent Tucker, who had reached for his gun. The SWAT team trainer sprawled on the ground and lay motionless. More engines growled from all directions, as three bikers churned circles in the grass around the Trio. The riders wore black from head to toe and aimed assault rifles at the trapped friends. David, Jordan, and Mitchell raised their hands over the heads, while David's heart rate shot heavenward.

"Dear God," he prayed. "Don't let us die here!"

A rider dismounted, tall and muscular. He motioned with his rifle. "On the ground!" he yelled, his gruff voice muffled by his full black helmet. "On the ground!"

The Trio complied and lay face-down on the grass. The rider slung his rifle over his shoulder and drew a large hunting knife from a sheath on his leg. Crouching on one knee, he gripped Mitchell by the head. *Oh, my God,* David thought, closing his eyes. *He's going to slit his throat!*

"No, please," Mitchell begged, "don't hurt me!"

David couldn't bear to look. There came a loud rip and then another, the sound of tearing fabric, not flesh. David opened an eye.

The rider inserted Mitchell's backpack into a pouch on his chest and mounted his bike again. Then, with a loud roaring of engines, the bikers sped off into the night.

CHAPTER 15

"Who took the eggs?" Special Agent Marco Hernandez yelled again. He had lost his patience even before they'd returned to the interrogation room.

David said, "We already told you, we don't know. We were working for you!"

Hernandez slapped the desk. "Bullshit! You're the only civilians who knew about the heist. You sold us out!"

"No, no, no," David said. "We were just doing our part to clear our names."

"He's right," Jordan seconded.

"Yeah," Mitchell thirded. "You're barking up the wrong tree. We're as stumped as you are."

Hernandez glared at the smirking Mitchell. "Tree? Stump? Are you busting my balls again? Because if you are, I'll throw you in a cell."

"No, Special Agent Hernandez," Mitchell said, failing to keep a straight face. "We're *rooting* for the same team." Hernandez lunged at Mitchell, but Special Agent Worth held him back. Mitchell did not interpret this as a sign that he should tone things down. He said, "Maybe if you'd given us guns we could have nipped those bikers in the bud!"

"Mitch," Jordan said, "if we'd had guns, we'd be dead."

The door opened, and Special Agent Amy Smith entered the room. It was three o'clock in the morning, and she looked tired and dazed. Armed thugs had intercepted the entire collection of imperial Fabergé eggs and escaped on motorbikes. The FBI had no clue who the culprits were or how they had discovered their covert operation. The agents would lose their jobs over this and, unlike most of the Trio, the agents needed their paychecks. David wanted to help Amy save the day more than anything.

"Agent Tucker woke up," she said. "The doctors say his condition is stable and they're transferring him out of the ICU." She gave them a brave grin. "Gentlemen, tell me more good news."

Special Agent Worth said, "No news is good news?"

Amy blinked at them and swallowed hard. "We've lost over fifty million dollars' worth of golden eggs. For now, NYPD thinks the bikers broke into the Met. They know nothing of our operation or how badly it went wrong. But unless we can retrieve the eggs in the next few days, we'll be in a whole new world of trouble. If we embarrass the Bureau, management will hang us out to dry."

Jordan said, "There must be a way to track the case."

"There was. We planted a GPS transmitter in the case, but the signal died soon after the interception. These people know what they're doing." She glanced at David and his friends. "Guys, now's the time to come clean. Because if we go down, you're going down with us."

David stared at her, open-mouthed. Was she going to scapegoat the Trio for the FBI's botched mission?

"Whoa," Jordan said. "We did our part. We played your game, broke into the Met, and stole the eggs. How are we to blame for any of this?"

"It's not stealing if they let us," Mitchell said.

Hernandez rolled up his sleeves. "I'll show you how you're to blame."

"Marco," Amy said, placing her hand on his shoulder. Her touch had the magical effect of calming him down. The lion tamer had just stepped into the ring. "He's right. They were acting on our instructions, and they have no reason to double-cross us." She sighed. "Criminal elements might have shown interest in the eggs as soon as the Met announced the exhibit. They might have followed the Trio and learned of our plans."

"Or," David said, eager to be of use, "maybe it's the Elders? They might have sent other operatives to steal the eggs."

"Right," Jordan said, "Maybe they told us to steal the eggs so we could take the blame? We were just decoys."

"We're not decoys!" Mitchell said.

"Mitch!" David and Jordan said as one. They were already knee-deep in trouble, and there was no need to keep digging.

"Maybe you're right," he conceded. "We were just a diversion. Who'd send a bunch of new recruits on such a risky mission, right?"

The agents stared at them in silence. The scenario made sense.

"OK," Amy said. "You're free to go." She turned to her colleagues. "We should all get some rest. Soon we'll need it."

The Trio changed back into their civilian clothes and returned their equipment. David hung around to say goodbye to Amy, but she'd already left.

The Trio piled into Jordan's Roadster and headed home.

"Phew, what a relief," Jordan said. "We're finally off the hook."

Mitchell shifted around on the cramped back seat but kept his complaints to himself.

"Yeah," David said. He had a hard time mustering enthusiasm for their operation's failure. Not only had he sunk his only opportunity to combat anti-Semitism, but he'd also let Amy down. His hopes for a future with the FBI team leader skipped further away. He'd always remind her of the worst bungled operation in her law enforcement career.

"We screwed that up, didn't we?"

Jordan chuckled, stopping at a red light. "Yeah, I guess we

did."

Mitchell spoke up from the backseat, a smile in his voice. "I wouldn't say the operation was a total loss." He leaned forward, extending his arm between the two front seats. In his hand, he held a shiny golden egg with an intricate silver lattice pattern and an immense diamond at its base.

David jumped. "What the hell, Mitch?"

Jordan said, "You stole an egg?"

"*We* stole them, remember? I just saved one of them. Imperial Coronation." His voice filled with wonder. "Do you want to see the chariot?"

"Put that away, Mitch!" David said, shoving his hand out of view of passersby. "What, are you crazy? How do you even still have that? The bikers took the briefcase."

"Calm down. It was just a joke. I slipped it into my pocket in the museum. I wanted to see their faces when they saw an egg was missing. That turned out well, don't you think?"

A horn blared behind them. The light had turned green. At 4 AM, some angry dude was waiting behind them. Welcome to Manhattan.

Jordan stepped on the accelerator. "You're taking that back."

"What? No way! My granddad had a chariot like this one."

"Mitch," David explained, "I don't think that'll stick in a court of law. It's not yours."

"I'll hang onto it for a while. The FBI thinks the eggs are gone. Who's it going to hurt?"

Reasons stampeded David's brain and got stuck in the bottleneck of his mouth. "Whatever. I can't handle this now. It's too late, and I'm too tired to argue. We'll speak later and work things out."

"If you say so. But you'll thank me for this one day."

David doubted that. Jordan dropped David outside his building. David took the elevator to his apartment, showered, and collapsed onto his bed.

He awoke in the early afternoon, still wrapped in his towel. He'd been so tired, he'd fallen asleep before dressing for bed.

He felt jet-lagged and shell-shocked. What had just happened? Had he really broken into the Met and stolen the Fabergé Imperial Collection? Had he really almost kissed Amy Smith?

He fixed a meal of scrambled eggs—a late brunch or an early dinner, he couldn't decide—then noticed the envelope peeking out from beneath his front door.

Making sure nobody was lurking in the corridor, he collected the envelope. A Zelig Pictures logo appeared on both the envelope and the letter within, which in terse and brutal terms warned him to vacate the apartment within three weeks.

David swore under his breath. Preston Clancy, the president of Zelig Pictures, had sent him another eviction notice. David liked his apartment. He liked his life in Manhattan. But the apartment belonged to Zelig Pictures, the company that bore his name, the company Preston Clancy had stolen from David's family. Preston had admitted as much to David's face, but without solid proof, David could do nothing. And with his bank balance depleting every day, soon he'd have to return to Los Angeles and move back in with his mom.

David trudged back indoors and tossed the rest of his breakfast in the trash. He'd lost his appetite. He pulled on his running shoes and hit the sidewalk to burn off the adrenaline and hurt that pumped through his veins.

Amy Winehouse sang "Valerie" in his earphones and helped clear his head. This proved to be a mistake. On autopilot, his legs took him to Central Park. He turned back only when he encountered the yellow police tape around the Met.

Back on his home block, he slowed to a walk, his shirt soaked in sweat. Sad reality hit him in the face. He'd blown his first and last FBI operation; he'd blown his chances with Amy Smith. The Trio was over. He needed a vacation and a change of scenery. A very long vacation, far away from Manhattan. The calming sandy-white beaches and turquoise conspiracy-free waters of the Maldives beckoned.

David leaned against a wall to stretch his tendons and remembered his recent financial woes. The vacation would have to wait. What he needed now was a job.

"Hey," a woman said. She had olive skin, intense dark eyes, and a tight black braid. "Good job," she said, unsmiling.

"Have we met?"

"The eggs," she said.

David almost peed his pants. "Wh—what eggs?" His slow recovery didn't fool her.

"What's the matter—don't you recognize me without a cloak?" she said.

Holy crap! The Islamic Elders of Zion had found him. Their operative had accosted him right outside his apartment building!

"My name is Nasim," she said. "Drop off the eggs at twelve PM this Sunday, corner Sixty-Fifth Street and Fifth Avenue. You got that?"

"Yes, but how did you...?"

David didn't get to complete the sentence. The woman walked off and disappeared into the flow of pedestrians.

CHAPTER 16

"They know where I live!" David said, trying not to yell. The Trio had gathered that afternoon in an FBI conference room to discuss their predicament. David's nightmare chickens had come home to roost in the form of Nasim, the Elders operative, outside his apartment building. His delusions of walking away from the secret society debacle unscathed had crumbled along with his plans for an exotic vacation.

"Which means," Jordan said, "they know where the rest of us live too."

"Jesus," Mitchell said. "What do we do now?"

Special Agents Amy Smith and Eddie Worth pondered the development with concern. Only Marco Hernandez seemed to enjoy the Trio's discomfort. At last, the rich kids were feeling the heat too. David held his breath, hoping Amy would wake him from this nightmare. Seeing her again was the only silver lining. *Enjoy her company while you can, David. You're a dead man walking.*

Eddie Worth said, "Well, we now know the Elders didn't take the eggs. They seem to believe the Trio pulled off the burglary."

"Unless this is a trap," Jordan said, the eternal optimist. "If they know where we live, they know our names. Zelig,

Brody, and Joffe. They know we're Jewish."

"Not necessarily," Hernandez said. "Maybe they followed David to his building but don't know which apartment is his."

"OK," Jordan conceded. "Let's suppose they aren't out to murder us yet and they expect us to deliver the eggs on Sunday. That's three days from now! What are we supposed to do?"

Jordan gave Mitchell a meaningful glare, his cue to confess to pocketing Imperial Coronation. Mitchell responded with a threatening glare of his own. Their wordless struggle went unnoticed by the FBI agents.

Amy said, "It's time to activate Plan B."

"There's a Plan B?" Jordan said. He sounded as surprised and relieved as David felt.

"Operation Evil Twin," Amy said.

First Humpty Dumpty, now Evil Twin. The operation code names did not inspire confidence in the Bureau.

Amy explained. "Before the heist, we created digital scans of the eggs, both inside and out. Operation Evil Twin involves creating exact replicas of the eggs and their surprises using the latest 3D printing technology. We started the process two days ago. The eggs will be ready in time for the drop-off."

"'Two days ago?" David asked.

"You didn't think we were planning on handing the Elders the real eggs, did you?"

David felt his cheeks redden. "No, of course not," he lied. The FBI regained some of its lost prestige in his eyes. Perhaps David would wake from this nightmare, after all?

"Are you serious?" said Jordan, the eternal pain-in-the-ass. "I don't think plastic eggs will fool the Elders."

"The printer uses lead along with fine layers of gold and silver. The printed eggs will match the real eggs in every scratch and imperfection. Only an expert jeweler will be able to tell them apart. And the Elders won't suspect foul play. You've started to win their trust. The visit from an undisguised operative proves that. It's likely you'll meet other Elders of Zion members, perhaps even the Grandmaster."

David's heart jumped in his ribcage. The Grandmaster had picked on him during their first meeting, and David was not looking forward to a replay.

"This is the opening we've been hoping for," Amy continued and looked at David. "A chance to plant a tracker on the inner circle of the Elders."

"To plant a tracker?" David said. That sounded risky. "How are we going to pull that off?"

"The Bureau will provide training, and we'll guide you every step of the way."

David's insides squirmed. The Trio had bungled the Fabergé heist, despite the controlled environment and no small amount of FBI hand-holding. This time, they would perform alone, in public, and without a safety net.

"I don't know," he said. "This is way over our heads."

Amy held his gaze. "I know this is difficult, David. Believe me, if I could go in your place, I would. But the Elders are expecting you. Once you've provided the eggs and planted the trackers, the Bureau will take over and dismantle the Elders. You'll all be home free."

David turned to his friends. Jordan frowned but inclined his head in reluctant consent. Mitchell's head bobbed up and down, almost drooling with anticipation. David raised his hands in surrender. "OK, one last operation."

"Great! Eddie, please notify Operations."

"Will do." Eddie Worth hurried out of the conference room.

Mitchell said, "This time we get guns, right?"

Hernandez said, "No guns, Mitchell."

Mitchell rolled his eyes. "Whatever."

"Wait a minute," Jordan said. "The drop off is twelve PM this Sunday, right?"

"Yeah."

"Corner of Sixty-Fifth Street and Fifth Avenue?"

Amy shrugged. "That's what David said."

"*This* Sunday?" Jordan looked to his friends with expectation. They disappointed him. "C'mon, guys, *this* Sunday?"

"Just spit it out," Mitchell said.

Jordan shook his head at their abysmal ignorance.

Amy said, "Is there a problem?"

"A problem. No, no problem." They had activated Jordan's passive-aggressive streak. "I just think you might have trouble guiding us among all the crowds."

"Crowds? What crowds?"

Then David understood, and he swore under his breath. They were doomed. "This Sunday," he said, "is the Israel Day Parade."

CHAPTER 17

"I've got a bad feeling about this," David said, Sunday morning. The Trio waited in an empty Bureau apartment on Sixty-Fifth Street, where the FBI had walked the three friends through the plan one final time. The Israel Day Parade had started an hour ago and the band music of the approaching marchers grew louder through the second-floor window. "A drop-off in the middle of the Israel Day Parade—that can't be a coincidence."

"It isn't," Amy said. "Crowded streets are harder to observe. And the Elders know law enforcement will hold back to prevent civilian casualties."

"Jewish casualties," Jordan said.

"Exactly. For the Elders, Jews are expendable."

"Just follow our instructions," Hernandez said, "and you'll be fine. We have snipers on the rooftops and a dozen plainclothes agents in the crowd."

Eddie Worth chuckled. "Along with the rest of the NYPD." He peered out the window. "I've never seen so many beat cops in one place."

Amy raised a small black dot between her forefinger and thumb. The dot was paper-thin. "This is the tracking device. Nanotechnology, state-of-the-art. You get two each. Slip them into the targets' pockets or attach them to the inner linings of their clothing as we showed you. The Velcro fibers allow easy attachment."

She handed the dots to the Trio while the other two FBI officers pulled black Kevlar jackets over their civilian clothes.

"Do we get those too?" David asked.

Amy shook her head. "Protective vests will only raise suspicion. You're meeting with an ally, remember? The same goes for earbuds. And no, Mitchell," she said, as he opened his mouth to speak, "no guns today either."

"All set?" Eddie asked them.

David eyed Jordan and Mitchell. They had passed the point of no return. Everything rested on their performance today. But unlike their previous operation, the Trio was on its own. They drew deep breaths and nodded.

"Don't forget the eggs," Hernandez said. He hefted a metallic briefcase identical to the one the black bikers had stolen outside the Met.

David drew near. "Can we have a look? Our lives depend on the quality of those eggs."

Hernandez shrugged. "Trust me, you've got nothing to worry about."

He opened the briefcase on the table. Nine golden eggs lay in their padded beds of black foam. David extracted the replica of Imperial Coronation, the egg Mitchell had pilfered. As far as he could tell, the egg, which had the weighty feel of the other eggs he had handled, was indistinguishable from the original.

"Here, Mitch," David said, holding out the egg. "You've held the real ones. What do you think?"

Mitchell eyed David with suspicion, then accepted the egg. He studied the silver patchwork exterior and the diamond at its base. Opening the egg, he extracted the golden chariot. "It's perfect," he said. "Great job." He placed the egg back in the designated cutout.

Hernandez shut the briefcase, closed the latches, and handed the eggs to David. "There's no lock or code," he said.

Amy said, "We'll observe your progress from here then support you from the street if necessary. Help is only a few steps away. Any questions?"

David studied her eyes. One question had buzzed in his head ever since he'd met her. Was she interested in him? During the past few days, they had shared a few more brief moments together. To demonstrate the technique of slipping the practice trackers on a target, she'd stepped behind him, so close he could feel her breath on the nape of his neck. Again, an electric charge had passed between them, making his skin prickle. He could have sworn her hand had lingered in his jeans pocket a moment longer than was necessary. Now the buzz of that question was impossible to ignore. But this was neither the time nor the place for an intimate conversation.

The friends shook their heads. They had no questions.

"Then good luck, and see you on the other side."

The other side. The phrase triggered David's premonitions again.

"Thanks."

The friends filed out of the apartment and started down the stairs.

David halted at the sound of his name. Amy stood in the passageway, her face tight with concern. Was she worried he'd get hurt? David walked back to her. They stood very close, gazing into each other's eyes, an irresistible gravitational field pulling them closer. *Kiss her, you fool!*

Amy broke eye contact and stared at her feet, suddenly fidgety and vulnerable. "I just wanted to say I'm sorry you got mixed up in all this."

David swallowed hard. "I'm not."

Gravity took over. They lunged at each other, their lips meeting, their bodies pressing together for two stolen, ecstatic seconds until Amy pulled away.

"Go," she whispered, her voice raw with the effort of restraint.

David nodded, then rushed to the stairwell. A smile cracked his face from ear to ear. "Yes!" he wanted to shout.

"She's into me!" A cloud of bright butterflies exploded in his core, shattering all ominous gut feelings. Amy wanted him! No number of gun-toting secret societies could stop him from nailing his mission and returning to her, victorious.

He burst through the doorway and onto the street. The world raged with color and sound. People thronged the streets, waving American and Israeli flags. White tents and canopies stood over the sidewalk, covered in the blue Star of David. The mayor of New York linked arms with a line of dignitaries and marched behind a banner that read "Celebrating Israel." Smiles greeted David wherever he turned. This was a great day. A most wonderful day. David would ace this operation and return to Amy's arms. They would never be apart again.

"What's with him?" Jordan asked Mitchell, who shrugged. "Dave, you do realize we could all die soon?"

"Don't be silly, Jordy. The FBI has got our backs."

"Our six," Mitchell said. "They've got our six. That's what the Marines say. I heard that on TV."

"Yeah, guys!" David declared. "Today we're marines. We're heroes. Now let's take those anti-Semites down. They won't even see us coming."

"What has he been smoking?" Jordan asked Mitchell, despairing of a sober response from David. "What did you give him?"

"C'mon, guys. Let's get into position."

The friends put on their identical pairs of sunglasses and waded through the sea of people toward the corner of Sixty-Fifth Street and Fifth Avenue. The sunglasses had been Mitchell's idea.

David scanned the crowds for Nasim's dark braids. He scanned for black cowls. A handful of men in dark glasses stared back at him. Were those Elders of Zion operatives or the FBI agents Hernandez had mentioned?

His wristwatch read 12:02 PM. *Crap!* They had arrived late at the rendezvous point. Had the Elders split when the Trio didn't show on time? Did they suspect a trap? High overhead, helicopter blades sliced the air. David imagined FBI snipers tracking them in their crosshairs from the rooftops. Amy and her colleagues waited, ready to spring at any moment. David resisted the urge to glance back at the FBI apartment. *Just stay calm, Dave. Stay cool.*

A finger tapped his shoulder. A young Middle Eastern woman with black braids and glasses brushed past him and marched up Fifth Avenue, against the stream. David elbowed his friends and hurried after Nasim. Pushing against the flow of smiling faces and waving flags, he struggled to keep up with her.

The Elders operative turned left onto Sixty-Sixth, and the Trio followed at a trot. David rounded the corner. The crowds thinned off Fifth Avenue. Nasim was a hundred yards ahead and showed no sign of slowing. David broke into a jog, the briefcase swinging at his side.

"What the hell is this," Mitchell grumbled between breaths, "the New York City Marathon?"

"She's drawing us," Jordan said, huffing and puffing, "away from our team."

Crap! He was right. The Trio had slipped away from the FBI apartment. Any covert agents following them would blow their cover. David hoped Amy's snipers still had eyes on them and would send their support team in the right direction.

Just as they were catching up with Nasim, she turned left onto Madison Avenue, then left again into Sixty-Seventh Street. David, the street jogger, had no trouble keeping up, but he could not say the same for his friends. If they survived today, he'd legislate regular exercise at the Trio's next meeting. But there would never be another Trio meeting, would there?

"We're heading back," Jordan said, "the way we came. Two... blocks down."

Two blocks. Would that throw off the FBI snipers?

At the end of the street, the crowds thickened again. A white tent with a blue Star of David occupied a square of sidewalk near the street corner. Nasim slowed, allowing them to close the gap, and then she slipped through the overlapping tent folds. David gave his friends a surprised glance as they followed her inside.

Nasim faced the panting Trio in the empty tent. She hadn't broken a sweat. "Government agents followed us," she said. "I think we threw them off."

David hazarded a smile. "Good," he said. The tip of an electronic earbud poked out her ear. The Elders had operatives of their own in the field, and they'd gotten the better of the FBI.

"I'm Nasim," she said, removing her sunglasses and eyeing the other two members of the Trio. "And you are?"

The Trio dispensed with their sunglasses too. They had discussed this question with Amy, who had assigned them each a fictitious name. The ploy would tell them how safe their true identities were.

"Dean," David said. Nasim didn't argue but gave Jordan an expectant look. The gamble had paid off. There really was a chance they'd kept their real identities safe.

"Jake," said Jordan.

"Mitchell," said Mitchell. He wasn't trying to screw them over. The FBI had recommended using Gentile-sounding names, and Mitchell's given name fit the bill.

Nasim glanced at the briefcase in David's hand. "That the eggs?"

David nodded.

She held out her hand, and David handed over the briefcase. She unlatched and opened the case, then examined the contents, gold glinting in her dark eyes.

"The tracker," David's inner spy yelled. *"Now's your chance!"* He looked her up and down, but her clothing had no pockets or sleeves. Slipping his hand into his jeans pocket, he snagged a small dot between the tips of his fingers. Attaching the tracker required physical contact, and Nasim did not seem like the touchy-feely type.

Nasim shut the briefcase and dangled it by the handle.

"Good work," she said. Their meeting was coming to a close. *Don't let her go! Plant the tracker!* But how? He made eye contact with Jordan, who gave his head a subtle shake. *Chickenshit!* Mitchell blinked at him, feigning stupidity. *It's up to you, Dave.*

He was about to lean in for a very awkward hug, when she said, "The Grandmaster is pleased with your performance. He wants to congratulate you in person."

David gulped. "What, now?" Amy had been right—the heist had gained them access to the secret society's inner circle. Why waste his tracker on Nasim when he could hook the big fish. David's knees threatened to buckle.

On cue, the back flaps of the tent parted and two men entered. Both had dark Middle Eastern complexions and wore, not black cloaks, but jeans and T-shirts. Otherwise, they looked nothing alike. The stocky henchman with the pockmarked face trailed a grinning bald man with perfect teeth and a well-trimmed goatee.

Nasim bowed low. "Grandmaster, I give you Dean, Jake, and Mitchell."

"Ah, the Trio," the Grandmaster said, his Arabic accent both undeniable and familiar. "My name is Abdul. You have proven yourselves critical to our cause. On behalf of the Elders, I thank you."

Imitating Nasim, David bowed his head. "The honor is ours, Grandmaster."

The secret society leader turned to Nasim. "The Imperial Collection?"

Nasim held the briefcase out and opened the lid for inspection. Outside the tent, a saxophone played the Israeli anthem, The Hope, and voices in the crowd sang along.

The Grandmaster's smile widened as he gazed upon the Fabergé eggs. "Very good." Nasim closed the case and handed it to her leader.

"You'll be happy to know," he continued, "that the plans for our major operation are complete. With this," he hefted the case, "soon we will turn those plans into actions."

David used their new familiarity to learn more. "Grandmaster, if you don't mind me asking, what is this major operation?"

Abdul searched David's eyes with renewed interest, and David groaned within. Had he pushed his luck and aroused the cult leader's suspicions?

"But of course," the Grandmaster said. "It is only fitting that you should know the meaning of your hard work. A week from now, the Jews will gather at their infamous JAPI Convention. This year, the Elders will also attend—with fire and brimstone." He chuckled at the thought. "Imagine— thousands of Jewish powerbrokers snuffed out in one deadly attack!"

David's face went cold. Despite the balmy weather, ice flowed in his veins. The eggs were fake, he reminded himself. But if the copies had duped the Elders, would their black market buyers accept them as the genuine article too? David had wanted to keep Jews safe, but now he had just helped fund the most devastating slaughter of Jews ever plotted on American soil!

"Congratulations, Dean of the Trio!" Abdul held out his hand. David stared at it. His limbs had turned to Jell-O and so had his mind.

A soft, distant voice in his head said, *The tracker, you numb-skull. The tracker!*

David gripped the little dot between trembling forefingers. He reached for Abdul's evil hand, squeezed it—*my palms are clammy, has he noticed?*—then he stepped forward and gave the Grandmaster a brotherly pat on the shoulder.

Taken aback, Abdul glanced at the hand on his shoulder and released his grip on David's own hand. "What is this?" The joy had fled his voice.

His henchman leaned closer, squinting. His thick fingers picked a small black speck from his leader's white T-shirt and handed the tracking dot to the Grandmaster.

A number of excuses jumbled in David's mind—a fleck of fabric; a particle of stray confetti—but none exited his mouth.

Abdul crushed the dot between his fingers, and metallic components cracked. The broken tracker dropped to the sidewalk. An enraged snarl twisted the Grandmaster's visage. "Traitors!" he declared, a judge delivering a death sentence. "Traitors!"

In a flurry of activity, two large handguns appeared and pointed at the Trio. "On your knees!" Nasim yelled. "Now!"

David waited for the FBI to burst in. He waited for a sniper to shoot through the canvas tent and waylay the terrorists. Two excruciating seconds later, nothing had changed.

"I said, 'On your knees!'" David's knees finally buckled. Jordan and Mitchell joined him. "Hands behind your heads."

"Finish them," the Grandmaster growled, "once I'm clear." With that, he disappeared through the tent flaps, briefcase in hand.

"Any last words, traitorous scum?" Nasim hissed.

True to form, David had prepared none. He thought of his mom and how sad she would be. At least his dad had not lived to see this. He thought of Amy Smith and how he'd never kiss her again or find out what their future together might hold. His two best friends were about to die because of him and his stupid, stupid ideas. Haters had butchered Jews around the world and throughout history. Their senseless deaths had grieved and enraged David, but never for a moment had he seriously considered that he might suffer the same fate. David had lived a comfortable and good life. Pity he'd thrown it away. Nothing could save him now.

David closed his eyes and braced for the worst.

CHAPTER 18

"What do you mean 'They're gone'?" she yelled at him.

Special Agent Marco Hernandez had served over twenty operations with Special Agent Amy Smith. Through them all, she'd been unflappable. But today, she had flapped.

Marco repeated the information the sniper had relayed on the communications radio. "We have no eyes on them. They were last seen heading up Fifth Avenue."

"What about Nasim?"

"They spotted a woman of her description but they're not sure it's her."

Amy swore. He'd never seen her so riled up. Even when the heist at the Met had ended in disaster, Amy had kept her cool, calling in reserve agents and directing search teams. But this was their second mission in a row to slide out of control, and their team would not survive another spectacular failure.

Special Agent Eddie Worth said, "Let me speak with them." He took the receiver from Marco and pressed Call. "Doppelganger, this is Superwoman Base. Do you read me?"

Their team's call names, thick with pop culture references, were why many other law enforcement teams liked to work with them. Operation Evil Twin had inspired some memorable ones.

Amy listened, her arms folded over her chest while he waited for a response on the radio. Amy buffered her team from the crap the higher-ups offloaded on her whenever an operation went sideways. Marco wished she'd open her heart and share the burden. In their years of service together, he'd grown to care for her. Often, he wished to be more than her friend and colleague. But Amy was professional to a fault and pretended not to notice his advances. Romantic relationships with subordinates were out of the question. Now a hot spark of jealousy fired within Marco. Was her abrupt change in demeanor the result of their recent failures or because of the source who'd fallen off the grid?

"Superwoman Base," the radio crackled. "This is Doppelganger. Reading you loud and clear."

Eddie said, "Do you have eyes on Dick Tracy?"

Translation: Had the snipers spotted the Trio?

The speaker crackled again. "That's a negative."

"What about Grendel?"

Grendel meant Nasim or other Elders of Zion operatives.

"That's a negative too."

Amy swore, and the hot spark within Marco burned brighter. Amy and David might think nobody had noticed their personal interactions over the past week, but Marco had. A pool of boiling bile rose in his gut whenever he saw the pretty, rich kid. Marco had worked long and hard to get here. The world might bow at the privileged feet of David Zelig, but Marco wouldn't let him steal his girl.

"What if there's no Grendel?" Marco said as soon as the idea struck.

"What do you mean?"

"The only information we have on Nasim comes from the Trio. What if they've set us up?"

"Oh, come on, Marco."

"What if they're working for the Elders? Think about it, Amy. How did the bikers know exactly when and where to intercept the eggs?"

Amy scoffed. "You're not making any sense. If the Elders

already have the eggs, why the wild goose chase?"

She had stumped him. "I don't know. Maybe they want the duplicates too? Maybe they just want to make us look stupid?"

She scoffed again. "We don't need any help with that." Her face stiffened. "What was that? Did you hear that?" Marco had—the unmistakable staccato of gunfire. As the shots ended, cries of panic took over as the Israel Day Parade dispersed. "How many shots was that—five, six?"

"Jesus," Eddie said. "We should've given them guns."

Amy grabbed the receiver. "Superwoman Base to Doppelganger. What the hell is going on out there?"

"Superwoman, we have multiple rounds fired on the corner of Sixty-Seventh Street and Fifth Avenue. We're getting eyes on the location as we speak. It's a mess out here. People are running in all directions and we have multiple friendlies with weapons drawn."

"Any sign of Dick Tracy?"

"Negative."

She released the talk button. "Marco, are the trackers moving?"

He knew what she was asking. If the Trio had planted a tracker on the Elders, the signal would reveal their target's location. If they'd failed, a moving signal would mean the Trio was alive.

Marco pulled up the tracking application on his open laptop. He swore. "We have five of six signals on the corner of Sixty-Seventh Street and Fifth Avenue."

Amy looked over his shoulder. "They're not moving. Why aren't they moving?" she asked, but she knew full well. "Eddie, we're going out."

"Yes, ma'am." He grabbed his semi-automatic rifle.

The situation was spiraling out of control. "Don't do this," Marco pleaded. He couldn't let her risk her life for those entitled brats. "We don't know what we're up against."

Amy slung her rifle strap over her head. "I sent them out there. I'll bring them back."

"Amy, they're probably dead already. Running around with guns out there, you'll draw friendly fire too."

She tossed the receiver to Marco. "Stay with Doppelganger. Get a bird in the sky."

"From where?"

"I don't care, just get it done."

Amy and Eddie rushed out of the apartment in their Kevlar jackets.

"Wait," Marco called, but it was too late.

He grabbed the receiver and switched the frequency to that of the New York State Integrated Command. "Superwoman Base to Command, we have agents in pursuit of an ongoing incident and we need an eye in the sky."

"This is Command," a man's voice answered, irritated. "Who the hell is this?"

"Superwoman—"

"Cut the mumbo jumbo. Who is this?"

"Special Agent Marco Hernandez, sir. FBI."

"FBI? We don't have any FBI on the war board. Did you clear this with Central?"

Marco had been afraid he'd bring that up. "This is an unscheduled op." He winced. Unlike many special teams in the FBI, Amy's worked beneath the radar of interagency coordination. They were desperate to keep this operation under wraps until they could either take down the Elders or return the eggs or both.

"You're out of luck, son. All our birds have flown. We have a situation on Fifth Avenue."

"That's where we're at, sir. Corner of Sixty-Seventh Street and Fifth Avenue."

The silence on the line could have sliced a metal rod. A different voice broke the silence, and it spoke with annoyance and authority. Marco cringed. "This is Chief Evans of the NYPD. Who am I speaking to?"

Marco wanted to crawl under a rock and die. "Special Agent Marco Hernandez."

"Special Agent Hernandez, who shot up our Israel Day

Parade?"

"Hard to tell, sir."

Outside, the staccato of semi-automatic gunfire erupted again.

"Because if you had anything to do with this—"

"Be right back, sir." Marco switched back to their operational frequency. They had requested separate radios for multiple frequencies, but the duplication of the Fabergé eggs had drained their team's budget.

"For the tenth time," Amy's voice yelled, "do you read me?"

"Superwoman Base here, I read you."

"Where the hell have you been?"

"Ordering that bird, ma'am."

"We're taking fire!"

The floor fell out of Marco's stomach. His worst fears had materialized. In the background, bullets ricocheted off asphalt and concrete. "How many perps? What weaponry?"

A man cried out in the background.

"Eddie's down! I need a medevac. Call it in."

Marco forgot all about radio call names. "Amy, get out of there!"

"I have eyes on Dick Tracy."

"Are they alive?"

"I can't tell. Where the hell is that medevac? I'm going in." She was going to risk her life for those spoiled, rich bastards.

"No, Amy, don't!" Her response was an earful of static. "Amy? Amy!"

Marco grabbed his rifle and ran down the stairwell.

CHAPTER 19

On his knees in the tent and with his eyes closed, David flinched as three shots rang out in the dark. A body thumped to the ground. His body. His death had been loud but painless. He floated there, a disembodied spirit.

Another barrage of shots followed, even louder than the first volley. Something metallic clattered to the ground, and a pair of feet ran away. The afterlife was noisy and confusing. His spirit could hear but not see.

David opened his eyes. He knelt on the sidewalk, his hands still behind his head. The henchman lay on the ground in a puddle of blood. Dots of red spatter covered the white wall of the tent like spray paint. Nasim had disappeared, leaving a small pile of spent casings on the floor and a gap in the flaps at the back of the tent.

David stared at the dead man. He'd never seen an actual corpse before, certainly not one so recently and messily deceased. Even at his father's funeral, he'd only seen the casket. As the terror of the sight faded, another thought arose in his mind. He was not dead.

He turned to his friends on either side. "Guys, they saved us!"

"Who?" Jordan asked, his eyes transfixed on the bloody

corpse.

"The FBI, who else?"

Mitchell stared into vacant space, for once speechless.

A rifle barrel poked between the flaps at the side of the tent. The barrel grew into an assault rifle held in black-gloved hands. Two armed men in black tactical gear and balaclavas entered the tent, rifles at the ready. Amy's FBI team had worn Kevlar jackets over their clothing. This must be SWAT. The first officer, tall and ripped like a bodybuilder, glanced at David.

"Oh, thank God you're here," David said. He pointed at the other flap. "She went that way."

In return for David's willing cooperation, the bodybuilder punched him in the face. David toppled over. He was about to ask, "Hey, why d'you do that?" when a hard black boot kicked him in the gut, winding him and emptying him of follow-up questions.

Gloved hands pulled his arms behind his back, zipped his wrists together with cable ties, and yanked him to his feet. Outside the tent, a black van idled, similar to the FBI van that had carried the Trio to the Met. In the streets, pandemonium reigned. Men and women ran and shrieked. Most ran away from the Trio and their black-clad captors.

"Get in," the man said. David obeyed, climbing into the van and sitting on the low, hard bench along the interior wall. Jordan and Mitchell joined him, their hands tied behind their backs.

"I don't think they're FBI," Jordan muttered.

"I think I'm going to puke," Mitchell said, as the body-builder gunman climbed into the back of the van and closed the doors.

The van lurched forward without warning. The friends slammed into each other, then slid off the bench and onto the hard floor. More shots sounded outside, a long spurt of automatic fire. David could see little in the darkness. Black paint obstructed the windows. *Who are these people, and why have they taken us?* David had no idea what was happening or where they were going.

The driver hit the brakes, and David's friends pressed against him on the floor of the van. Something hammered the side of the van, and long fingers of sunlight pierced the darkness through holes above David's head.

"Stay down!" he cried, as another row of bullet holes peppered the wall of the van. Who the hell was firing at them, and would they please stop?

The gunman in their van had survived the attack. He swung open the back doors and fired his rifle. The air was alive with the ping and pong of rounds fired and bullets ricocheting off walls and asphalt. The gunman jumped out of the van and hurried away, abandoning his captives, as the whine of unseen motorcycle engines tore the surrounding air.

David stole a glance out the back of the van. A smaller van, another black GMC, had crashed into a barrier on the edge of the sidewalk. Balaclava-clad gunmen poured out of the sliding side door and fired their weapons at unseen targets. Return fire chipped the road's surface and sent bits of street flying. One fighter fell to the ground and twitched on the asphalt. The others ran for cover and disappeared out of view. The drop-off had turned Manhattan into a war zone, with the Trio caught in the middle.

"Is this real?" Mitchell said, his voice monotone, his eyes glazed over.

"Just keep your head down," David said. He didn't know whether to stay put or take his chances outside. Police sirens wailed and helicopter rotors purred high overhead.

Two figures crept along the city block at the foot of the tall buildings. They wore Kevlar jackets and gripped rifles. Amy and Eddie! David lifted his head and waved. Could they see him? The FBI agents took cover in a recessed doorway, as unseen gunmen fired on their position. Amy peeked around the corner, her rifle drawn. She peered at David and, for a moment, relief flashed over her face. She'd seen him! The FBI was here to get them. David knew he could count on her. But they were two agents against dozens of well-armed criminals.

David had to get to Amy and prevent her from exposing herself to enemy fire. He crept toward the open doors at the back of the van.

"Dave, what are you doing?" Jordan said.

David pointed. "Amy and Eddie are over there."

"Yes, but that's a battlefield."

"If we can just—"

Gunfire ripped the silence and tore chunks from the walls of the building. The FBI agents dived back behind the wall, but not fast enough. Eddie lay on his back, yelping, and Amy dragged him out of view.

"Jesus," Mitchell said. "They shot Eddie. I liked Eddie."

"He's OK," Jordan said, with little conviction. "He'll be OK."

"He's screaming."

"Screaming means he's still alive!"

David backed away from the rear door of the van. He had no Kevlar vest, no assault rifle, and the barrage of shots had come from behind their van. He'd be a sitting duck. "C'mon, Amy. Call in the big guns." David didn't know what big guns she had on call, but that option sounded better than running into a firing squad.

Amy poked her head around the corner.

"No," David said aloud. "Don't do it."

But she did. Head down and her rifle blazing, Amy charged toward the second bullet-riddled van. David couldn't watch; he couldn't take his eyes off her either. *Come on, Amy. You can make it. You have to!* When this was over, she'd get a medal of honor, a Purple Heart or whatever the FBI gave agents who went above and beyond the call of duty to save lives.

Miraculously, Amy reached the other van unscathed as bullets pelted the street around her. But the vehicle offered little protection. Spraying another burst of bullets at her unseen attackers, Amy dived into the side of the van and slid the door shut.

The gunfire settled, smoke wafting in the air along with the acrid smell of burnt powder. Amy had reached the van, but the shooters had trapped her, just like David. The van jiggled on its suspension as she moved around inside. What was she up to?

Of course! The smaller van was one large interior compartment. Amy could climb into the driver's seat and back up the van toward the Trio. Once inside, they would all speed away to safety.

"Guys," David said, "get ready to jump ship."

"What, are you crazy?" Jordan said.

"Amy's going to back up the other van. When it gets near, be ready to—" But he didn't finish the sentence.

A bright cloud of flame blinded David for a moment. Heat scorched his eyebrows, and a shockwave shoved him backward. The burning hulk of the other van bounced on melting wheels as flames licked through empty holes where the windows had been. The other van—Amy's van—had exploded.

"No," David said. "No!"

Feet stomped the street. The bodybuilder gunman climbed back into their van. This time, he'd brought a friend. David stared past them at the flaming carnage on the street. The floor of the vehicle shifted once more as the driver returned and revved the engine. Then, as David's heart lay smoldering on the asphalt, the back doors closed, shutting out daylight, and the van sped off.

CHAPTER 20

Marco jogged along Fifth Avenue to Sixty-Seventh Street in his Kevlar jacket. He might have wandered onto the movie set of *Godzilla*. American and Israeli flags littered the streets, sidewalks, and islands as civilians fled in every direction. He stepped over abandoned posters, banners, shoes, and shopping bags. But that pandemonium was nothing compared to what waited around the corner.

Sixty-Seventh Street was a war zone. Motionless bodies in black tactical gear sprawled on the ground amid the detritus of cement chunks and broken glass. Blood flowed into the gutters. Gunfire had riddled the street with bullets and shattered the windows of hotels and apartments. In the distance, a GMC burned, and two black motorbikes lay on their sides.

SWAT officers walked among the ruins and inspected the fallen bodies. Marco had missed the battle. He offloaded his panic and fear on the nearest law enforcement officer.

"FBI," he yelled. "Where the hell are the perps?" The stocky SWAT officer looked like he could flatten Marco with one beefy hand, but right now Marco didn't care.

The officer glanced at Marco's badge. "Choppers lost them in Central Park," he said, "but not before we took a few of them down." The officer didn't seem upset about the gunmen's escape. With his heavy boot, he prodded one of the prone bodies. "This one won't tell us much, but we caught a whole vanload of black terrorists on Sixty-Eighth."

"Black terrorists?"

"Mm-hm. Like the ones who shot up that kosher store in Jersey City. They're an extremist faction of the Black Hebrew Israelites. Armed to the teeth, they were about to attack the parade when all hell broke out on the street."

Marco considered the dead white gunman, who looked more like a well-trained European assassin than a trigger-happy black supremacist. But he couldn't tell the NYPD man about the Elders of Zion.

The SWAT officer wrinkled his brow. "I didn't know the FBI was operating here today."

"You still don't," Marco said, already walking down the street.

Two paramedics wheeled a stretcher toward the back of an ambulance. The man on the stretcher groaned, and Marco ran to him.

"Eddie! What happened?" The paramedic pressed his hand to Eddie's shoulder, which seeped blood.

"Too many," Eddie said, his face a grimace of pain. "Couldn't stop..."

"Eddie, where's Amy?"

Eddie pointed with his good hand and winced. "She... She went to get the Trio. The gunmen took them. I told her it was too dangerous." He teared up.

"Eddie, where is she?"

"The van. She went to the van."

"Sir," a paramedic said, "we need you to step aside. This man needs medical attention."

Marco backed off, and the paramedics loaded the stretcher into the ambulance.

The gunmen had taken the Trio. Marco could understand why they'd take the eggs, but why capture the Trio? Why not kill them instead?

He had warned Amy against trusting those rich kids. They

thought they were above the law. For all Marco knew, David and his friends had been working with the Elders all along. To think he'd helped them break into the Met and steal the eggs. Marco ran his hand through his hair. Ever since they'd teamed up with the Trio, their operations had nosedived.

He had to find Amy and make her take his suspicions seriously. If she had feelings for David Zelig, her love would turn to hate once she saw how he'd swindled them all.

Marco trudged down the street, his rifle slung over his shoulders. Amy had gone to the van, Eddie had said, but the only van Marco could see was a flaming wreck. The tires gave way as he approached and the doors slipped from their hinges. The windows were gaping holes. Something had torn through the back, leaving a large crater-like gash. What a mess. The Elders must have launched a bazooka at the vehicle.

He glanced up and down the street. Where was Amy? She was not among the dead, and she'd never abandon an injured agent. *She went to the van.*

Dread piled in his chest. No, it couldn't be. Marco stepped closer to the burning wreck. Shielding his eyes from the searing heat with his arm, he peered inside through the crater.

His arms dropped to his sides. Inside the van lay a charred human figure. Like the luckless residents of Pompeii, their last moments preserved in the ash of Vesuvius, the form of a woman crouched on the floor of the van. Her hands clutched a semi-automatic rifle, and smoke rose from her Kevlar jacket.

"No," Marco said aloud, fighting back the truth. Special Agent Amy Smith, his team leader and the only woman he loved, was now a lifeless lump of charcoal. "No!"

Even as the pain of her loss hollowed out his heart, Marco's hands curled into hard fists. David Zelig had done this. And David Zelig would pay.

CHAPTER 21

"This is all your fault!" Jordan hissed, later that afternoon.

"My fault?" Mitchell hissed back. "How is this my fault?"

David slumped cross-legged on the hard, uneven floor of the dungeon. There was no other word for their new accommodations. When the thugs had shoved him forward and the blindfold had come off, David had still found himself in darkness. Ragged rocks formed the walls of the cramped chamber. Ancient hinges had groaned as the thugs, now wearing gray cowled robes, had slung the heavy wooden door shut and turned the key in the lock. The bad guys sure liked their cloaks.

In the murky darkness, water dripped. David had no strength left for arguments. Seared into his mind's eye was the image of a burning van.

Amy was dead. She had died trying to save David and his friends. He would never kiss her again. They would never build a life together. He had lost her forever. *Amy was dead.* Nothing mattered anymore.

"You couldn't just do as you were told, could you?" Jordan said. "No, you had to steal that effing egg." He performed a high-pitched and not very accurate impersonation of Mitchell. "'Chill out, dudes. One day, you'll thank me for this.' Well, look where that got us. Thanks a lot, *dude*!"

Mitchell said, "The egg has nothing to do with this. We gave the Elders a complete set of Ferrero-Rocher."

"Fabergé, you imbecile. It's *Fa-ber-gé*. And these guys aren't the Elders. You saw the uniforms and guns. They're the bikers who jumped us outside the Met. Why do you think they're still on our backs? Why do you think they kidnapped us and locked us in a cell? Could it be they're looking for the missing ninth egg?"

Mitchell said nothing for three seconds. He'd been running out of words a lot lately. "Crap," he said.

"You can say that again."

"Crap," Mitchell said.

"You think this is funny?"

"Guys," David said. "Just cut it out already, will you?" He rode the momentum of the silence his outburst had created. "This isn't about us anymore. People have died, OK? Amy is dead." He let that sink in.

"I don't know," Mitchell said, "she could have slipped out before—"

"I saw her get in," David said, cutting him short. The feeble attempt at comfort wasn't helping. "I saw it explode. She's dead, and no amount of bickering will bring her back."

"I'm sorry about Amy," Jordan said.

"We're both sorry," Mitchell seconded.

David had more anger to vent. "More people could die soon. You heard what the Grandmaster said. They're going to attack the JAPI Convention. That's thousands of people— Jewish community leaders and philanthropists among them. We've got to let the FBI know so they can stop them. Beating each other up won't help."

"You're right," Jordan said. "So how are we going to get out of here?"

Mitchell said, "We could dig a tunnel."

Jordan scoffed. "Yeah, right. All we need is twenty years and a poster of Rita Hayworth."

David said, "Why didn't they kill us?"

Mitchell said. "I guess they want us to die slowly."

"Or," David said, "they want something from us. What if Jordy's right—what if they're after the ninth egg?"

"See!" Mitchell said. "If I hadn't kept the egg, the bikers wouldn't have stopped the Elders from killing us. Imperial Coronation saved us. I knew you'd thank me one day."

Jordan groaned. "Don't, Mitch. Just don't."

David said, "What I mean is that we can use the egg as leverage. The egg for our freedom."

Jordan said, "Why would they trust us to hand over the egg once we walk free?"

"I don't know. They could ghost us until we hand it over. That sounds reasonable."

"These are not reasonable people, Dave. They kill to get what they want."

"And," Mitchell added, "they wear those weird robes."

"Thanks, Mitch," Jordan said, oozing sarcasm. "The bottom line is this—once they get the egg, I doubt they'll just say thanks and send us on our merry way."

David threw his hands in the air. "Well, I'm open to suggestions."

Jordan shrugged. "For all they know, the last egg is still in the Met. We should wait it out. Let them make the first move."

"How long do we wait? A week? There are thousands of lives at stake, Jordy."

"Our lives too," Jordan countered. "We won't help anybody if we're dead."

"But how will we live with ourselves knowing we could have saved the Convention?"

"OK," Jordan said. "Let's vote on it. By a show of hands, who thinks we should tell them we have the egg?"

David raised his hand. "Come on, Mitch. Put up your hand."

Mitchell seemed wounded. "Dave, I know you want to be the hero and all, but the thing is, I really like that egg."

"Quit messing around, Mitch. Don't you want to get out of here? It's not yours to keep."

"I gotta admit, it looks great on my mantelpiece."

Jordan said, "That's one vote in favor, two against. We say nothing. God, I love democracy."

"Mitch, come on. Put your hand up, *now!*"

A key turned in the lock and the heavy door swung open. Three figures in gray robes stood in the doorway. The middle and tallest robe held a flaming torch. Light danced on the long, upturned blades of the broadswords in the hands of his two companions. Had they overheard the Trio's conversation? Had they come to kill them?

The middle robe, his face hidden in the shadow of his cowl, pointed at David. "You, come with us."

CHAPTER 22

Deep in the dark belly of the earth, the Father waited. His hands caressed the carved orbs on the armrests of his throne, worn smooth by the hands of his many predecessors. Soon, he would make them proud. Their order had waited patiently for centuries. Now the time for waiting was at an end. Victory was so close, he could taste it. But triumph in this Final Holy War would require sacrifice. In the latest skirmish, he had a lot to lose. Too much, perhaps? Soon he would learn what sacrifices Providence had claimed today.

The shuffle of sandaled feet on the cavern floor displaced the rhythmic drip of ancient waters. A gray-robed figure separated from the gloom, stopped at the foot of the raised throne, and bowed his cowled head.

"Luke," the Father said. "Is the battle over?"

"Yes, Father."

The Father's fingers trembled with anticipation. "Were we victorious?"

"Yes, Father. In almost every way."

The Father's fingers trembled on the orbs. The tension ate away at him, but he could not betray his feelings.

"Are our chief assets safe?"

"Yes, Father. All except the fake eggs. The Elders of Zion

intercepted them."

Thank the Lord! The Father breathed at ease. He could shoulder many burdens, but as the Merciful Lord knew, some losses were too heavy to endure. His main concern laid to rest, he turned to the others.

"Did the Mohammedan fools bleed?"

"Oh, yes, Father. Many infidels paid with their lives."

"And what of our poor brothers?"

The cowled head dipped. "Three martyrs succumbed in the fighting."

The Father grunted. "May the Lord bless their immortal souls." He got back to business. "And the *Trio?*" The name of the upstart society tasted bitter on his tongue.

"In the dungeons, Father."

"Good. Kill them."

Luke cleared his throat. "Father—"

"Yes, Luke," the Father interrupted. "I know what I promised, but still. We have the real eggs; the Jews have outlived their utility. Their very existence makes my skin crawl."

"As you wish," Luke said. "And yet Your Holiness might consider enduring them a little longer."

"Longer? These vile and filthy creatures are demon spawn, every last one! Will you have me pity them?"

The Father had put a lot of trust in his captain; perhaps too much trust. Had he too succumbed to the Jews' sorcery?

"Not pity, Father—"

"Their ilk breathes greed and deception," the Father interrupted again. "They have caused enough trouble as it is. Thanks to their evil machinations, we lost a key weapon in our arsenal!"

"You are right, Father. But let us remember that the eggs in themselves are of no use to us. To obtain the true object of our desire, we will need the help of other agents. Especially considering recent developments."

The Father did not like the sound of that. "How so?"

"The Mohammedans know of our quest. We have remained one step ahead, but they will only intensify their efforts to thwart us. The final step in this quest will be extremely dangerous. One could call it a suicide mission. Why risk losing more holy souls?"

The Father gripped the armrest of the throne. The prospect of more dead soldiers unsettled him, but clearly Luke was heading somewhere with all this. "Go on."

"According to our latest intelligence, the Jews will have a distinct advantage in this final stage. Vile and filthy they may be, but their unholy feet may tread where ours may not."

The Father clenched his jaw. "Are you proposing we send the Jews to do our bidding?"

Luke shrugged. "Provided with the right incentives, even demon spawn might serve a holy purpose. And if they fail, well, we won't shed any tears for dead Jews, will we?"

The Father inhaled deeply. The suggestion repulsed him, but Luke had a point. To vanquish the forces of evil in this Final Battle, the forces of good would have to leverage every available resource.

"What does this plan of yours require?"

"Faith," Luke said.

The word had never sounded more displeasing to the Father. "How much faith exactly?"

The cowl shifted. "A great deal, I'm afraid. A very great deal."

CHAPTER 23

David trudged down the rough tunnel of hewn stone. Heavy iron chains clinked at his wrists and ankles and hampered his movement. Behind him, the two henchmen held their naked swords at the ready. His captors, who seemed to be stuck in the Dark Ages, had dressed him in a thick gray cloak, and he struggled not to trip on the low hem. But he was in no position to complain.

Keeping his mouth shut, he followed the tall man with the flaming torch. Despite his loose robe, the man reminded David of the bodybuilder gunman who had saved—then captured—the Trio earlier that day. His deep, gruff voice had reminded David of the black-clad rider who had stolen the Fabergé eggs from Mitchell. Were they the same man? He was in no position to ask questions either.

Would his captors respond to rational self-interest and strike a deal? David clung to that hope. He could use the ninth egg as a bargaining chip, despite the Trio's decision. Surely, he could defy the democratic process to save his life? But his dilemma was both theoretical and optimistic. The thugs were probably leading him to his execution, not a parley. He wouldn't get a word in edgewise. *I'll see you soon, Amy.*

The gray cloak ahead unlocked another heavy wooden door and proceeded down another dark corridor. Beyond the ever-present drip of water, David heard the distant hum of male voices, like the Gregorian chant of a church choir. If Jordan was right and their captors were not the Islamic Elders of Zion, who were they?

The corridor ended in yet another heavy door, which opened onto a large cavern. Flaming torches rested in sconces on the walls of rough stone. A flight of stone steps climbed to a dais with an imposing wooden throne, where a gray cloak sat beneath an immense crucifix.

David's escort stepped aside to join the swordsmen behind him.

"David Zelig!"

The voice had boomed not from the robed figure on the throne but from the man at his side. The cloak stepped forward and descended the steps until he stood three feet from David. He lifted the cowl from his head. With his crown of short salt-and-pepper hair around a circular bald patch, he looked like a Franciscan monk.

He smiled at David. "My name is Luke." David nodded, unsure whether his captor would permit him to speak. "You stand before the Father of our Temple. Very few have merited this honor."

David swallowed hard. The monk had confirmed David's suspicions. He had fallen into the clutches of yet another secret society, this time a Christian one. Although his grasp of Christian history was spotty, he understood that the religion's bloody treatment of helpless Jews rivaled that of Islam. The monk knew David's name, and he probably knew all about his friends too. David should learn as much as he could about this second society. He tried his luck.

"What Temple is that?"

"Who were the first international bankers, David?"

David scanned his spotty grasp of history once again. The task did not take long. Was this a trick question—or worse, a leading one? "Um, the Rothschilds?"

David braced for a verbal attack. Would Luke condemn him for the crimes, imagined or otherwise, of a mythical global Jewish conspiracy? Luke surprised him.

"No, David," he said. "The first multinational bankers conducted their business centuries before the Rothschilds. During the Crusades, the need arose to move currency and to honor promissory notes across large territories. That task fell to a group of believers of impeccable honor and devotion. I am referring to the Poor Fellow-Soldiers of Christ and of the Temple of Solomon, also known as the Knights Templar. We prefer 'the Temple.' It's shorter."

"You're the Knights Templar?" David tried to cleanse his voice of all sarcasm and failed. The Knights Templar was a well-worn trope of conspiracy theories. He'd expected something more original.

"Officially," Luke said, "a papal decree disbanded the Knights Templar in the fourteenth century. But *unofficially*, the Temple continued to operate underground. The sacred knights waged secret crusades against infidels wherever they gathered power and threatened Christendom. To this very day. And today, the danger has never been greater. The Mohammedans have arisen again, aping fictional global Jewish conspiracies, and conspiring to overrun Christian America. They sink their claws into our land, spreading their tentacles, waiting for the right moment to strike. But we've got news for the so-called Elders of Zion. Their evil schemes all feed into the Lord's plan for the End Times and the Final Crusade. And this time we will vanquish them forever!"

Luke had spoken with exhilaration, his eyes bulging, his arms interlocked in the loose sleeves of his robe. Now he regained his composure. "And the Trio has a role to play in the Divine Plan."

David swallowed hard. Luke knew about the Trio. Whenever the Crusaders set forth, they slaughtered the Jews in their path, and this Temple seemed eager to repeat that bloody chapter of history, starting with him.

"Um," he said. "I, ah, I'm not sure, ah…"

Luke didn't seem to hear him. He gestured, and another gray robe emerged from the shadows. This one carried a familiar metal briefcase. The robed Templar Knight opened the case in his hands to reveal eight golden Fabergé eggs.

"The Fabergé Imperial Collection," Luke announced.

"You have the eggs?" David said. He feigned surprise.

"The genuine eggs, yes." Luke nodded at the robe, who closed the case and held it out to David.

David glanced at the case, then at Luke. He had not mentioned the missing ninth egg. Was this a trick—a test?

"Take it, David. Do not be afraid."

David accepted the case. "Why are you giving me these?"

"Did the Elders tell you why they wanted the eggs?"

"They need them to fund a major operation, an attack on a Jewish target." David kept the details of that operation to himself for now.

Luke waved the words away. "Lies!" he yelled. "The Mohammedans ooze oil money. A few golden eggs are peanuts to them. They went after the eggs only once they learned that the Temple desired them."

"Again," David said, "why are you giving them to me?"

"The eggs are a means to an end. Our true goal is a holy relic that has eluded us for decades and is sure to bring us victory in this Final Crusade!"

David's chest tightened at the talk of holy relics and Final Crusades. The metal briefcase felt heavier by the second. A quick summary execution no longer seemed to be the worst outcome for this meeting.

"How do I fit in?"

"David, we want you to acquire this holy relic for us. And to do so, you will need the genuine eggs."

David still didn't understand. "What relic is that?"

When Luke told him, David almost burst out laughing.

CHAPTER 24

Mitchell scrunched his nose. "The Holy Prepuce?" he repeated. "What the hell is a prepuce?"

David had returned to their cell, the case of authentic imperial Fabergé eggs in hand, and updated his friends about his meeting with the Temple Father.

Jordan gripped his stomach, trying not to keel over from the fit of giggles. "It's," he said, gasping. "It's a foreskin!"

"A foreskin?" Mitchell still looked confused. "You mean like this?" The King of Subtlety gripped his crotch.

"No, you idiot. It's the part removed during circumcision. The *fore*skin."

"I don't get it. Christians don't do circumcision."

David stepped in to explain. "But Jesus was Jewish, right? When he was eight days old, he had a circumcision, and somebody kept the foreskin."

"Ew, that's gross!"

"It gets better. Somebody preserved the foreskin and handed it down through the generations. They believe the Prepuce has magical powers and can help bring the Second Coming."

"Second Coming!" Jordan said, surrendering to another tearful fit. David tried to keep a straight face. Mitchell did not seem to have noticed the double entendre.

"Come on, that's baloney, right?"

"Baloney!" Jordan said. The mental image of a smoked sausage set him off again.

"Shh! Keep it down, Jordy. To answer your question, Mitch, who knows, and frankly, who cares. The Prepuce is our ticket out of here. After decades underground, the relic has surfaced again in the private collection of an eccentric multimillionaire. He's obsessed with imperial Fabergé eggs and anything connected to Tsar Nicholas II. The Temple figures he'll trade the Holy Prepuce for the complete set of imperial eggs."

"What's his name?"

"Peter Zheltkov."

Mitchell shrugged. "Never heard of him."

"But why us?" Jordan said, overcoming his hysterics. "They've had the eggs for a week. Why can't they just steal it or make the trade themselves?"

"They don't know where he keeps the Prepuce. Zheltkov is paranoid and has alarm systems to rival the Met. Besides, they have no access to the collector. He hates Christian relic hunters with a passion. But he might trade the Prepuce to a well-known wealthy Jew."

Mitchell said, "Meaning you?"

David hesitated. He was approaching the difficult part of the bargain. "We have family friends with connections in the art world. They might be able to arrange a meeting."

Jordan said, "Did they ask about the missing egg?"

"No. They don't seem to have noticed. That's the catch." David tapped the metal case. "Zheltkov *will* notice that the Imperial Collection isn't complete. He'll want the full set."

Two pairs of eyes turned to Mitchell.

"No," he said. "Can't do. The egg has sentimental value."

"Mitch, if Zheltkov refuses our offer, we're screwed."

"What are they going to do—kill us?"

"Yes! That's exactly what Luke said."

"The chariot," Mitchell said. "Let me keep the chariot and

we have a deal. We'll say it got lost."

"Mitch, this is our lives here!"

"OK, Jesus. I'll get the egg and you can give them all away for an old foreskin. Happy now?"

"Getting there. Where did you put the egg?"

"That's my business."

"Mitch?"

"I'll drop the egg at your place, Dave, and we can speak with this Peter guy together. I'm a great negotiator." Mitchell paused when he saw David's expression. "There's another catch, isn't there? There's always another catch."

David nodded. "They're sending me. Alone. Until I come back with the Prepuce, you guys are the insurance policy."

CHAPTER 25

TOP SECRET
FEDERAL BUREAU OF INVESTIGATION
OFFICE OF PROFESSIONAL RESPONSIBILITY
Transcript of interview with Mr. Hyman Schneider
Also present:
Special Agent A. Maynard
Special Agent in Charge M. Reed

HYMAN SCHNEIDER:
David Zelig dropped by on a Tuesday evening smelling of booze and fast women. Later, I learned the reason. His good friend Mitchell had hidden Imperial Coronation where nobody would think to look—with a friend of dubious virtue who tended bar at a downtown strip club of dubious legality. I've never frequented such establishments myself, but the effort seemed to have drained the young Zelig's enthusiasm for his mission.

"Hymie," he said. "I need a favor,"

"Anything," I said and let him inside. He declined my offer of a stiff drink.

I had been wondering about him since the evening he'd pitched me a Jewish secret society, but I decided against asking any probing questions. There was no need to encourage such foolishness.

"David, what's on your mind?"

"You have connections in the art world, right?"

I said, "Is the Pope Catholic?" I own a few galleries in the city and like to think of myself as a patron of the arts.

He asked me if I knew Peter Zheltkov. "Now there's a name I haven't heard in some time," I said.

"You know him?"

"Sure, I know Peter Zheltkov. In our circles, who doesn't? We did some business a while ago. He's of Russian extract and as straight as an arrow. What was our deal? I remember! A painting by Laurits Tuxen, *Leaving the Table*. We tracked it down to an auction in Denmark. A very unusual man, Zheltkov. What do you need from him?"

I admit he'd triggered my curiosity but not my suspicions. In retrospect, I should have sensed that something was off. Only a week ago, thieves had broken into the Met, and Sunday's Israel Day Parade had ended in a shootout between police and terrorists. The world was going to hell, and anything was possible.

David said, "I've been learning about Imperial Russia."

"Then Zheltkov is your man. He's obsessed with Imperial Russia. And you're in luck! The Met is exhibiting the imperial Fabergé egg collection this week." Then I remembered what I'd read in the papers. "Scratch that. The museum closed temporarily after that burglary. I'm sure Peter would have shown up for that exhibition, though."

"He would?"

"Sure, he has a Fabergé collection of his own, though none of the imperial eggs, as far as I know."

"Actually, I saw the imperial eggs," David said, choosing his words with care. "Before the Met closed. I'd love to discuss them with Zheltkov."

"Why don't I call him," I said, "and see if he's in town? It's a great excuse to catch up."

And that's exactly what I did. I put on my reading glasses

and found his number in my old Rolodex. You're too young to know what a Rolodex is. Dinosaurs like me still use them. I dialed the number and what do you know, Peter answered.

We had a nice chat. I told him about my friend's son, practically a nephew, who was interested in imperial Fabergé eggs, and would he be willing to meet with him. Our timing could not have been better.

I covered the phone's mouthpiece with my hand. "David, what have you got planned tomorrow?"

"Nothing."

"Feel like a trip over the pond?"

"Where?"

"Peter's flying to London tomorrow. He can show you his Fabergé collection at his home. Are you in?"

David was so excited I thought he would kiss me. A few scribbled details later, I put down the phone.

"The deal is done. Meet him tomorrow morning, at nine AM."

"Thank you so much, Hymie. This means a lot to me."

"It's my pleasure," I said. "I'm glad you found something constructive to do with your time. Now all you need to do is find that nice young woman."

I regretted the little joke the moment I saw his face. He looked like somebody had just died. Of course, somebody had, but I only learned about Amy Smith later.

"Can I ask one more favor?" he said.

"Sure, David."

"Can you hold on to this for me?" He meant the metal briefcase he'd brought with him.

"No problem."

"Just promise me two things: you'll keep it safe, and you won't open it."

If I hadn't smelled something fishy before, now I did. "There are no drugs in there, are there?" I had to ask. You never know with kids these days.

"No drugs."

"No human heads or other severed body parts?"

That one got a laugh out of him. "No, Hymie, no body parts, human or otherwise."

"Then we're good. I'll throw it in my safe and I will not open it."

We shook hands, and I wished him well. He had some packing to do. I like to think he left my apartment in an optimistic state of mind, despite all he'd been through in the past twenty-four hours.

If so, that optimism must have died when he walked out of the building and straight into the FBI. Special Agent Marco Hernandez picked him up and this time he used the cuffs.

CHAPTER 26

"Am I glad to see you!" David lied. He shifted uncomfortably on the back seat of the unmarked FBI cruiser, his arms cuffed behind his back, while the night lights of Manhattan panned by the window. Special Agent Marco Hernandez was not the last person David had wanted to see, but he was on the shortlist. David could not afford to miss his meeting with Peter Zheltkov the next morning. He had to convince the wealthy collector to trade the Holy Prepuce for the imperial Fabergé collection, or else the Templars would kill David's friends.

Did the FBI know about the Temple, or would Hernandez think David had created the secret society out of whole cloth? Telling the FBI agent the truth about his new mission would only raise doubts about David's sanity or his reliability or both.

"I was just about to call you." This was David's second lie. He had returned to his apartment to shower and pack a travel bag for the next day. That had been a big mistake.

"The Elders will attack the JAPI Convention in Washington next week," David continued. "The Grandmaster told us himself. You were right—he showed up in person at the drop-off. We have to warn the convention organizer, Gerry

Cantor. I know him personally. He'll be very grateful."

Hernandez said nothing. He had not said a word since he'd arrested David, and now the agent's silence worried him. David really was in deep trouble this time, and no amount of negotiation would save his ass. Hernandez would have a lot of questions for David, and this time, he'd throw David in a jail cell until he got answers. David's friends were as good as dead. And David would not be far behind.

David leaned back, his hands digging into his back, and closed his eyes. He deserved this. No, he deserved worse. Because of him, Amy was dead. Nothing he said or did could bring her back. He knew this. Hernandez knew this too.

The car stopped, and Agent Hernandez got out. David opened his eyes. They were on a dark street. This was not the FBI headquarters.

Hernandez opened the back door and pulled him from the cruiser. The horn of a tugboat honked on the Hudson. The Statue of Liberty was a lone, distant figure glowing white in the thickening night.

"Where are we?" David asked.

Hernandez said nothing. David got his bearings. While he'd simmered in self-pity, the car had crossed the Brooklyn Bridge and veered into the old docks west of Borough Park. Hernandez grabbed a duffel bag from the trunk, then waved David toward a warehouse with red brick walls and shattered windows.

"Inside."

David trudged ahead of Hernandez to the warehouse, his hands still cuffed behind his back. Why the hell had Hernandez brought him here? Was this part of yet another secret FBI mission—Operation Big Bad Wolf?

Hernandez unlocked the door of the warehouse but still said nothing. He had seemed to hate David's guts from the start. Did he blame David for Amy's death? David did. At least now, he and Hernandez had something in common.

Hernandez slid the door open and shoved David inside. The warehouse was empty. No FBI team, no fancy equipment, just a stained cement floor and a steel-framed chair.

"Sit," Hernandez said.

David did as he was told.

Hernandez dropped the duffel bag on the floor behind the chair. After rummaging around inside, he zip-tied David's wrists and ankles to the steel frame of the chair and removed the steel cuffs. Then he stood before David, admiring his handiwork.

"Is this necessary?"

Hernandez spoke his first full sentence. "I've got one agent with a bullet in his arm, another burned to a crisp. You and your friends disappear, and then you show up at your apartment eight hours later as though nothing happened. Yeah, I think this is necessary."

"I can explain."

"Oh, I'm sure you will."

"Special Agent Hernandez, I had nothing to do with those gunmen. They're not even with the Elders. They belong to a rival secret society."

Hernandez emitted a bitter laugh. "And they just knew where and when the drop-off was going down?"

David opened his mouth to explain, then realized he had no answer. How had the Temple known about the Trio's every move? "They know everything about us," he said, thinking aloud. "Our names. They know about the Elders too."

"You spoke with them?"

"They took us prisoner and put us in a dungeon. I don't know where."

"OK, then. Who are they?"

David hesitated. He had to come clean. There was no other way. "They call themselves the Temple. They claim to descend from the Knights Templar."

Hernandez raised his hand to ask a question. "As in the Crusader knights? Let me guess. They wear dark robes and carry flaming torches?"

"Yes! Do you know about them?"

David's head snapped sideways as a hand connected with his cheekbone. For the second time that day, somebody had punched him in the face. He hadn't seen this one coming either. Hernandez was left-handed, and now David would have matching bruises on each side of his face.

"Ow," David said.

"Do I look like a clown?" Hernandez yelled.

"You hit me!"

"File a complaint. But you might want to wait on that. There's more where that came from."

The FBI agent did not seem concerned about having assaulted a civilian. A small, primal corner at the back of David's lizard brain raised a red flag. The rest of David's brain ignored it.

"Listen," he said, aiming for a common bond. "I'm sorry about Amy. I never wanted—"

David's head snapped in the other direction. The agent had hit him again.

Hernandez danced on the spot like a boxer, warming up. "Oh, no you don't. Don't you dare speak her name! You don't deserve to. She's dead because of you."

David hung his head. He was right. Amy had died trying to save David's life.

"Because of you and your games and your little secret societies. Did you ever stop to think about the people you'd hurt, the lives you'd ruin? But I'm on to you, David Zelig. I. Am. On. To. You. You won't get away with it. Not this time."

That red flag rose in his brain again, and this time the warning got his attention. His head felt hot and wet. *He's going to kill you, David. No matter what you say or do, he brought you here to die.*

"I figured you out," Hernandez continued. "You were working with the Elders all along. Leading us on, feeding us disinformation, using us to get at the eggs. You got into Amy's head. She didn't see what you were doing. But I did." A tear slipped down his cheek, and he stopped dancing. "I saw it, but I didn't stop you. I should have plugged you a long time ago. Now I'll fix that mistake."

"No," David said, through trembling lips, trying and failing to stay calm. "That's not true. I told you the truth. I led no one on. I never dreamed of hurting anybody, much less Amy. I loved her."

"No, you didn't!" Hernandez yelled. "Not like me. But that doesn't matter anymore. All that's left is justice. That's the least I can do for her."

Hernandez sprang into action, leaping forward like a demon. David closed his eyes and braced for the worst, but the rogue FBI agent had not lunged at him. Instead, he rummaged around in the duffel bag on the floor behind David.

"You don't have to do this," David said. "This is all a big mistake. They have my friends—Jordy and Mitch. You know them. If I don't do what they told me, they'll kill them both."

Hernandez wasn't listening. He reappeared holding an orange two-gallon jerry can. "You enjoy burning people to death, don't you? You're gonna love this." He twisted off the lid, and the heady smell of gasoline filled David's nose.

"No! Please, no!" David shifted on the chair and pulled at his restraints.

Hernandez inhaled deeply and chuckled. "You smell that? That's the smell of your future, David. And your future is very, very bright."

He tilted the can. Gasoline splashed over David's lap, trickling over his jeans and into his Rockports. A full-blown panic attack racked David. His limbs pulled and writhed, but the zip ties held fast.

Hernandez made to pour the highly flammable liquid over David's head, then thought better of it. "No need to overdo it," he said, his eyes already afire with hatred. "We'll roast you nice and slow. You'll enjoy every moment. And so will I."

He stepped away, placing the jerry can at a safe distance behind him. Then he pulled a square, silver cigarette lighter from his shirt pocket. "You smoke?" he asked. David shook his head. "Soon you will." He grinned at David and cackled.

The man had lost his mind.

David's hair was damp with sweat. He turned from side to side and pumped air through his mouth. *Think, David! You've got to get out of this. There must be a way. Think!*

Time slowed to a crawl. Hernandez stepped closer, a leisurely moonwalk. *Think, David!* The duffel bag was behind David. If he shifted backward, he might reach it. But his arms and legs were tied to the chair. The fall might break the chair under his weight. Then again, the fall might break his wrists too. Back to square one.

Hernandez snapped open the lid of the lighter. David searched the warehouse for an escape route. Red-brick walls. High, broken windows. One wall was made of fiberglass. An old boat hangar sealed off and converted into a warehouse. The fiberglass was old and grimy. A good ramming with his shoulder might break through. But he'd need his legs to run, and Hernandez was no amateur. He knew how to secure a prisoner.

The agent's thumb rolled the flint wheel of the lighter and pressed down on the fork. A spark flickered as gas hissed through a tiny tube, and the flame ignited above the lighter. Hernandez held the lighter above the puddle of gas at David's feet. Then the lighter fell, the flame still burning.

No! No! No!

With a sickening whoosh, the puddle of gasoline ignited. The flames swept over David's shoes and up the legs of his jeans.

This was the end of the road. Game over. David hadn't said goodbye to his mother. He hadn't called her in weeks. This was not the bright future she had envisioned for him. *Dad, I'll see you soon.*

The flames raced onto his lap. Hot tongues of fire licked up at his shirt. A deep growl rumbled in his head, the growl of an angry animal. Demons were lining up, eager to drag David to the Netherworld.

He gasped, turning his torso this way and that, trying to escape the hot flames. His legs felt hot as the gasoline burned and the fabric of his jeans caught fire. The growling grew louder. The fiberglass wall opposite him bulged and splintered. Shards of grimy material scattered in explosive trajectories around the form of a shiny, black motorbike. The rider crouched low, the warehouse's fluorescent light gleaming on his helmet. Feet above the warehouse floor, the rider extended an arm and fire belched from the barrel of a handgun.

David turned away as chunks of bone and brain burst from Hernandez's head, and blood sprayed from his back. The dead agent's body flopped to the floor, as the motorbike landed heavily, swerving and screeching to a halt at David's feet.

Time caught up. David's jeans were on fire. Flames danced over his crotch and spread to the hem of his shirt. He yelled. He shrieked. Gloved hands slapped at David's shirt, smothering the blaze. The hands reached for David's waist, pulled at his belt, and yanked his jeans down to his feet. The rider dragged him and the chair out of the fiery circle, then stood over him, panting.

A realization coalesced like melting snowflakes. His savior was a she. She pulled off her helmet, releasing a tumble of auburn curls. Sad, intelligent eyes considered him above a small, delicate nose. The face belonged to Amy Smith.

CHAPTER 27

"Do you want a beer?" Amy asked.

The dead woman opened her fridge and peered inside. In his underwear, David sat at the kitchen table of her Soho apartment and watched her. From her calm voice, one would never have guessed that only minutes ago Amy had crashed a motorbike through a warehouse wall and gunned down her former colleague. David wasn't sure he should drink anything she handed him.

Amy kept a tidy and minimalist apartment. The chrome stove and white countertops looked unused, the refrigerator close to empty. She had removed her biker jacket, and the sight of her leaning over in a T-shirt made his heart pound. But the trembling in his fingers had more to do with the singed hair on his legs and the pile of weapons on the kitchen table than sexual attraction.

She placed a beer on the table. David looked at the bottle as though it might bite him.

"I have wine too," she added.

"Who are you?" David asked.

Amy gave him a sad, regretful look as though she'd hoped to avoid a confrontation but knew that was impossible. She closed the fridge, stepped closer, and leaned her hands on the back of a kitchen chair. "My real name is Mary Rudolph. But I prefer Amy."

Mary Rudolph. An ironic laugh escaped David's lips. He'd felt bad after their first meeting for not using his real name. Now she'd settled that score.

"I suppose you're not really with the FBI."

"I am with the FBI. Or I was."

"Well, you just killed an FBI agent, and I'm guessing that's against Bureau policy."

"Marco had gone rogue. He was about to murder you in cold blood."

David nodded. She had saved his life. He had to give her that. After putting out the flames on David's clothes, she had pulled a survival knife from the sheath strapped to her leg. She sliced through the zip ties, releasing David from the steel-framed chair. Luckily, the flames had not reached his skin. Then she'd doused Hernandez, the motorbike, and David's charred clothes with what remained of the gasoline and lit them up. They'd left in the unmarked sedan with Amy in the driver's seat. Neither of them said a word all the way to her apartment, and now the unanswered questions burst through the dam walls.

"How did you know where to find me? How are you still here, breathing and talking? How does any of this make sense?" David doubted his own sanity.

"I didn't start out in the FBI," she said, her voice soft and contrite. "I was born into the Temple. From an early age, I had trained to be a warrior in the Final Crusade. Joining the FBI was part of the plan. Infiltrate the Bureau and climb the ranks. I did better than expected. One day I would have made upper management. But then I met you."

David scoffed.

"What, you don't believe me?"

He gave her a sarcastic grin. "The trained killer, brainwashed from birth by a powerful secret society, sees the light after she meets David Zelig? With all due respect for my ego, you have to admit that's quite a stretch."

She stared him squarely in the eye. "It's true. They raised me to believe Jews are Devil spawn, that you feed on greed and lies. Then I met you, a real-life Jew. You could have hidden behind your money but instead, you risked your life. Not for greed or conquest, not for power or to spread an ideology, but to save innocent lives. That was a major crack in my blind loyalty to the Temple. There were others."

She looked away. "A few months ago, my mother disappeared. The Temple accused her of heresy and treason. They suppressed the details, but everybody knows the Temple killed her. The Temple isn't very open-minded about women either. I'm one of a handful of female operatives and the only one to have risen so high. My family came from a respectable Temple bloodline. Since I was a kid, I had served the Temple and fought the Holy War. But after my mother's disappearance, I began to ask questions. Wherever I looked, I found contradictions and hypocrisy. And I wondered—would I be the next Temple woman to disappear?"

She turned back to him and her eyes brightened. "Remember the night we first met?"

David smiled wistfully at the memory. How could he forget? "The Grand Hyatt," he said. "At the bar of the Cyber Summit. I was Guest One."

Amy smirked. "The one and only."

David sighed. That seemed like a lifetime ago. "I really thought we'd hit it off. But I guess that was just part of the plan."

"No, David, it wasn't. Yes, I was staking out the summit, searching for Elders operatives. But I had no idea who you were. We only put the details together later. But that didn't stop me from liking you."

David wanted to believe that so much, his eyes watered. But the past week had made him suspicious of stories that sounded too good to be true. "Liking me doesn't bring people back from the grave."

Amy drew a deep breath. "After the Temple intercepted the eggs at the Met, I was supposed to blame the Trio to cover my tracks. You would take the fall for the heist and lost eggs. Believe me, Marco would have gone along with that gladly. But I couldn't bring myself to frame you. The Temple pulled me in for a review. I had disobeyed orders. They said I was losing my edge. When I confessed my feelings for you, they decided to pull me from the FBI. The drop-off at the Israel Day Parade was to be my final operation. The Temple wanted to intercept the fake eggs to prevent the Elders from using them to get the Holy Prepuce. They used that operation to fake my death. But they also kept you three alive. That was my only condition."

"But I saw you get into that van. I saw it explode."

"We rigged the van with explosives and removed part of the floor. We'd practiced the maneuver and timed it to perfection. The driver parked the van over a manhole. Temple operatives in the sewer system pushed a corpse through the hole in the floor of the van. I had ten seconds to pose the body, slip out, and cover the manhole before the charges detonated."

David couldn't hold back. The tears trickled down his cheeks, and his body quaked. He was not hallucinating. Amy was alive. She was here and she loved him.

"I'm so sorry, David. I knew my death would hurt you, but I had no choice. The Temple Father had wanted you dead. This was the only way to save us both."

David blinked back his tears. Chair legs squeaked as Amy sat down beside him. She laid her hand on his shoulder. "When I heard the Temple had released you to make the exchange, I couldn't stay away. I used the tracker they'd planted on you to follow your movements."

"Tracker?"

She smiled. "The FBI isn't the only organization with advanced technology."

"Yeah, but, you know…" He lowered his voice. "Are they listening now?"

"A location tracker, silly. It burned with your clothes."

"Right." The Temple had kept tabs on him, and David

had been oblivious. Talk of the FBI reminded David of an urgent task he'd neglected.

"The JAPI Convention," he said. "The Grandmaster said they're planning on attacking the JAPI Convention in a week. That's why they wanted the Fabergé eggs—to fund the operation!"

"That's disinformation, David. The Elders don't need the eggs to attack anyone. They have plenty of money. The Elders only wanted the eggs to screw the Temple."

Luke, the Temple monk, had told David the same story, but this fact only intensified David's suspicion of Amy. "The Grandmaster said—"

"David," Amy interrupted. "Did you think the Grandmaster would give away his grand plan to a bunch of new recruits?"

She made sense even if she hadn't convinced him.

Her voice dropped to a whisper. "Tonight, let's forget about the Temple and the Elders. It's just you and me now." She leaned in and kissed him on the lips, long and slow. David wanted this. He needed this. He'd almost died today. Now he wanted to live—to embrace life with all his senses.

David pulled away.

"What's the matter?"

"What's the matter?" He didn't know where to begin. "Until a few minutes ago, I thought you were dead, and now we're making out?" She smiled guiltily. Was this a game to her? She'd just killed her old FBI buddy. "Amy, this is too much. I mean, how do I know the Temple didn't send you to keep tabs on me?"

Amy studied his eyes, sad again. "I don't blame you for being skeptical, but I'm no longer on the Temple's side. I'm on *our* side."

"What does that even mean?"

"It means I'll never hurt you. I'll never betray you." David shook his head, so she continued. "Don't you see? The Temple was grooming me for leadership. I had risen higher in the FBI than any other Temple operative. I would be the first female on the Temple's council, and the Temple isn't big on change. The point is, I had my dream future lined up for me but I gave it all up to be with you."

David wanted to believe her, but she'd lied to him before. "How do I know that's true? Maybe this is all part of their plan, and once I've delivered the Holy Prepuce, you'll turn on me?"

"I'll prove it." Now she had his undivided attention. "When the Temple interrogated you, they didn't mention the missing ninth egg, did they? The egg the Trio stole."

David swallowed hard. "You know about that?"

"I'm the only one working for both the FBI and the Temple on this operation. I know you took all nine eggs from the Met, but the Temple only received eight. If the Temple knew you'd held back on them, they'd have put you on the rack."

"I don't know what that is," David said, "but it doesn't sound pleasant."

"No, it isn't. The Temple doesn't know about the missing egg because I didn't tell them. I'm guessing Mitchell took it. Typical. But to be honest I don't care. I just want to keep you safe. So you have to trust me now, just as I trust you."

"I don't understand."

"You've got leverage on me, David. If the Temple ever finds out I've hidden that little detail, well, let's just say the rack would be too good for me. I'd get special treatment. In a bad way. I've put my life in your hands."

She inched closer and nudged his lips with hers. "Don't ever betray me, David," she whispered.

"I won't."

"Good, 'cause if you do, I'll kill you."

"Oh, I believe you."

She pressed her chest against his. Amy or Mary—her name didn't matter. Neither did the Elders of Zion, the Temple, or the FBI. All that mattered was here and now—this girl and this moment.

Their lips met again. His hands slipped under her shirt. Her fingers raked his back. They rose to their feet and dispensed with the gaps between them. She eased him backward.

"Bedroom," she whispered, coming up for air and guiding him in the right direction. Then she moaned with pleasant surprise as her hands moved to his behind and discovered he was already in his underwear.

"That's convenient," she purred in his ear.

"You know me," he said, shuffling toward the bedroom. "Always one step ahead."

CHAPTER 28

Sunlight seeped through the slatted shades of Amy's bedroom window. Car horns blared outside as the reluctant city rose to face another Monday morning. David watched Amy as she slept in bed. Yesterday, he'd been set on fire and almost shot in the head. Even now, he was far from safe, a Sword of Damocles still hanging over his head. But lying there next to Amy, he'd never felt more content. He wished he could freeze-frame this moment and stay in bed with Amy forever.

Guilt disturbed his tranquility like a boulder dropped into a still pool of water. What right did he have to these stolen moments in a warm bed while his friends rotted in a tiny dungeon cell? He had no right to Amy's love either. He had told her he'd founded the Trio to protect his fellow Jews. But his real motivations were far less noble. Would Amy still admire him if she learned the truth?

He reached for his wristwatch on the bedside table. The time was 8:04 AM. His heart jumped. *Holy crap!* He was late.

David leaped out of bed and searched for his clothes. He found his underwear under the bed and slipped them on. On the way to LaGuardia Airport, he'd stop by his apartment and grab some travel essentials.

"Where are you going?" Amy said, yawning.

"I'm late for my flight."

She sat up. "What flight?"

"With Peter Zheltkov. He's got the Holy Prepuce." David found his undershirt and a sock. "Have you seen my jeans?" Then he remembered. Amy had burned his clothes last night in the abandoned warehouse. "Never mind. I'll improvise. I'm sure New York cabbies have seen worse things than a man with no pants."

Amy got out of bed, making no attempt to find her clothes. "Don't go."

"Don't go? The Temple set me free to get the Holy Prepuce, the same Temple that—"

Amy interrupted. "Screw the Temple and screw the Holy Prepuce. I'm not interested in foreskins."

David flashed a mischievous grin. "You demonstrated that last night."

"I'm serious, David. This has to stop. It's too dangerous."

"It's not a big deal. An old family friend arranged the meeting. Zheltkov is an art collector. He's not with the Elders."

Amy did not look convinced. "The Temple cares only about its Holy Crusade, no matter how many people die. Our lives mean nothing to them. But we don't have to take orders from anyone anymore. Let's just walk away."

"Walk away?" David wished that were possible.

"We'll get new identities, leave the country, and start a new life together."

David hesitated. She was right. Sooner or later, the Elders, the Temple, or the FBI would lay hands on them. The likelihood of their story leading to a happy ending approached zero. But what if they just disappeared off the face of the earth? His mother wouldn't like that!

"I wish I could," he said.

"Why can't you?" Her voice was small and vulnerable.

"The Temple has Jordy and Mitch. Their lives depend on me delivering the goods, Amy. What will the Temple do to them if I just run away?"

Amy lowered her eyes to the floor. Would she ask him to sacrifice his friends for her? And if he agreed, what would that make him? "Then I'm coming with you. From now on, I'm not letting you out of my sight."

David shrugged. "Fine by me."

Amy's gorgeous smile returned, then faltered. "Will the collector be OK with that?"

"Probably. It's his jet. I'll text him to be sure." David had recovered his phone from Hernandez's car. "There's only one problem."

"What?"

"I'm out of trousers."

CHAPTER 29

David and Amy got out of the taxi at the steps of the private jet where a smiling blonde flight attendant waited for them. David paid the taxi driver, and the latecomers hurried toward the Dassault Falcon 7X, its triple jet engines already humming and ready for takeoff.

"Welcome to Zheltkov Air," the flight attendant gushed. The bubbles in her voice were as fake as her smile and thick makeup. "Mr. Zheltkov's little joke," she said, by way of an apology. "Mr. Zheltkov has already boarded. May I have your passports?"

David and Amy handed them over. "Mr. David Zelig," the attendant read. "And Ms. Amy Anderson?"

She gave David a questioning glance. "My girlfriend," he said.

"Wonderful! Please make yourselves at home while I get these stamped for you. My name is Zina. You can leave your bags here. Mr. Zheltkov is *so* looking forward to meeting you both!" She smiled at them as they climbed the staircase to the open cabin door.

"Do we need to tip her?" Amy asked.

"Can't hurt, but I don't think so."

"Wow, we didn't have to wait in line for anything. Have

you flown in one of these before?"

"A few times. Charters mostly."

Amy flushed. She drove motorbikes through walls and gunned down thugs without flinching, but she got all excited about a ride in a private jet. Go figure.

A sobering thought entered his mind. *Enjoy the ride too, Dave. The way your finances are heading, you might never board a private flight again.*

Mr. Peter Zheltkov's welcome was chillier than that of his flight attendant but warm enough considering the circumstances of their meeting. Fit and trim at seventy and with his mane of gray hair combed back, Mr. Zheltkov shook David's hand and flashed his pearly teeth.

"Nice to meet you, Mr. Zheltkov," David said. "Thank you for fitting us in on such short notice."

"Remind me of your name?" Zheltkov said. He had a British accent.

"David Zelig. This is my girlfriend, Amy Anderson."

"A pleasure to meet you," Zheltkov said. The multimillionaire was more enthusiastic about welcoming a beautiful young woman aboard than an unfamiliar young man. "Any nephew of Hymie is welcome."

"A family friend," David said, correcting the mistake.

"How's that?"

David raised his voice and talked slower. "I'm not a nephew, just a family friend. Hymie and my late father were very close."

"Oh." Zheltkov seemed taken aback by the misunderstanding, as if concerned that the stranger he'd welcomed into his home might leave with the silverware stuffed in his coat pockets. He pointed to the pair of armchairs in soft cream-colored leather opposite him. "Please have a seat. We'll be taking off shortly."

David and Amy settled on the armchairs, admired the lacquered wood finishes, and breathed in the satisfying scent of expensive leather.

"Seatbelts," David said to Amy, and they buckled up.

Within minutes the aircraft had taxied, taken off at a sharp incline, and reached cruising altitude. Zina served snacks and drinks and hurried off to prepare brunch.

"I understand you're a student of the Russian Empire," Zheltkov said, a mischievous glint in his eye.

"Yes, sir."

"Please, call me Peter. Personally, I find the Romanov dynasty fascinating. All that pomp and ceremony, not to mention that vast wealth and power concentrated in a single man."

David swallowed hard. He needed to turn the conversation to the subject of their exchange but without mentioning his Templar sellers, whom Zheltkov apparently abhorred. Insulting one's host was undesirable when suspended in a high-speed pressurized tube forty thousand feet above the ocean and six hours from London. Now he seized his opening. "Did you see the exhibition at the Metropolitan Museum?"

"Of course I did. Magnificent, aren't they? What workmanship and attention to detail! Such extravagances were possible only in the Imperial Era. Did you know that Fabergé was my great-grandfather?"

David traded impressed glances with Amy. "No, we did not."

"Peter Carl Fabergé, Goldsmith to the Imperial Crown. That's my grandmother's side of the family. We didn't inherit the House of Fabergé, but I've acquired a good number of the Fabergé eggs. They belong to a different world." He seemed nostalgic for the empire that had ceased to exist long before his birth.

"Yes, it was," David said, aiming for rapport. "A lost age."

"And good riddance!" Peter said, his outrage surprising David. "Tsar Nicholas II was a bumbling fool. Had he embraced political reforms and open markets, his empire would have thrived. The Romanovs would have kept their wealth and lived on as the pride of their nation, like the Windsors of Great Britain. Instead, the stubborn goat dug in his heels. If he'd spent more time solving his country's problems and less entertaining conspiracy theories and charlatans the likes of Rasputin, he wouldn't have ended up in a pit along with his entire family. What folly!"

Peter Zheltkov shook his head. "His people would have thanked him too. Nicholas was so obsessed with the imagined evils of democracy and capitalism, but his obstinacy opened the door to a much worse system—communism. Do you know how many Russians died in the Communist purges and genocides that followed? The average estimate is a hundred million. One hundred million people! The Nazis only killed twenty-five million with their war and Holocaust. It beggars belief."

Zheltkov sipped his tonic water. "Capitalism has proved itself time and again, the world over. But my friends, you didn't come here to listen to a lecture on ancient history, you came here to talk business."

David and Amy shared a startled look.

"Don't be coy, my dears, I wasn't born yesterday. Nor the day before that. The entire Imperial Collection goes missing and only a week later, I receive a mysterious visitor interested in Fabergé eggs."

David cleared his throat. "What makes you think they're missing?"

"The director of the Metropolitan Museum is an old friend." The mischievous glimmer returned to his eye. "I expect your anonymous seller has sent you with a most aggressive offer."

"Well, the thing is—"

"I'll remind you and your master that the market for stolen artifacts is very, very small."

David said, "The, ah, sellers don't want money. They propose a trade."

"A trade? How interesting. What could I possibly offer them in exchange for the Imperial Collection?"

"Um. They want the Holy Prepuce."

The smile dropped from Zheltkov's lips. "Oh," he said.

"*They* sent you. But how could they possibly know I'd have the Prepuce?" he added, talking to himself. "That is not public knowledge."

His reaction confused David. Did he know who *they* were?

"You have the Prepuce?" Amy said.

Zheltkov smiled again. "I'll show you."

Using a key on a necklace underneath his shirt, he unlocked a cabinet of polished wood and extracted a vacuum-sealed square of transparent plastic. He placed the item on the narrow table before him. In the center of the square was a small tapered piece of brown leather.

"May I?" Amy said.

"That's why you're here."

Amy picked up the Prepuce and studied it from all angles.

"Looted during the Sack of Rome," Zheltkov said, "venerated for centuries in the village of Calcata, the Holy Prepuce disappeared in 1983, never to be seen again. Until now."

"How do we prove its authenticity?"

"Traditionally, the faithful have used a taste test. But I'd advise against that, my dear. You never know where that thing has been."

Amy grimaced. "We'll take your word on that." She placed the Prepuce back on the table.

"It's fake, of course," Zheltkov said, and he seemed to relish their surprised expressions.

"It is?"

Zheltkov leaned forward. "Tell me, how many foreskins did the baby Jesus have?"

David shrugged. "One?"

"Then how did twelve Holy Prepuces materialize in churches during the Middle Ages? The Prepuce is fake, and so are all similar religious relics. None of them have any magical properties, I assure you. The very idea of a Holy Foreskin is ludicrous, if not repulsive. Leo XIII excommunicated anyone who dared to talk of the Holy Prepuce, and most self-respecting Christians would agree with him. Not all believers have such self-respect, I'm afraid."

"But you'll trade the Prepuce for the eggs?"

"Without question. Idiots are idiots, but I'll still take their treasures. That's why I got into the relic trade. Nothing gives me greater joy than to batter the gullible over the head with their own stupidity."

David couldn't believe his good luck. The Temple had told him that Zheltkov wouldn't deal with Christians. Were they mistaken—or had they lied to him? Why, then, would the Temple not send their own operatives to make the trade?

Zheltkov returned the plastic envelope to the cabinet and locked the door.

"So do we have a deal?"

David met Amy's eager glance. "We have a deal."

David reached out to shake Zheltkov's hand when a woman's voice said, "I wouldn't do that if I were you."

The woman who stood in the aisle wore a pilot's uniform and aimed a handgun at the seated business party. David swore under his breath. He recognized her tight braid and intense, dark eyes. The last time they had met, she'd held a gun on him too. Her name was Nasim.

CHAPTER 30

"He's lying," Nasim said. She gripped the handgun in both hands. Her chest heaved with tension—or was that righteous indignation?

"Who, me?" David said, although he had no desire to argue with a gun-toting extremist at forty thousand feet.

"Yes, you." She glanced at Peter Zheltkov. "He doesn't have the eggs; we do. David Zelig handed them to me himself."

Zheltkov turned to David. "Is that true?" The presence of a gun in the pressurized cabin did not seem to faze the old man.

David cleared his throat. He needed Zheltkov to know he had the real Imperial Collection. But he'd already angered Nasim. Revealing the truth might push her over the edge. David hoped honesty was the best policy in this situation. "I gave her replicas of the eggs," he said. "The genuine eggs are still in my possession."

"Liar!" She turned the gun on David again.

Amy said, "Her eggs are made of lead. I oversaw their production myself."

The gun moved between David and Amy, and Nasim's eyes widened with panic as she realized the Trio had duped her.

"Two sets of imperial eggs," Zheltkov summarized. "Only one of them is genuine. How interesting. What is your name?"

The question snapped Nasim out of her panicked confusion. "Nasim."

"Well, Nasim. I take it you are also interested in exchanging the eggs for the Prepuce?" Nasim nodded. "Very well. The matter should be easy to settle. You will both bring your eggs to a meeting place of my choosing and I shall examine each set. The provider of the authentic eggs will receive the Holy Prepuce in return. Does that sound satisfactory?"

Amy whispered to David, "Fasten your seatbelt."

"What?" Strapped to his seat, David would make an easy target. "Why?"

"Just do it."

"But please, Nasim," Zheltkov continued. "Put the gun away. That's no way to do business."

David reached for the straps of his seatbelt and brought the ends together.

"I'm not here to do business," Nasim said.

The click of David's seatbelt drew the terrorist's attention. Amy tensed, ready to spring into action. Had she brought a gun or had she expected a pre-flight security search? He hoped she had a gun. But a shootout inside a plane at high altitude did not seem like a good idea.

The gun barrel turned back to Zheltkov. "Give me the Prepuce," Nasim said. If she couldn't buy the eggs, she'd take them by force.

"My dear," Zheltkov said, insulted. "That's a poor way to negotiate, and we have many miles to cover until we reach our destination."

Nasim seemed to relax for the first time. "This plane will land when and where I choose. So either you hand over the Prepuce or I'll take the key from your dead body and help myself."

Zheltkov's lips twitched. "All right then. We'll do it your

way." He gave David an apologetic grimace and reached for the key on the chain around his neck.

A woman shrieked in the aisle. David whipped his head around, watching as Zina threw her hands in the air, sending a tray of sliced fruit tumbling to the floor, spilling silver cutlery and kiwifruit on the carpet. As Nasim's aim shifted to the flight attendant, Amy launched from her seat. She grabbed Nasim's hands and shoved the gun upward.

"Dear God," Zheltkov exclaimed. "Don't fire that in here! Zina get back!"

Zina didn't seem to hear him. She screamed her lungs out as the two female operatives struggled for control of the gun. Amy stomped a high-heeled foot onto her opponent's flat pump. Nasim cried out. Her arms swung sideways—Zheltkov ducking out of the way—and a shot rang out. A bullet tore through Zheltkov's leather armchair and buried itself in the wooden cabinet.

"Fools!" Zheltkov yelled. "You'll kill us all!"

David, strapped to his seat, watched the struggle. Should he unbuckle and help Amy, or would he just get in her way? The aircraft banked to the right and tipped downward. What was going on? Then the cockpit door opened and an olive-skinned man with a captain's peaked hat and a thick mustache appeared in the doorway, a gun in his hand.

"Amy!" David yelled. "Behind you!"

Amy head-butted Nasim on the nose and turned the gun toward the new threat. Another blast sounded, and the captain fell backward onto the floor.

Nasim roared, her nose pouring blood, and swung her arms around toward David. *Holy crap!* David sank into the chair's soft upholstery. He flinched as a third shot exploded. There was a shattering of glass and a whirlwind blasted the inside of the cabin. David had trouble keeping his eyes open.

The jet's descent sped up into a sickening dive. Oxygen masks dropped from the ceiling, their supply hoses curving toward the gaping hole where a window had been. The escaping air pulled at David's body, which strained against the seatbelt strap. Papers, knives, and cocktail glasses—anything not nailed to the floor—circled in the air and sped toward the sucking hole like bathwater down a drain.

Zina, still shrieking, sped past David's head, rump first. For a moment, her body blocked the window, and the floating objects dropped to the floor. Then, with a sickening crunch and squelch, her body folded, squeezing through the hole, and the whirlwind raged again.

Nasim and Amy, still entwined and struggling for the gun, flew toward the window like skydivers. David reached out and grabbed Amy's legs. Her skirt flapped in his face. Her goose-fleshed skin slipped through his fingers until he held onto her by her ankle. The pilot's body crashed past the human chain and disappeared through the hole.

Nasim's feet tapered toward the sucking window. Amy's grip on the gun was Nasim's only anchor to the inside of the cabin. Realizing this, Amy let go. But Nasim had seen that coming. She grasped Amy's fingers with her other hand and struggled to bring the gun back around. Amy was Nasim's lifeline, but that wouldn't stop Nasim from blowing Amy's brains out.

With a grunt of effort and just as the gun barrel found its target, Amy chopped at Nasim's hand and the Elders operative slipped free. With a familiar crunch and squelch, the terrorist exited the cabin.

David's burden had grown lighter, but he groaned at the effort. His head spun from the vertigo of the jet's dizzying plummet and the lack of oxygen. His fingers went numb around Amy's ankles as stars flashed before his eyes. He had to hold on to her, but how much longer would he remain conscious?

Without warning, Amy dropped to the floor, and David slumped back in his armchair. Cabin pressure had equalized, and David's head cleared with every panting breath. Peter Zheltkov lay back in his armchair, his hair in disarray, exhausted but conscious. During the excitement, he had somehow fastened his seatbelt.

Amy climbed to her very unsteady feet. The jet was still dropping fast. "There's no pilot!" she yelled over the noise of the gusting wind.

She hurried toward the cockpit. David unbuckled and joined her, sitting down in the copilot's seat. A panel bristled with dials and levers. Red lights flashed across the board. The Atlantic Ocean filled the narrow windows, close enough that David could see the white crests of waves. "Can you fly one of these?"

"I trained on a Cessna, but it's been a while."

For the first time since Nasim appeared with her gun, David thought they might get out of the plane alive. "Same idea, right?"

Amy stared at the flashing dashboard. "Not even close."

David's optimism fled. Amy pulled back on the joystick. Nothing happened.

"It's not responding."

"How can that be?"

"I don't know. Something broke during the descent, or the pilot locked the controls."

"Can you unlock them?"

"I'll try." Her fingers traced over the array of buttons and levers, and she toggled a few of them. "It's not working." The ocean raced toward them.

"Can we make an emergency landing?"

"We're in the middle of the ocean."

"What about Bermuda?"

"Too far south. We're heading to London. There's nothing but blue seas between here and Nova Scotia."

David swore. This was a high-end private jet. What were the guidelines for surviving this contingency? Maybe Zheltkov had an idea?

A loud crash came from the main cabin. That did not sound good.

"What was that?" Amy asked.

"I don't know. I'll have a look."

He got to his feet and hiked back to the cabin, holding onto the chairs and hand grips for support. Sunlight poured into the cabin from a large hole where the cabin door had been.

Zheltkov's hair spun as he stood at the open door. The old man had a contingency plan, after all. His plan was to jump out of the plane wearing a yellow life vest and with an orange parachute strapped to his back.

"Peter!" David yelled.

Zheltkov turned. "Sorry, friend. Last parachute."

"What?" He couldn't be serious.

"The others are away for a safety review. We weren't expecting company. Good luck!" And with that, he stepped out the door, and air friction swept him up and out of view.

Bastard! David hurried along the aisle and checked the storage cabinets. Zheltkov hadn't lied. There were no more parachutes, only three yellow flotation vests. David grabbed them and lumbered back to the cockpit.

How long did they have before impact? Was it better to jump out the door or to strap himself to a seat? He'd read somewhere that the rear end of a plane was the safest place to sit in a crash. He had to get Amy out of the cockpit. As he stumbled onward, the floor rose and began to level out.

Joy flooded his heart. She'd done it! Amy had unlocked the controls. She'd turn the plane around, and they'd head back to New York. Air traffic control could talk them through the landing. He made a mental note to extract the Holy Prepuce from the cabinet before they left the plane.

"Zheltkov bailed out," David said, back in the cockpit. They were only a few hundred feet above the waves. Amy had gained control not a second too soon.

"He bailed out?"

"Yeah, with the only parachute."

"Son of a bitch!"

"Yeah, well, that's his problem now. Good job on leveling out. That was a close call!"

"I didn't do anything. It's on autopilot."

Again, David's optimism met an ugly and untimely death. "Where's it taking us?"

She pointed. On the horizon, a small forested island loomed. It couldn't be more than two miles wide.

"What is that?"

"I have no idea! But I can't see a landing strip."

She grabbed the radio communications receiver and flipped a switch. "Mayday! Mayday! Can anyone read me?" Only the sound of the windy cabin answered. Amy repeated her call for help.

"How are we going to land?"

"Hard. Sit down and buckle up."

"Shouldn't we move to the back?"

"There's no time."

She was right. The distant island was now a rocky bulk covered in leafy trees. There was no landing strip. No buildings or boats either. David dropped the lifesavers, sat down in the copilot's seat, and fastened the seatbelt. Something loud and mechanical churned inside the plane.

"What was that?"

"Landing gear. Hold on."

David grabbed the seat and tried not to wet himself. The forest rushed at them, way too fast. "If we don't make it," he said, "I want you to know I was looking forward to getting to know you."

Amy turned to him and smiled. "Same here, David. But we're going to make it. We have to. OK?"

The jet shuddered as the landing gear skimmed the tops of the trees. They dropped sharply, large white trunks battering the aircraft's nose, slicing through the wings and spinning the cockpit from side to side. The plane plowed through the forest, branches smashing the windows and swiping at David's face.

David shot forward, pressing against the seatbelt straps. The plane had ground to a halt. Then the nose shifted downward at a precipitous angle. Metal groaned and creaked. The cockpit had become a treehouse.

David looked at Amy. She looked back. They dared to smile. They laughed too. "We made it. We made it!"

Metal groaned again, and the treehouse shifted. "Oh, no. No!"

The cockpit turned nose down. The ground far below disappeared in a blanket of green and shadow. With a horrific crunch, the latticework of branches that had supported their weight gave way.

CHAPTER 31

David opened his eyes. A pair of yellow reptilian eyes stared back. A forked tongue tasted the air.

David jumped and pain shot down his leg. His sudden movement spooked the thick, slimy snake, which slithered out of the battered cockpit, seeming to decide that the human would cause indigestion.

Birds cawed and flies swarmed. The air was hot and moist. David's heart drummed in his chest. The cockpit had landed face-first in a bed of lush undergrowth on the forest floor. Jungle would be a more accurate term. The seatbelt had prevented David from falling out the cockpit window, now empty of glass. Amy slumped forward in her seat, the seatbelt strap stretched tight at her waist.

"Amy," he said. "Amy!"

He shifted around and discovered he could not move his right leg. The force of the drop had ripped the dashboard down the center, shattering the dials, popping levers from their sockets, and crumpling the metal chassis over his leg.

He shook Amy by the shoulder. "Amy!"

"Mm?"

Oh, thank God, she's alive! "Amy, wake up!"

She smacked her lips. "Mm."

"Amy, we have to get out of here."

She yawned. "I had such a bad dream. We were in a plane crash." She opened her eyes. "Oh." She looked about her. "Are you OK?"

"My leg is stuck, but besides that, I think so."

She raised her legs, rested her feet on the dashboard, and unfastened her seatbelt. She fiddled with the equipment. "The radio's dead," she said. "So much for calling for help. Here. Take my hand and open your seatbelt."

Gravity pulled David downward, putting pressure on his knee. He lifted his leg onto the dashboard to avoid falling out face-first, but his right leg remained trapped. "It's no good."

Amy stepped along the dashboard. "I had to wear heels today, didn't I?" She climbed through the window and slid down the jet's broken nose, landing on the ground. "Hold tight, I'll look around." She disappeared from view.

"I'll just wait here," he said, as though he had any choice in the matter.

How long had they hung there? Judging by the dull hint of sunlight filtering down through the trees, David guessed it was early afternoon. The vegetation shifted nearby, and he hoped the unseen mover was Amy. He had to free his leg by nightfall or he'd be in trouble. If he had no broken bones, he'd be OK.

Amy returned with a long, thick branch, and David helped her climb back into the cockpit. She inserted the branch along David's stuck leg and planted her feet against the far side of the cockpit for traction. Then she levered the dashboard upward, using her entire body weight. The metal creaked. Sensing a decrease in pressure, David slipped his leg out, sacrificing a shoe in the process. Amy helped him squeeze out the window and slide down to the jungle floor.

David gasped. The cockpit was just that—a cockpit. The crash had decapitated the jet, and the fuselage was nowhere in sight.

"I suppose we won't be flying out in that."

"Nope." Amy examined his leg. The crash had ripped his

trouser leg and bruised his skin. "Can you walk?"

"I think so." The pain in his leg was already fading. He shifted his weight to his injured leg and limped a few steps. "I'm good to go." He stared around at the dense jungle. "Which way is New York?"

Amy laughed. "Let's find some water and shelter. We might be here a while."

David shivered at the thought. Jordy and Mitchell were counting on him. Would the Temple give him the benefit of the doubt if he disappeared for a few days or would they assume he'd run away?

Amy stalked off, picking through the undergrowth with the broken branch.

David slapped a mosquito on his cheek and followed. "I hate camping."

They found the main body of the Falcon in two parts two hundred feet away. The path cleared by the crash was easy to trace. The wings had separated early on, leaving shredded, stumpy shoulders. A destroyed luxury jet was a sad thing to behold. Three plastic water bottles and a half-dozen tomato juices had survived the impact.

They took small sips of water, rationing their meager supplies, not knowing when they'd next find potable water. Then they flopped on the remaining leather armchairs.

"Do you think anyone's looking for us?"

"Not yet. We didn't send a distress signal and we're only expected in London around now. It might take some time until somebody realizes Zheltkov's plane is missing."

David got up and moved to the wooden cabinet. The lock held. Zheltkov had taken the key with him. David would have to break it open to get to the Prepuce.

"Try this," Amy said. She handed David a length of metal from the jet's wreckage. He shoved the thin edge into the gap behind the door of the cabinet and leaned on the rod with his full weight. The wood splintered around the hinges, and the door fell out. David handed the plastic-wrapped Prepuce to Amy.

"Do you think he survived?"

"Zheltkov? He's shark food by now. Talking of being eaten alive, we should stay here tonight, gather wood for a fire. The predators will come out after dark. We'll be safe once we seal the openings."

A twig crunched nearby. The talk of predators had heightened David's sense of hearing.

"What was that?" Amy whispered.

"A deer?" David guessed. What other friendly animals lived in forests?

Quietly, Amy got to her feet and raised her branch like a baseball bat ready to swing. David fell in behind her. They stepped out of the torn fuselage. Amy moved in the sound's direction, then stopped, listening.

Something moved behind them. David turned around. A shadow slipped between the tree trunks, then another—lithe forms as tall as men. Again, leaves crunched behind them and they spun around.

Four nearly naked men stepped out from behind the trees. Each carried a long spear with a sharp stone edge. The warriors crouched low, their elbows bent, poised for attack. The stranded couple turned to flee, but another five tribesmen approached from behind, surrounding David and Amy.

As the armed men drew closer, David's mind itched. Something about the jungle warriors looked wrong. They wore the skimpy, furry loincloths one would expect of a primitive indigenous tribe, but their skin was the milky white of Europeans. Their eyes were green and brown and blue, their hair blond and tawny brown. He and Amy seemed to have landed on a live-action set of *The Flintstones*.

Amy dropped the branch in surrender. Forget the wild animals, tonight they'd end up in the stewing pot of this yet-undiscovered tribe of pale-skinned cannibals.

The tallest of the warriors drew near, his hair and beard wild and red. Ice-blue eyes drank in the newcomers and their broken vehicle with deep suspicion. He poked the stone-edged spear toward David's chest and spoke to them, his voice full of curiosity laced with malice. To David's surprise, he understood their language. The warrior had spoken English but with a strange Russian accent. The question he asked startled the couple.

"Did the Jews send you?"

CHAPTER 32

"Ouch!" David said. The tribesmen prodded him with their stone-tipped spears whenever he slowed down. "I'd walk faster if you'd untie me, OK? Ouch!"

Despite David's assurance that "the Jews" had not sent them, the warriors had tied his wrists together with twine and chained his ankles with a two-foot rope. They let Amy walk unrestrained, not seeming to consider her a threat. They were in for a surprise.

After a ten-minute march through the jungle, the party arrived at the narrow opening of a cave. They entered in single file and assembled in a rounded antechamber. Light from a hole in the cave ceiling fell on a pile of stone-age equipment on the dusty floor. One warrior struck two flinty stones together, the sparks igniting homemade torches of dried leaves. Holding the flames aloft, the party entered a dark tunnel.

David had fallen into the hands of yet another torch-bearing secret society. At least this clan had dispensed with the robes, though he wasn't sure the loincloths were an improvement.

The cave floor descended into the rocky belly of the island. Millennia of rainwater had formed the rough, angular walls. But here and there David saw signs of chiseling with crude implements—widened passageways and removed outcrops to prevent nasty bumps on the head. They passed through large chambers lit by skylights far above. Stalactites formed grotesque chandeliers. Stalagmites created natural partitions on the dusty cave floor, behind which small, grimy faces stared at the aliens who had fallen from the sky.

Finally, they entered an immense cavern lit by flaming torches on the walls. A dozen tribesmen stared at them as they entered, but also women. David could not help staring at them. They wore elaborate Victorian ballroom gowns made of dried leaves and twine and had plaited their hair into demure braids. His attention turned to the large throne at the center of the subterranean hall. An oversized armchair—a jumble of driftwood held together by lengths of twine—formed a Frankenstein throne.

The tribal leader who sat on the throne wore no shoes or socks but a black tuxedo and top hat. Or what remained of them. Twine stitches had patched the countless holes and tears in the faded material. His beady eyes studied the strangers with imperious suspicion. David had seen that impressive mustache and tidy beard before. But where?

The red-haired warrior separated from the crowd, approached the throned leader, and whispered in his ear. Then he stood beside the throne, facing the audience.

"You stand in the presence of Nicholas, Warden of Tsarlandia. Present yourselves."

Nicholas. Tsarlandia. David's brain connected the dots. The mustache and beard belonged to the photo of Nicholas II at the Met. But even if the last tsar of the Russian Empire had somehow escaped the Bolsheviks a hundred years ago, there was no way he'd still be under thirty!

Amy nodded at David, a cue for him to do the talking. David cleared his throat.

"I'm David Zelig, and this is Amy Anderson. We're from New York."

"New York?" Nicholas's eyes brightened, and his manner

softened. His accent matched that of the wild-haired warrior. The islanders all spoke the heavily accented English of Russian immigrants.

"Yes, ah, Your Highness." Unsure how to address this so-called Warden, David had erred on the side of flattery.

Nicholas waved the words away with his hand. "One man alone is worthy of that title—the man we all serve." David swallowed hard but said nothing. Who was he talking about? "The Emperor," the Warden said, sensing David's confusion.

David shifted on his feet. He sensed that a word out of place might land him in the stew pot. Best to let Nicholas fill the silence, which he did.

"The Emperor who sent you to us." A smile broke out on his face, and he teared up. "We have waited many years for your arrival—generations! All this time, we remained stead-fast to the Emperor. Long live the Emperor!"

The room answered in chorus. "Long live the Emperor!"

"At last, the Emperor has sent you to rescue us and return us to the fold! We have made every preparation to be of maximal use to the Emperor in the New World. We have educated our children in English, as well as Russian and French. Like ourselves, our children know the Bible from cover to cover. All of us remain the Emperor's loyal servants to this very day." He turned to the wild-haired warrior. "Alexander, remove his restraints."

Alexander gave his leader a doubtful glance, then trudged forward, cut the ropes with a flint blade, and returned to his post beside the throne.

The island leader pressed his hands together, and his face filled with dread. "I beseech you, David Zelig! Apologize to the Emperor. Beg his forgiveness. We failed in our mission. But we are not to blame. The Emperor's enemies struck us down. They hound us day and night!"

David was adrift at sea. "Your mission?"

Nicholas nodded with enthusiasm. "Show them, Alexander."

Alexander bowed his head. He walked behind the throne

and dragged a small wooden table into view. On the table sat a wooden box. He opened the box, and David's breath caught in his throat. On a bed of straw sat a large golden egg.

"Open it," Nicholas said, and Alexander complied. The egg cracked open on golden hinges to reveal a golden trophy cup. A diamond-encrusted frame above the trophy contained a monochrome photo portrait of the royal couple, Tsar Nicholas II and his wife.

"Emperor Nicholas II entrusted my great-grandfather with this holy mission—to prepare a new home for the tsar in the United States of America. This was, of course, a mere precaution, in the event that the Empire's enemies brewed trouble at home. He gave my great-grandfather the newest egg in his Fabergé collection, Victory. Now, after over a hundred years of waiting, we bring the tsar Victory!"

"Victory!" the crowd chanted. "Victory!"

David could not believe his eyes or his ears. Amy stood beside him, her mouth agape. They had located the lost egg, the tenth imperial Fabergé egg, Victory. So many questions remained.

"But if the tsar sent you to the United States, how did you end up here?"

Nicholas's countenance clouded over. "Their ship sank. Only my great-grandfather and a few loyal members of his team escaped in a lifeboat along with the clothes on their backs and a bundle of Bibles. The sinking was a terrible tragedy. What a wonderful ship it was!" He caressed a lacquered plank of wood that comprised the throne. "The finest ship in the world. An unsinkable ship."

David gasped again as the realization hit. "The *Titanic*?" he said. "Your great-grandfather survived the *Titanic*?"

Nicholas seemed surprised. "You know of the *Titanic*?"

"Everybody does. It's the most famous shipwreck in modern history."

"1912," Nicholas said. "After two terrible weeks on the open seas, God delivered my great-grandfather's lifeboat to this island. It has been our home ever since."

Their century of isolation appalled David. "In all that time, nobody found you? Nobody discovered your beacons?"

"We lit no beacons. My grandfather hid the lifeboat as soon as he landed."

"But why would he do that?"

"Survival, that's why! You need to understand something about our enemies, the Jews. Their dark powers are limitless. Even an unsinkable ship was no match for those hateful demons! But sinking the world's greatest ship was not enough for their bloodthirsty appetites. They sent boats to finish off the survivors in the chilly waters. But my great-grandfather knew what they were up to. He directed his lifeboat away from the lights and the screams."

"What?" David said, unbelieving.

"Oh, yes. The Jews will stop at nothing until they've killed every last one of the tsar's faithful. That's why we chose to live underground. Only here are we safe from the Jews' evil nets."

David couldn't hold back. These poor survivors had spent a hundred years cut off from civilization because of an age-old, irrational delusion. "But Jews didn't sink the *Titanic*. It hit an iceberg."

Nicholas laughed, studying David with pity. "Don't be so naïve, David Zelig. Who do you think placed that iceberg in the *Titanic*'s path?" He tapped his forehead, as though he'd just shared a brilliant insight. "The Jews! Their eyes and claws are everywhere!"

David opened his mouth to speak, then closed it. He wanted to help them, but the tribe's lunacy was so profound, so self-reinforcing, he didn't know where to begin.

"No," he said in frustration. "Jews aren't evil or demonic. They're just people like you and me. Some are smart, but others are downright stupid. And they're always arguing. They couldn't put together a functional secret conspiracy if they tried. Trust me," he added under his breath, "I know."

Amy's hand touched his arm. He'd gone too far, and he knew it. But how was he supposed to crack those delusions and set them free? He searched for another angle.

"I'm sorry to be the bearer of bad tidings, but Emperor Nicholas II died a long time ago."

The man on the throne leaned forward and sneered. "Do you take us for fools? Of course Nicholas II has died by now. His son, Alexei, too. To our great regret and shame, we do not even know the name of the current tsar."

"There is no current tsar. There is no Russian Empire."

"Treason!" a voice cried behind them. "That's treason!"

David continued, doing a little math on the fly. "The last tsar, Nicholas II, was executed in 1918 along with his entire family, six years after your grandfather sailed on the *Titanic*."

"Enough of this!" Nicholas roared. "I will not have you spew lies in our court. We asked you if the Jews sent you, and you lied!"

"I didn't lie. Nobody sent us here!"

"Prove it, then. Show us the foreskin!"

"What?" David said. Did they know about the Holy Prepuce? He was about to ask Nicholas about the relic when a new chant rose among the assembled tribespeople. "Show us! Show us! Show us!"

Strong, cruel hands gripped David's arms. Yet others grabbed his legs, lifting him off the ground.

"No," David said, realizing what they were doing and resisting the indignity with every fiber of his being. "No!"

"Leave him alone!" Amy cried, but to no avail.

Hands pulled at his belt buckle and unzipped his trousers, pulling them down around his ankles. His underpants followed. The room sank in terrified silence, as David's circumcised penis flopped unceremoniously for all to see.

"Just as I suspected," Nicholas roared. "He's one of them!" Apparently, David was no longer worthy of being addressed directly. He had become a thing, not a thinking, feeling human being.

The hands dropped him to the floor as if physical contact with the Jew would contaminate them. David reached down and collected his trousers, along with what remained of his self-respect.

"Spies!" Nicholas raged on, turning a defamatory finger at them. "Assassins!"

A ring of spear-wielding warriors closed around them. "They'll die for this. Both of them!"

CHAPTER 33

"Where is he?" Jordan complained. He paced the cramped dungeon cell, stepping over Mitchell, who was doing push-ups on the hard floor. The Temple provided its prisoners with two daily meals of lentil soup, a bucket of cold water, and a chamber pot, but no means of entertainment.

"Say it again, Jordy. That'll speed Dave up."

Jordan rolled his eyes. Petty sarcasm during a crisis was typical of Mitch. His so-called friend got on his nerves at the best of times. Being cooped up with him in a tiny cell for days on end was driving Jordan out of his mind.

"You might be happy waiting around and doing nothing, Mitch, but I'm not. I've got companies to run, board meetings to attend. It's been three days already, and Dave hasn't shown."

Mitchell panted. "Yeah, maybe he's abandoned us."

"What? No! How can you say that?"

Mitchell rested on the floor and sighed. "In his shoes, I'd do the same thing. You would too."

Jordan would not allow that. "Maybe you would, Mitch, but Dave would never abandon us."

Mitchell snorted. "Don't be so sure. What if he couldn't get their Holy Foreskin or whatever they call it? Do you expect him to come back here so they can kill him too?"

"No, I expect him to get the FBI to rescue us."

"You're right."

Jordan opened his mouth to argue, then closed it. Had Mitchell just agreed with him? "I am?"

"Yeah. And seeing that the FBI hasn't shown up, either Dave abandoned us or he's dead."

Jordan's shoulders slumped. He'd been right to doubt Mitchell's sudden embrace of reason. "You don't really believe that."

"Why not, Jordy? I'm sorry to break this to you, but not every story has a happy ending. Superman doesn't swoop down and save the day."

Of course, Jordan knew that. He wasn't naïve. Terrible, tragic things happened every day and all over the world. But they happened to other people, not Jordy or his inner circle. Dying before thirty in a dank dungeon had never featured on his checklist of probable life outcomes.

Jordan hid his fear behind a mask of sarcasm. "Oh, so now you're an authority on how the world works?"

"Yeah, I guess I am."

Jordan balled his hands into fists. "Why are you so mean to me?"

"Mean to *you*? I thought the relationship was mutual."

"Not just the last few weeks, Mitch. You've been out to get me from the beginning—ever since we met."

"What are you talking about?"

Jordan hadn't wanted to regurgitate that memory, but Mitchell had forced his hand. "I'm talking about Aspen, Mitch, the winter of our sophomore year."

"What about it?"

"You don't even remember, do you?"

"The snow was great. What else was there to remember?"

"Melissa Baron, does that name ring a bell?"

"Melissa... Sure, I remember her. Great rack. What about her?"

"Don't pretend you don't remember. She was my girlfriend until you… stole her."

"Oh, please, Jordy. She wasn't girlfriend material. I was doing you a favor."

"A favor? I loved her!"

"Oh, come on."

"I loved her and you knew it, so you had to steal her."

"OK, whatever. You'd gone out for, like, two days."

"I'd had my eye on her for years. She was the first girl I'd ever asked out. It took me months to work up the courage. I was so happy. Until I walked in on the two of you in the hot tub."

Mitchell said nothing for a few seconds. "I'm sorry, Jordy. I was a dick."

Jordan stood there, his teeth clenched. He didn't want an apology. Words couldn't undo the hurt and betrayal he'd felt, the anger he'd carried all these years.

"I didn't think she mattered to you so much."

Jordan scoffed but Mitchell continued.

"Seriously, dude. You had everything going for you. Doing well at school, winning all those awards. All my mom could say was, 'Why can't you be more like Jordan Brody? You need to spend more time with Jordan Brody.' She drove me nuts." Mitchell's shoulders rose and fell as he breathed. "You'd be a success. That was clear to everyone even then. And I would coast along, letting everybody down. It felt good to beat you for once. Not that I could have bragged about Melissa to my mom."

Jordan didn't know what to say. Mitchell always seemed so self-assured, so impregnable. Jordan hadn't realized his old friend resented him. The anger subsided a little.

Mitchell sighed again. "I'm sorry I screwed Melissa Baron. We'll probably die here anyway, might as well patch things up. What the hell, right?"

Grudgingly, Jordan agreed. There was no point taking that heartache with him to the grave. "I forgive you."

"Thanks, buddy. If it's any consolation, she wasn't so good in bed."

"In bed? You mean you hooked up with her again?"

Jordan regretted dispensing his forgiveness so quickly.

"I might have."

"How many times did you sleep with her, Mitch?"

"I don't know. Four or five."

"Four or five?"

"Geez, Jordy. That was years ago. I've said I'm sorry, OK? And you said you forgave me."

Mitchell was right. He had apologized, and Jordan needed to let it go. He might never get another chance.

"OK, Mitch. Apology accepted."

He held out his hand, and Mitchell shook it. The time had come to move on.

"What now?" Mitchell asked. "Should we try to break out?"

Jordan had considered the possibility. "Nah. There's too many of them and they're all armed. I guess we just wait for Dave to bring them the Prepuce."

Mitchell nodded gravely. "I'm sure he's OK."

"Yeah, me too. He's probably on his way back already."

CHAPTER 34

A wet sensation woke David with a start. His hand shot from the water just as a flash of long serrated teeth broke the surface, followed by a dozen small fins. The flesh-eating creatures had risen from the murky depths the moment his hand had slipped over the edge of the watery prison.

He rolled onto his back, bumping into Amy. The tribesmen had herded the alleged spies into a large cavern and forced them to walk a narrow plank over deep waters to the slab of rock in the center.

Alexander, their red-bearded turnkey, had removed the plank, then dropped a bucket of entrails into the murky waters. The frenzy of teeth and scales that churned the water had dissuaded the prisoners from swimming across the moat to freedom.

David crouched on the clammy slab of rock, hugging his legs in a fetal position. The tribesmen didn't believe in quick deaths. David was tempted to dive into the waters and get it over with. Yesterday's trauma was too great to bear.

Amy stirred beside him. She rested a consoling hand on his shoulder, and he flinched at her touch.

"You OK?"

David shrugged. After witnessing his humiliation, would

she ever respect him again? Would she still love him?

"David, speak to me."

"You don't belong here," he said. "You're not Jewish. I should have told them right away."

Amy shifted closer. "David, you don't belong here either. You've done nothing wrong."

"Tell the men with the spears."

"I don't care what they think. They had no right to treat you like that."

David shivered in the dark. "You always hear the stories," he said. "About the Holocaust. How the Nazis shaved their victim's heads, stripped them naked, herded them like sheep to the slaughter. You think you understand how they felt, but you don't." Tears distorted his voice, but he was beyond caring about that. "Not until they do it to you." He shuddered. "I feel so... sub-human." She wrapped her arms around him.

"It's OK, David," she whispered. "I'm here with you. I love you and I'm not going anywhere without you. We'll get through this together."

David shook his head. "To them, I'm not human. I'm a diseased rat. They'll kill me without thinking twice. I've never felt so violated." David paused. He *had* felt this hurt before, and the time had come to tell Amy the whole truth.

"I'm not brave," he said. "You think I am, but I'm not."

"You are, David. I know you."

"No." He sucked in a deep, halting breath. He hadn't wanted to tell her but he owed her this much before the tribesmen slaughtered them both. "I didn't start the Trio to save Jews or to prevent the next synagogue shooting. I did it for revenge."

Even in the gloomy cavern, surprise glimmered in her eyes. David told her everything: about Preston Clancy and how the Zelig family had lost Zelig Pictures; how when David had turned to Preston to save his apartment, Preston had confessed to his betrayal of the Zelig family; how Preston had unmasked his intense Jew-hatred, telling David, the "filthy Jew," that he'd better "crawl back to Europe."

"Wow," Amy said, hugging him. "What a jerk. I'm betting his family didn't sail over on the *Mayflower* either."

David's laugh was a short gasp. "The Zeligs moved to America long before his family, that's for sure. But when have facts ever stopped an anti-Semite?" David's chest heaved at the memory. "I felt so enraged and helpless."

David relived the surge of righteous indignation. Tears trickled from his eyes in the damp darkness of the water-logged prison. Amy rested her head on his shoulder.

"I'd never felt so miserable. He'd said the name 'Zelig' as though it meant 'cockroach.' 'You're a Jew,' he seemed to say. 'You will always be inferior to me.' How could this happen in our post-Holocaust, civil-rights world—in the Land of the Free? This wouldn't happen if the Jews controlled the world. Oh, no. Preston wouldn't dare mess with the Zeligs if the fear of the Elders of Zion cast its shadow over the bigots of the world."

There, he'd said it. Amy would leave him now. A vindictive cockroach wasn't worthy of her love or admiration. She could do better than him. Assuming they got out of this mess.

But Amy only hugged him tighter. "I'm so sorry you experienced that, David. I can't imagine how that feels, but you're not alone."

David pulled away. "The thing is, Preston was right. I've done nothing special. I didn't create Zelig Pictures. I'm just the great-grandson who happened to be born into the right family. I didn't deserve any of it."

"David, you don't have to cure cancer to deserve to be treated like a human being. You don't have to apologize for being lucky either."

"That's easy for you to say. You're amazing. You did things in your life. You've gone undercover and saved lives— you drove a freakin' motorcycle through a wall! You're a real-life Superwoman."

Amy fell silent, and David realized he'd hit a raw nerve.

"I wanted none of that," she said. "I hated the lies and deception, living a double—sometimes triple—life. The people I've had to kill will always haunt me. I'm tired of being a pawn in a game run by old hateful men. All I ever wanted was to be ordinary, to do ordinary things, think ordinary thoughts, without worrying about who I'm supposed to be or how much everybody else knows. Most of all, I wanted an ordinary, honest relationship with a man I love and respect. And you've given me that."

She shifted closer and held him again. This time, he didn't pull away.

"Don't let the haters get to you. Look at them. This is the twenty-first century, and they still live in caves."

David laughed, a short, hot burst of released tension.

"The Temple isn't any better," she continued. "They're prisoners of their own hatred. They have no right to judge you or me or anybody. Don't waste your time and energy worrying about them. Oh, and in case you didn't notice, you saved my life too. If it weren't for you, I would have been sucked out the window like the others."

David was also the reason she had boarded that plane in the first place, but he gave that detail a free pass. She'd worked hard to cheer him up, and she deserved better than a puddle of self-pity and doubt.

"So you still want me around?"

"More than ever."

"Even after what they did to me?"

"David, I just blew my FBI cover *and* pissed off the Temple for you. It'd take a lot more than dropping your trunks in public to push me away."

She leaned in and kissed him hard. David responded in kind, losing himself in the moment. Soon, a tribe of anti-Semitic cavemen would execute them both, but for now, he'd snatch another fleeting moment of joy from this cruel, cruel world.

Wood scraped on stone at the edge of the cavern, and David and Amy disengaged. Alexander had returned with his henchmen, who slid the plank back over the treacherous moat.

"Jews," he said. "Time to meet your fate."

CHAPTER 35

To the slow and ominous beating of a drum, David and Amy followed Alexander through a dark tunnel, their hands restrained with twine. Spear-toting guards followed the spies in case they got any clever ideas about escaping. *This is it,* David thought. *These are our last moments in this life.* He'd had close shaves with death before, but this time was different. He and Amy had no friends on the island. No one back home knew they were here. There was nobody left to save them.

The tunnel emptied into the great hall, where they had met the clan's leader and earned his loathing. From his new throne—one of the leather armchairs from the crashed jet—Nicholas eyed the couple with disgust. A throng of onlookers had gathered for the big event.

How would the islanders execute them? David saw no nooses or guillotines, only a thick wooden stake, as tall as a man, sticking out of the dusty cave floor. The stone spears in the islanders' hands were sharp but rough. So much for a quick, clean death.

"Amy," David whispered. "They might grant me some final words. If they do, I'll confess."

"What?" Amy said, confused and alarmed. "Why?"

David didn't have time to explain, but he wanted to make

sure she wouldn't interfere with his plan. "They've made up their minds about me, but not you. I'll tell them you're not Jewish and that I deceived you into following me to the island."

"But David—"

"Please, Amy. It's the only way either of us will survive. I need you to deliver the Prepuce to the Temple and save my friends."

He faced forward again, cutting off further discussion. Amy didn't talk him out of it. She knew he was right. David had dragged her into this mess too, and he'd make sure she didn't go down with him.

But David didn't get to speak his last words. The guards prodded them to a stone slab before the throne and bade them face the leader.

"David Zelig and Amy Anderson, you stand accused of spying on Tsarlandia for the Jews. This crime is punishable by death. How do you plead?"

David almost laughed with relief. "There's a trial?"

"Yes, of course. We're not savages! You will receive a fair trial. How do you plead?"

David sucked in a deep breath. This was his chance. The crowd was baying for blood. By offering himself as their scapegoat, he'd save Amy from the same bitter fate. He opened his mouth to speak.

"Not guilty," Amy said, beating him to the mark. "Neither of us." Her mouth tightened with defiance. Her unspoken message to David: We're in this together, pal. Now get us the hell out!

David swallowed hard. How was he supposed to do that?

"Fine," Nicholas said, adjusting the threadbare top hat on his head. "Alexander, swear them in."

Alexander approached the defendants. "Place your right hand on the Bible," he told David, "and repeat after me."

The worn book looked too thin to be a Bible. David read the title on the flaking cover and almost swallowed his tongue.

"Hand on the Bible!" Alexander said. David complied and swore to tell the whole truth.

"That's no Bible," he whispered to Amy after Alexander had sworn her in and stepped away.

"What is it?"

"*The Protocols of the Elders of Zion!*"

Amy's face fell. "We're doomed."

"No," David said. "Not yet."

The Protocols had given him an idea. No wonder the islanders obsessed over Jewish conspiracies. Their only literature was an incendiary piece of anti-Semitic propaganda, a work that David had studied in depth. Hope sprouted in his heart.

"David Zelig," Nicholas boomed from his throne. "Do you deny that you are a Jew?"

"No, sir."

"And do you deny that you came here to spy for the Jews?"

"Sir, if I may. Why would the Jews want to spy on you?"

"I ask the questions, Jew!"

"Your Excellency, you promised us a fair trial, and we're at your mercy. What harm can there be in answering?"

Nicholas considered this and grudgingly gave in. "Very well. The answer should be obvious. Collecting information on those faithful to the empire will help you destroy them and the monarchy."

"Sir, why would we want to destroy the monarchy?"

Nicholas ground his teeth. David was stretching the leader's patience, but he had promised a fair trial and there were only so many opportunities for entertainment on the island. He humored the defendant once more. "Because the Jews want to replace the monarchy with democracy, a form of government they can manipulate easily to control the masses."

"And yet," David said, "when the Russian Empire ended, communism took over. If the Jews wanted democracy, they failed miserably. How powerful can the Jews be?"

Nicholas laughed. "Your lying tongue has ensnared you. Jews were among the founders of communism too. Was not Karl Marx a Jew?"

David shrugged. "True, but few Jews appeared among the Bolshevik leadership or the later Soviet Union." The assembled tribesmen shifted on their feet. David's reference to historical events unknown to them had unsettled them. David continued. "Now I'm confused. Do the Jews favor democracy or communism?"

"Both," Nicholas said. "Neither," he added, correcting himself. After a moment's consideration, he added, "They are opportunists. They employ whatever strategy is likely to give them control."

David had the cavern's attention. The Warden's change in tune had injured his case, and David searched the historical facts and trivia he'd learned over the past few weeks for more ammunition.

"People have hated Jews for being rich," he said, "and for being poor, for remaining separate from Gentile society and for trying to assimilate. No matter what Jews do, the irrational hate changes the target to fit the Jew."

Murmurs circled among the audience.

Nicholas raised his hand for silence. "Why should we believe a word you say, Jewish spy?"

"Because we're from out there." David pointed upward, in the general direction of the outside world. "We've seen what the last hundred years did for humanity. And trust me, those were a difficult hundred years. Two world wars claimed tens of millions of lives. The Germans murdered six million Jews throughout Europe. Where were the all-powerful Elders of Zion then? Communism led to the deaths of one hundred million people, whereas democracy and capitalism have allowed most of the world's population to escape poverty, increase life expectancy, and prosper."

David pointed to the worn copy of *The Protocols* still in Alexander's hand. "That so-called Bible is a well-known forgery created by the secret police of the Russian Empire."

Voices gasped in the crowd. Any moment now, Nicholas would cut David off and seal his fate. But he didn't. Either David's words had shocked him into silence, or the Tsarlandians' lifelong thirst for enlightenment had overcome their desire for blood. Peter Zheltkov's words rang in David's mind, and he knew they would resonate with the islanders too.

"Senseless hatred kills countless people around the world, not only Jews. But the real victims are the haters themselves. Instead of solving their problems, they blame scapegoats. But once all the scapegoats are dead, the problems remain."

David turned to address the crowd directly. "Look at yourselves. Living in caves, wearing leaves and rags. All because you fear some imaginary enemy. I've got good news for you. These demonic Jews exist only in your heads. The world outside has progressed. There's plenty of food and clothing for everyone. More people die from obesity than starvation. Medicine has improved by leaps and bounds. We've eradicated smallpox and many other deadly diseases. People live longer and better. We fly across the globe—for vacation! And we return home within hours. Don't even get me started on TV and the Internet. You'll have to see those to believe them."

The islanders blinked at him, mesmerized. The balance had tipped in David's favor. To close the deal, he spoke to their hearts. "Your great-grandparents locked you in a prison of hate and fear," he said. "That's in the past. But is that what you want for *your* children and grandchildren, or do they deserve better?"

CHAPTER 36

TOP SECRET
FEDERAL BUREAU OF INVESTIGATION
OFFICE OF PROFESSIONAL RESPONSIBILITY
Transcript of interview with Mr. Hyman Schneider
Also present:
Special Agent A. Maynard
Special Agent in Charge M. Reed

M. REED:

Mr. Schneider, let me backtrack again. As you told us, David Zelig's girlfriend, Amy Smith, was a Templar agent who had infiltrated the FBI. She used her position as a federal agent to embed the Trio in the Islamic Elders of Zion, the Temple's archenemy. The Elders, for its part, enlisted the Trio to steal the Fabergé eggs, hoping to prevent the Templars from acquiring the Holy Prepuce. The Templars believed the Prepuce would grant them victory in their Holy Crusade against the Elders. The Trio's involvement in the heist also allowed the Temple to intercept the eggs with little resistance. Both covert organizations ultimately wanted Zelig dead.

Meanwhile, Amy had fallen out with the Temple, which

faked her death to withdraw her, their rogue agent, from the FBI and to isolate her from David. But Amy just couldn't stay away. She intervened to save David's life. Effectively, Amy was working against everybody—the FBI, the Temple, and the Elders—by helping David get the Prepuce to save his friends so she could elope with David. Did I get that right?

HYMAN SCHNEIDER:
One hundred percent. Would you gentlemen like a cigar? Every man has a vice, so they say. Cigars are mine. They're Cuban, but imported for personal use, I assure you. Here you go.

M. REED:
No, thank you, Mr. Schneider.

HYMAN SCHNEIDER:
You don't mind if I smoke, do you?

M. REED:
No, of course not. This is your home, after all. Now Zheltkov's jet crash-landed on a small and apparently undiscovered jungle island in the Atlantic. David and Amy fell into the hands of—let me see—the Tsarlandians, a tribe of cave-dwelling Russian imperialists. The sinking of the *Titanic* had shipwrecked their ancestors on the island. Excuse me for being blunt, Mr. Schneider, but doesn't this all sound a little unbelievable?

HYMAN SCHNEIDER:
[PUFFING] Mm. Now that is a good cigar. Sorry, what was the question?

M. REED:
Isn't this story far-fetched?

HYMAN SCHNEIDER:
Which part—that Zheltkov's jet crashed on the island or

that the imperialists were living in caves?

M. REED:

The Atlantic is a very well-traveled ocean, Mr. Schneider. We would know by now about any lost jungle islands and their *Titanic* survivors.

HYMAN SCHNEIDER:

You're absolutely right, Agent Reed. I'd had my doubts about the story too. So I dug around. Did you know that merchant ships sail only a handful of fuel-optimized routes? I didn't either. And Tsarlandia is beyond the reach of lighter vessels. A few intrepid explorers may have visited the island. But colonizing a small, distant island would not be worthwhile for any nation or private individual. Of course, that's just the wild guess of one old man.

A. MAYNARD:

Mr. Schneider. Did the islanders let Mr. Zelig and Ms. Anderson go?

HYMAN SCHNEIDER:

Ha! You would think so, right? But no. Despite David's well-reasoned defense, Nicholas sentenced them to death.

CHAPTER 37

"I was sure that was going to work," David said. A tribesman wrapped lengths of twine around his chest, tying him to the upright tree trunk fixed to the dusty floor. The sound of drums reverberated through the cave—the sound of his imminent death.

"It was a good speech," Amy said, behind him. The captors had tied her to the other side of the tall pole.

"Thanks."

The Tsarlandians gathered around the doomed strangers to witness the execution. A row of warriors drew near, their sharp spears at the ready. David had survived death by gunshot and burning only to face impalement at the hands of cave-dwelling imperialist Russians. The scene was too bizarre to be real. His life couldn't end this way. Was that what Tsar Nicholas II had thought when the Bolshevik firing squad turned their guns and bayonets on him and his family? Now the tsar's long-lost countrymen were about to reenact those murders on David and Amy. History had a very dark and ironic sense of humor.

A shudder passed through the wooden trunk. Was Amy sobbing?

"Amy, I'm sorry."

"Buy me some time," she said. Her request confused him, but at least she didn't seem to be crying. "I'm cutting through the rope, but this piece of flint isn't very sharp."

"Oh! OK!" David wanted to palm his face. While he'd been bemoaning his death, Amy had been working to set them free. He didn't ask how she planned to deal with the roomful of warriors once she had severed their restraints. Unlike David, Amy could handle herself in a fight. He'd hide behind her and hope for the best.

The drums fell silent. Nicholas, the Warden of Tsarlandia, descended his throne and walked over to the doomed convicts while the Tsarlandians looked on.

"David Zelig and Amy Anderson, we have found you guilty of spying for the Jews. You will die for your crimes. Do you have any last words?"

"Yes," David said. He waited. The intensity of the shudder behind him decreased as Amy tried to hide her frantic work from the onlookers.

"Well?"

"There's been a big mistake."

The Warden grew impatient. "You have had your trial, Jew, and my decision is final. We will accept no further evidence."

"You are right, Your Excellency. But there's something I didn't tell you. You see, I am a Jew, but Amy isn't. She's a devout Christian. She only boarded that flight because of me. Please, I beg of you—spare her life!"

Nicholas considered David's words, his jaw clenched. He was eager to proceed with the execution but did not want to appear unmerciful before his followers.

The Warden walked around the stake to Amy. The shudder ceased, and David sagged with disappointment. His attempt to buy Amy more time had backfired and focused the Warden's attention on her!

"Is this true?"

"Yes, Your Excellency," Amy said. If the Warden pardoned her, she'd use her freedom to release David.

Nicholas said, "I wish we could execute you twice for your treachery! A spy and a traitor."

Scandalized murmurs circled the room, as grimy-faced women shook their heads and eyed the demon-helper with scorn.

"Alexander," Nicholas cried. "Execute justice upon them now! And start with the traitor."

The red-haired warrior trudged forward, his spear raised. He rounded the stump, disappearing from view.

"No!" David cried. He twisted his neck, trying to look behind him. He struggled against the ropes of twine, but the restraints held him fast. Amy hadn't severed the ropes in time. "Don't hurt her. Please—wait!"

But the warrior didn't wait. Alexander grunted, a javelin whooshed, and a knife blade burrowed into meaty flesh with a sickening, wet thud.

The onlookers gasped. Women covered their mouths and the eyes of their children. Amy had absorbed the blow without making a sound. Death must have been instantaneous. But David hadn't felt the impact of the spear.

A body collapsed at David's feet, and he hazarded a downward glance. Nicholas of Tsarlandia lay dead on the floor, the long shaft of a spear protruding from his chest.

One heartbeat later, pandemonium broke loose in the cave. Enraged tribesmen charged at David, their teeth bared and battle cries in their throats. David braced for the worst, but other fighters stepped in front of him and engaged the attackers with their spears and knives. Shrieking women fled with their children as the Tsarlandians clashed.

"Amy, what the hell is going on?"

"No idea, but I hope it keeps up. I'm almost done with the rope!"

Alexander stepped on the dead leader's chest and pulled the spear from his heart. Then he turned the blade on the doomed couple.

"Amy, watch out!" David shrank from the warrior's bloody spear, but Alexander only sliced the ropes that bound

David and Amy to the pole.

"Hurry," Alexander said, as the lengths of twine fell from their bodies. "Follow me."

The foreigners didn't need to be told twice. David and Amy rushed after the warrior as he parried blows and waylaid attackers. They made for a tunnel. Inside, a tribesman handed Alexander a flaming torch and a bag woven from dried leaves.

"Are we ready?" Alexander asked the man, who nodded. "Good. Hold them off." The warrior rushed back toward the melee with his spear.

Alexander shoved the bag into David's arms. "This is for you."

David peeked inside the bag. He held it open for Amy, and her eyes widened too. The bag contained Victory, the tenth imperial Fabergé egg and the Tsarlandians' greatest treasure.

"I don't understand."

"Payment," Alexander said.

"For what?"

"For taking us to America!"

CHAPTER 38

"How are we going to leave the island?" David whispered to Amy as they dashed after Alexander in the tunnel.

"Let's hope he has a plan."

The tunnel ended in a circle of daylight. Alexander dropped the flaming torch at the cave mouth and continued into the jungle. His pace slowed as he picked his way through the thick undergrowth.

"The Warden is an evil man," Alexander said. "He takes the best of our food and labor, the best of our women. For many years, we begged him to let us leave the island. But he refused. He'd rather die than let us escape his control. But your words opened our eyes. Our suspicions were true. The empire is lost. The world outside has moved on. We must move on too."

The jungle gave way to a stony beach. Two small boats bobbed in the shallow water of the small bay. Three young women, dressed in Victorian gowns of grass, cowered in the first boat. The second boat was empty. Alexander had a plan after all.

"You have boats?" David said.

"We built them in secret. The lifeboat of our ancestors rotted away, but we learned what we could. These boats are smaller but float well. All we lacked was a sign from God. You are the sign!"

David doubted that, but he'd be glad to leave the island all the same. Alexander helped Amy and David to board the second boat. Four more fighters arrived at the beach, bloodied and out of breath. They pushed the boats into the water, pulled themselves aboard, and rowed frantically with the simple wooden paddles attached to the sides.

"Which way do we go?" Alexander asked.

"West," Amy answered.

David wasn't sure the boats would survive an ocean voyage, but a risky boat trip beat immediate execution on the island. Alexander watched the shore, his spear poised for throwing. They were a hundred feet from the shore when a small crowd of Tsarlandians appeared on the beach. They jeered at the defectors and hurled insults but didn't enter the water.

Alexander chuckled, showing his teeth. "They can't swim," he said, elated. "None of us can. The Warden forbade it. Ha! That didn't stop us, did it?"

David doubted that too, for the pursuers on the beach raised their weapons and charged at the ocean. But they stopped short of the water and hurled their spears. A half-dozen thin lines climbed into the sky and arched toward the escaping boats.

Alexander's smile faded. "Get down!"

Amy shoved David sideways as the missiles rained onto the boats. A spear missed David by inches, burying its stone edge in the floor of the boat. Another projectile caught the warrior beside him in the back. He tumbled overboard, rocking the boat, and sank in the deep blue waters. David gripped the side of the boat, the urge to puke rising within him.

Alexander roared with grief and anger. He spread his legs and hurled his spear at the beach. The warriors in the other boat followed his lead. But the islanders scattered, and the missiles shattered on the stony beach.

Alexander reached for the spear buried in the boat's timber, but Amy cried out. "No, we'll sink!"

The warrior grunted with frustration. The defectors had spent their ammunition but were not yet out of range. In the boats, they had nowhere to flee or hide. Alexander grabbed the oars and rowed with a vengeance.

The Tsarlandians on the shore wasted no time. The warriors held their spear points, now wrapped in a cloth of dried leaves, to a flaming torch. Seconds later, fire descended on the other boat. Two of the flaming spears hit their mark. The untreated wood caught fire, turning the boat into a bonfire.

Yelping with terror, the three women and two warriors jumped into the ocean. Their arms flailed uselessly at the surface, and they gulped air as their bodies descended into the depths.

"No!" Alexander roared. He abandoned the oars and dived into the water. The last remaining fighter followed him, leaving David and Amy, the only ones who could swim, still onboard.

"I've got to help them," David said. He made to dive into the water when Amy grabbed him by the arm.

"Look." She pointed. The surface of the water rippled as countless silvery fins broke the surface.

"Alexander!" David yelled. "Get back! The fish are coming!"

Dog-paddling with little effect, Alexander turned around in the water, his arms reaching for the side of the boat as his head dipped under the surface. David grabbed their savior's hand. It was his time to return the favor. He gripped the drowning man's hand in both of his and pulled for all he was worth. Amy held him by his waist and pulled too.

The waters churned with frenzied activity, and David fell backward into the boat, landing on Amy. "Yes!" They had lifted Alexander to safety, and in the nick of time.

David opened his eyes. The hand he held ended in two long, exposed bones, picked clean by the island piranhas. Two toothy specimens still clung to the bone by their curved, needle-like teeth. David gasped and lobbed the severed hand

and fish overboard, where the red waters roiled with a thousand feasting predators.

"Oh, God! Oh, God! Tell me that didn't happen."

Amy grabbed the oars and rowed away from the island and the burning boat. The Tsarlandians watched them go. By the time the flaming boat sank in the ocean, the islanders were dots in the distance.

David took Amy's place at the oars. The work gave him something to do and distracted his mind from the piranhas and the hopeless journey ahead.

The island faded to a speck, then disappeared. They drifted on a vast, watery desert under the scorching sun. The boat rose and fell over the shifting dunes. Water surrounded them, but they could drink not a drop.

Amy located a sack of woven leaves at the bow of the boat. "There's food!" She rummaged inside, retrieving plastic bottles David recognized from the downed jet. "I hope you like tomato juice."

"I'll drink just about anything now."

She handed him a bottle. "Make it last. We only have three. The islanders had been optimistic about the duration of the voyage."

"I guess the rest of their supplies went down with the other boat."

David drank half the bottle. He hadn't eaten since the boiled piranha the islanders had served in the moated prison. Now the very thought of fish made his stomach turn.

"How long do you think it'll take to reach the coast?" David asked.

Amy had removed her shirt and draped it over her head as a hat. "Weeks, if we're lucky."

Weeks. They'd never survive weeks on the ocean. David searched their bleak situation for a positive thought.

"At least there are no tigers on board."

"What?"

"Never mind. I read a book about a boy stranded in a lifeboat with a Bengal tiger." An idea struck. "How good are you with a spear? We could try to catch something."

"I'd leave the spear in place. The edge is buried deep. Removing it might spring a leak."

She was right. Did flying fish roam the Atlantic? David hoped so.

He pulled at the oars. His shoulders ached. The sun beat down on him overhead. No matter how hard he rowed, the boat seemed to stay put. Sweat soaked his shirt.

"I need another drink," he confessed before he finished the bottle of tomato juice.

Amy glanced around at the horizon—three hundred sixty degrees of identical panoramas. "It's too hot," she said. "We must conserve energy. Row by night, rest by day."

David welcomed any excuse to take a nap. He and Amy hunkered down, making the most of the sparse shade offered by the raised side of the boat.

David dozed off. Spear-toting warriors filled his fitful dreams—their bones stripped clean of flesh.

He woke to the sound of lapping water. Night had fallen. Stars crowded the sky in a dazzling cosmic display. Even his empty stomach and parched mouth couldn't detract from the awe that overwhelmed him.

Amy stopped rowing. "Beautiful, aren't they?" She pointed. "That's the Big Dipper. And up there, Polaris—the North Star."

The moon rose over the ocean, large and pale, its silver glow sprinkling the waters with fairy dust.

David shifted over to Amy and wrapped his arms around her. "Don't say I never take you anyplace romantic."

She laughed. When had they last laughed? A lifetime ago, it seemed. They might as well enjoy these last moments before dehydration or the elements claimed them.

A thought formed in his head. He reached for the woven bag and lifted the Fabergé egg toward the stars. Golden dots of reflected moonlight danced over the waves and Amy's smiling face. She leaned in, and they kissed. David put the egg down. Their bodies took over, shedding their clothes with an urgent need while the brilliant heavenly bodies winked at them from above. They seized this last opportunity to make love in this life. Suddenly, Amy disengaged.

"You're right," David said, with regret. "We should save our strength."

Amy said, "Look!"

Three yellow lights wavered on the dark horizon. One light pulsed and lengthened—the sweeping glow of a search beam.

Still half-naked, David shot to his feet. The boat rocked as he waved his arms over his head. "Over here!" he yelled. "Over here!" In his excitement, his arm hit the shaft of the spear stuck in the boat.

"Use the egg!" Amy said.

Amy handed him the Fabergé, and he angled the golden dots at the ship. Could they see them? The three lights became one.

"They're turning our way," Amy said, tears of joy in her voice. "They've seen us!"

"Over here!" David yelled, and he whooped for joy. Then he paused and lost all sense of celebration. "Did you spill tomato juice?"

"No."

"Then why are my feet wet?"

"Stay with the ship," Amy told him. She dropped to the floor of the boat, then swore. "We're taking on water."

He believed her. The chilly seawater rose above his ankles and climbed his calves. "Can you plug it up?"

"I'm trying!" The boat sank deeper with every passing second. "It's no good. The water's almost over the rim. We need to flip the boat."

"What?" Was she serious?

"Upside down, it might float."

"What about the piranhas?"

"I think we're out of range."

"You think?!"

"If we sink, it won't matter!"

Out of options, David bagged the egg, then slung the strap over his head and one shoulder. Placing their combined body weight on the rim of the side of the boat, they capsized the small craft. For a few terrifying minutes, they clung to the side of the boat, treading water as the swells battered them. Vertigo gripped David, as the unfathomable murky depths sucked at his dangling legs. Attack scenes from every shark movie he'd ever seen looped through his mind over the terrifying soundtrack of *Jaws*.

Battling the icy water, they clambered onto the overturned hull. Amy had been right about the boat, which floated at the surface, buoyed by trapped air bubbles and the lower density of the wooden beams.

Soaked through and panting, David got to his feet. He straddled the keel of the boat and raised the golden egg over his head, his arms shivering. And he hoped to God the ship could still see them.

CHAPTER 39

"Sir?" said a voice behind them. "Ma'am?"

The next afternoon, David and Amy descended the ramp of the USS *Detroit* at New York harbor. They were hurrying toward the exit of the military terminal building when the voice forced them to stop and turn. A young African American in a gray suit bustled after them. He flashed his identity badge. "Officer Damien Brown, CIA. Please come with me."

Last night, an inflatable motorboat had ferried the bedraggled couple aboard the USS *Detroit*. The captain provided them with basic clothing, a hot meal, and a cabin on the navy combat ship. The crew's search-and-rescue mission had aimed to find debris from Zheltkov's missing jet. Rescuing two survivors had surpassed their best expectations.

Back on dry land, David and Amy found themselves at the table of another white-walled interrogation room. David's hands fidgeted while the clean-cut CIA officer studied them.

"Coffee?" Officer Brown said, sitting opposite.

"No, thanks. We had some onboard."

The officer seemed cordial and professional, but David, now familiar with law enforcement interrogation techniques, kept his guard up.

Officer Brown produced a thin manila folder. "I apologize

for the inconvenience. You've been through a lot and must be eager to go home, but we'd appreciate your help to answer a few questions."

"Sure," David said, brightening. They did not seem to be suspects in whatever the CIA was investigating.

"Thank you." Officer Brown opened the manila folder and glanced at a printed page. "I understand you were aboard a plane belonging to a Mr. Peter Zheltkov. Is that correct?"

"Yes," David said.

On the USS *Detroit*, he and Amy had rehearsed their story of how they were plane-wrecked in the ocean. Telling the whole truth was not an option. The ship's captain had taken them at their word. But if the CIA had discovered Amy's FBI affiliation and faked death, they'd have trouble talking their way to freedom.

David repeated the story now. The jet had lost cabin pressure for reasons unknown to them. Losing consciousness, they had awoken on the island, alone among the debris. Fearing jungle predators and despairing of rescue, they had set sail on a raft of wooden beams that had washed up on-shore. He made no mention of the Tsarlandians. Officer Brown took notes in silence.

"On our second day at sea," David concluded, "the USS *Detroit* appeared on the horizon."

Amy said, "We've never been so happy to see a ship!"

Officer Brown nodded. "And how did you come to be aboard Mr. Zheltkov's private plane?"

David answered. "He invited me. We share an interest in imperial Russia, and he was going to show me his collection of memorabilia." David did not mention the Fabergé eggs in case the CIA had learned about the eggs taken from the Met.

"And you, Ms. Anderson?"

"I'm David's girlfriend." She placed her hand in David's. "I just came along for the ride."

"And what a ride that was! Quite a bonding experience."

"You can say that again."

They chuckled.

"You are both very lucky to be alive."

"Yes, we are."

David said, "Has anyone found Peter?"

"Peter Zheltkov," Amy added. "We last saw him aboard the plane before the crash."

"No, we're still looking for him. We instructed the USS *Detroit* to search for wreckage as soon as we learned that the plane was missing. Let's hope he was as lucky as you two."

"Please let us know when you find him or the rest of his crew," Amy said. "He's such an extraordinary man."

"I'll do that, ma'am."

"I still can't believe we landed on that island—with nobody on board to fly the plane!"

The question had troubled David too. If the CIA officer was so interested in Zheltkov's missing jet, maybe there was more to the story than met the eye.

The CIA officer cleared his throat. "To be honest, ma'am, that wasn't pure luck. In the event of an emergency, our officers were to set the jet's autopilot for the island's coordinates and await a rendezvous with the ship."

"Your officers?"

Officer Brown hesitated. Then, seeming to decide there was no harm in opening up, he continued. "We've had our eye on Zheltkov for some time now. We have reason to believe he had criminal connections. To gather more information, we planted two of our officers on his jet."

The officer extracted two profile photos from his folder and lay them side-by-side on the table. David pressed his lips together to hide his shock. The faces of Nasim and the mustachioed pilot stared back at him.

"Did you see either of them on board the plane?"

David and Amy shook their heads.

"There was a flight attendant," Amy offered.

"Yeah," David seconded. "She was very nice. We didn't see her after the crash either."

"I see." Officer Brown seemed disappointed. He returned

the photos to the folder. "Our operatives replaced the jet's regular pilot and copilot at the last minute, so you probably never had the chance to meet them." He closed the folder. "Thank you for your time. I'll ask you to keep this information confidential. Our investigation is still ongoing."

"We understand," Amy said, getting to her feet. The men followed her lead, and Officer Brown held out his hand.

"Here's my card in case you remember anything that might be of help."

"We'll call you if we do," David said.

In the hallway, David and Amy walked as fast as they could without looking like fugitives.

"The CIA?" David whispered. "Nasim was working for the CIA? She'd tried to kill us!"

Amy kept her eyes on the exit. "Not CIA—Elders. She infiltrated the CIA for the Elders."

"The way you infiltrated the FBI for the Temple?"

"Exactly."

"Wow," David said. The operatives of religious secret societies had compromised two major US intelligence agencies. The state was a wooden edifice hollowed out by hordes of worms. It was a miracle the whole intelligence community hadn't collapsed in a cloud of sawdust.

David slowed. "The Prepuce!" he whispered. In the rush for survival, he'd forgotten about the vacuum-packed piece of leather. "How are we going to free Jordy and Mitch without it?"

"Keep going," Amy said, pulling him by the hand. "I have it."

"You do? Thank God! Wait, didn't the islanders search you too?"

"They did," Amy said. "I hid it well."

They walked on in pregnant silence.

David gave in to his curiosity. "Where?"

Amy grinned. "I have my ways."

CHAPTER 40

Deep in the dark belly of the earth, the Father waited. Again. The carved orbs of the throne no longer consoled him. His patience was wearing thin. David Zelig had taken the Fabergé Imperial Collection and fallen off the Temple's radar along with Amy, once the Temple's most valued intelligence asset. Luke had counseled the Father to have faith, but his faith too had worn thin, and his fingers trembled. Had he made a terrible mistake?

A buzzing in the deep pocket of his robe startled him. The Temple's ingrained suspicion of change had bred a distrust for newfangled technologies, but the Father had submitted to cellular communications. In this global Holy War, physical meetings were impractical. Only one person had the number of this cellphone, and the unscheduled call sent his blood pressure soaring.

He thumbed the button to accept the video conference, and a cloaked figure appeared on the screen. The face of the speaker disappeared in the brown cowl's shadow, but the familiar gravelly voice and French accent sent shivers down his spine. Every Father has a Father.

"Do you have it yet?" the voice said, skipping any pleasantries. He was referring to the Holy Prepuce.

"Soon, Grandmaster. Our brothers will return with good tidings at any moment."

"I hope you are right. Your Temple has failed us before."

"I assure you, Grandmaster, everything is going according to plan." He hoped his voice had not betrayed his doubts. The calls unnerved him. The European Temple used to grant him carte blanche. Now the Grandmaster kept him on a tight leash, and the Father chafed under his scrutiny. What had changed?

"I need not remind you," the voice continued, "of the traitors we found in your midst." The Father suppressed a snarl. The Frenchman seemed to enjoy pouring salt on his wounds. "Heresy is a poisonous weed. We must root it out without mercy."

"As we have. No matter what the cost."

"Then why do you employ this Jew, David Zelig?"

The Father was glad for the deep cowl of his cloak, which hid his hot flush. Was the Frenchman spying on him? Did he have informers among the Father's ranks? The plan had been Luke's idea, and now the Father wished he had listened to his own intuition.

"The Jew is a tool. Nothing more."

"I trust you will dispense with this *tool* when it has served its purpose?"

"Of course, Grandmaster."

"Beware, Brother. Jews have a talent for sowing heresy in the hearts of the faithful, and this Jew is of particular concern to us."

The revelation surprised the Father. David Zelig might descend from a rich and famous family, but he had not struck him as dangerous. "How so?"

The brown cowl remained silent for two full seconds. "Our sources need not concern you." The Father bristled with annoyance. The European Temple kept many cards up its deep sleeves.

"Do not underestimate this Zelig. We will not tolerate failure this time."

The Father bowed his head. "We will not fail you again."
The brown cowl grunted, as though not quite convinced.
"I hope so. For all of our sakes."

CHAPTER 41

Amy donned a gray robe and stood before the Temple throne room. Long centuries had warped and hardened the large wooden doors. The throne room had once filled her with awe. Now, she felt only resentment... and dread.

She pulled the cowl of the robe over her head. Most Templars required special permission to enter this place, but Amy was unlike most Templars. She drew a deep breath and knocked twice. The Temple robes would offer her little protection today, the day she needed it most.

"Well, well, well," the Father said as she entered. "The prodigal daughter returns home."

Amy ignored his sarcasm and approached the raised throne. As always, Luke stood at the Temple leader's side, poisoning his mind against her.

"And where have you been these past few days?" Luke asked.

"Keeping an eye on our investment."

The Father chuckled, but his voice was cold. "Your orders were to stay away from the Jew, David Zelig, and his cronies. His demonic presence has curdled your mind. Thanks to him, we had to withdraw our greatest FBI asset—you. Have you forgotten that already?"

"I made a mistake, Father. But at least let me earn back your trust. I will not fail you again."

Luke said, "Your old partner at the FBI, Special Agent Marco Hernandez, was shot dead a few days ago. You didn't happen to have anything to do with that, did you?"

Amy swallowed hard and was glad for the privacy the cowl offered. She must show no doubt, no weakness, or the Temple would have her head, regardless of her past service and noble bloodline.

"Hernandez was about to kill Zelig. I had to intervene or we'd never get the Prepuce."

"Amy," the Father said, his voice softening. "I told you years ago—the front lines are no place for a woman, no matter how... skilled. The time has come for you to retire from fieldwork and contribute to the cause in more suitable ways."

"Like making babies?" She spat the words.

The Father's robe shrugged. "The Temple needs soldiers. This Final Crusade will be the longest and bloodiest of all. We have already selected a suitable match for you. Step forward, sir."

Behind her, a robed figure emerged from the shadows. Tall and muscular, she recognized the henchman.

"I would be honored, Father," the figure said in his deep baritone. "Our children will be strong and loyal."

Amy gasped, filling with rage at the Father's audacity. Sir George "The Razor" was a reliable and ruthless Temple soldier, but the thought of sleeping with the dumbbell-brain made Amy want to retch.

"Zelig has the Holy Prepuce," Amy said, steering the conversation away from her future marriage. That shut them up for two seconds.

"Where?"

"I don't know. Does it matter?"

After they'd returned to her apartment and made love, Amy had given David the vacuum-wrapped foreskin for safekeeping. She didn't care where David stashed the Holy

Prepuce. The less she knew, the better. That way, the Temple could not force her to reveal its location and double-cross her lover.

Once the Temple obtained the relic, David and his friends would become expendable. She had to free Jordan and Mitchell before that happened.

"Have you seen it?"

"Briefly."

"And?"

"It looks authentic to me. Zheltkov vouched for it. Soon we will have the Prepuce of Calcata. David proposes an exchange at Times Square tomorrow at noon and—"

"Silence!" the Father roared. "The Jew will not dictate terms to the Temple."

"Father, he refuses to provide the Prepuce until we free his friends."

Luke said, "He sent you? He knows you are of the Temple?"

Amy held her head up high. "I had to improvise to save his life. David thought I had died at the Israel Day Parade, and I had to explain that away somehow."

"And you just had to see him again, didn't you?" Luke taunted.

"Revealing Temple secrets to a Jew is treason. Unforgivable! And to consort with one... vile and repulsive!"

"There was no other way," Amy shouted back. "I did what I did for the Temple."

Her words hung in the air. The beating of her heart filled her ears. Amy had presented her argument. The rest was out of her hands. Her fate depended on the Temple's decision.

Luke's cowl turned toward the Father. "She speaks the truth. If Hernandez had killed Zelig, the Prepuce would have remained forever beyond our reach."

The Father's robes expanded as he drew a deep breath. "Very well. We will proceed with this exchange but on our own terms."

Luke said, "The exchange will take place this Sunday in

Washington. At the JAPI Convention."

Amy smelled a trap and her heart sank. "The JAPI Convention?"

"The Convention is a public event where all parties can conduct business without drawing unwanted attention. And if Zelig tries anything stupid, there will be plenty of Jewish collateral damage and no lack of hostages."

Amy considered her options. She could work with the Temple's drop-off plan. But even so, her gut tingled.

"I'll let him know," she said. "I'll make sure things go smoothly. Thank you, Father, for your trust." She almost choked on the words. This man had destroyed her mother, and Amy felt anything but gratitude toward him.

"Don't thank me yet. You have grown too close to this Jew."

"Father, I have not—"

"Do you take me for a fool? You have disobeyed the Temple and polluted your soul. We have terminated other brethren for lesser perfidies. I cannot make exceptions for you, not after what happened with your mother."

Amy ground her teeth at the mention of her mother. Was the Father implying that perfidy was in her blood? Maybe he was right.

"Father, I am not my mother."

"So you say. But the Old Temple is watching us closely now. We cannot afford another mistake. I am giving you one final chance to clear your name and redeem your spirit. Luke, tell her."

Luke said, "Considering your recent track record, we have come to doubt where your true loyalties lie. We can tolerate no weakness on the battlefield. You will have to prove your fealty beyond all doubt."

Amy's heart sank deeper. "What will you have me do?" she asked, but she had already guessed.

When he told her, Amy felt sick to her stomach. The Father had given her no wriggle room, no loophole through which to crawl back to David. He had forced her to make an impossible choice, and she had to make it now. What had she expected? She couldn't play both sides forever. The Temple had existed for nine hundred years. The Temple knew how to protect its interests. A secret cult did not survive long without demanding great sacrifices.

Luke said, "Sir George will monitor the operation to make sure you comply."

Tears welled in Amy's eyes and spilled down her cheeks, as her world came crashing down around her. She nodded her head, hot spite burning within.

"I will do as you say, Father," she said, her voice subdued and defeated. "You have my word."

CHAPTER 42

"I'm starting to feel like a bank," Hymie Schneider joked. David had turned up at his Fifth Avenue penthouse Thursday evening with another package for safekeeping. "Do you want to put that with the briefcase?"

"Yes, please," David said.

Hymie led David to his office, turned the dial of the large combination lock on a steel door, and opened his vault. Jewelry boxes and thick, sealed envelopes sat on the shelves of the walk-in safe. Large paintings in elaborate gold frames leaned against a wall. The metal briefcase with the Fabergé eggs lay on its own shelf.

"I'll give you some privacy," Hymie said, shuffling back to the expansive living room. "Just shut the door when you're done."

David opened the metal briefcase. Nine imperial eggs nestled in the snug cutouts of the black interior. Glinting in the blue light of the LED in the vault's ceiling, the golden eggs seemed to wink at him. David extracted Victory from its cardboard box and placed the egg beside the others.

He considered the ten imperial eggs, united for the first time in over a hundred years, and the hairs on the back of his neck bristled. Again, he sensed that a hidden hand was moving him like a pawn on a very large and very complex chess-board.

David retrieved the Holy Prepuce from his pocket and straightened the creases in the vacuum-sealed square of plastic. His conscience twinged. The Tsarlandians had given him Victory. But now that he had acquired the Prepuce, how did he justify holding onto the other nine eggs?

Three days from now, this ordeal would be over. Amy had spoken with the Temple Father. At the JAPI Convention this Sunday in Washington, David would exchange the Holy Prepuce for his friends.

The JAPI Convention. Why had the Temple chosen the JAPI convention for the exchange—the same event the Islamic Elders of Zion planned to attack?

Both Luke and Amy had assured David that the Elders wouldn't dare storm the convention. The Elders only wanted the eggs to gain the Holy Prepuce. But still, the convention made a very tempting target for anti-Semitic terrorists. And now the Temple had chosen the JAPI Convention for their prisoner swap. The coincidence did not bode well. Did the Temple think the venue would guarantee David's good behavior or was something darker brewing beneath the surface?

One grim thought led to another. Once the Temple had the Prepuce in hand, would they honor their side of the bargain or would they see the Trio as a large loose end? David hoped Amy's exit strategy would not land them all in shallow graves.

David tossed the Holy Prepuce inside and closed the briefcase, then returned Victory to its box. He exited the safe and shut the door, and unseen mechanical bolts whirred into place.

When David returned to the living room, Hymie had poured two whisky glasses of that thirty-year-old Balvenie he loved. "Have a seat, David."

He did. The velvety single-malt, casked years before his birth, tickled his taste buds. Murmurs of Manhattan traffic drifted up from the streets far below. The sky turned pink as the evening horizon faded. In the penthouse, the chaotic workings of the bustling city seemed calm and well ordered.

"How is Peter Zheltkov?"

David almost snorted whisky out his nose. He chose his words with care. "He was fine the last time I saw him."

"And how was your trip?"

"Successful, on the whole."

Hymie grunted with satisfaction.

"Did you find what you were looking for?"

"Yes, I did."

"That's good." Hymie was feeling David out, searching for answers but not wanting to pry. He took another sip of his drink. "To be honest, David, I'm worried about you." Before David could object, he added, "You look exhausted. Worn out. Your mother called me the other day."

"She did?"

"She's worried about you too, says you haven't called her in weeks."

Ever since losing Zelig Pictures, David had dodged his mother's calls. Did he feel guilty for letting the family down? Or was he trying to avoid telling her that Preston had stolen the company from under them? David still had no game plan for facing their financial troubles.

Hymie continued. "Then there's this business of mysterious briefcases and packages. Are you in trouble?"

"No, Hymie. No! Thank you for asking, but I'm good."

"Because if you are, maybe I can help? I know a lot of people, people who might sort things out."

David's conscience twinged yet again. He was in over his head. But sharing his troubles with Hymie might put the kindly old family friend in mortal danger. David had dragged enough innocent friends through minefields already. But another lame denial would not console the old man. He had to give him more.

"Hymie, if I tell you something, will you promise not to tell anyone, not even my mother?"

"Of course, David. My word is my bond."

David paused for dramatic effect. "You see, there's this girl."

The smile on Hymie's face was worth the half-truth. "A girl? Well, that's wonderful news!"

"The thing is, she's not Jewish and she has a complicated past. I'm not sure I'm ready to share that with my mom just yet."

"I see. I see," Hymie said with gravitas. "I understand completely." He zipped his lips. "I'm just glad you've found a nice young woman. You deserve to be happy."

David presented a brave smile. He knocked back the rest of the whisky to mask his shame. "One more thing, Hymie. I need to pick up the briefcase on Saturday night."

"No problem, David. But not too late. I have an early flight on Sunday morning. I'm going to Washington for the JAPI Convention."

"You're going to the JAPI Convention?"

Hymie groaned. "You know Gerry Cantor. He's been pressing me for years to give that keynote speech and finally, I gave in."

David felt the blood drain from his face. The JAPI Convention might be a death trap.

"Hymie, don't go!"

"Don't go? Believe me, I wish I didn't have to. I can't stand those conventions. Haven't attended one in years."

"Then skip this one too."

Hymie stared at him, confused. "What's gotten into you, David?"

"Nothing, it's just..." David couldn't believe he was about to do this, but he saw no other option. "This year is my turn."

"Your turn?"

"You know Gerry Cantor. He's been pushing me to speak at the convention since my bar mitzvah, and I said I'd give the keynote speech this year."

Hymie gave him a doubtful glance. "Gerry didn't say anything about that."

"Must have slipped his mind. But trust me, I've got this one covered. The speech is ready and everything."

Hymie's consternation turned to relief. "Oh. That's just as well. I was going to wing it, and those large crowds always give me indigestion."

"Then it's settled. I'll go to Washington and do the speech. I'll call Gerry Cantor myself."

Saving Hymie from a speech—and potentially from getting killed in a major terrorist attack—was the least David could do for his trusted friend.

"OK, then," Hymie said. "But on one condition."

"Name it."

"When you come by next, I want to meet this mystery lady of yours."

David hesitated. He and Amy had planned to travel to the airport separately in case either of them got held up by airport security. He hadn't shared with her his family's inner circle, and an irrational thought warned that such a meeting would jinx their chances for a happy ever after. But how could he deny Hymie such a harmless request? He owed Hymie that much.

David shook Hymie's hand. "That's a deal."

CHAPTER 43

Later that night, David unlocked the door of Amy's dark Soho apartment and slipped inside, when the barrel of a gun pressed against the base of his skull.

David's breath caught in his lungs. Had Nasim somehow survived her freefall and hunted him down? He raised his hands, the bag of Double Dragon takeaway rising into the air.

Wait a minute. He recognized that perfume.

"Amy, it's me." Why was she holding him at gunpoint?

A switch clicked, and light flooded the apartment.

"Geez, David, we spoke about this. Two knocks before you enter."

She was right. "I'm sorry. I forgot."

Amy slammed the door and put the gun away. "I almost blew your brains out!"

"I know. It won't happen again."

He placed the bags of Chinese takeaway on the coffee table, his fingers trembling. The aromas of fried chicken and sweet-and-sour sauce filled the air, but the gun had ruined his appetite.

Skirts and dresses filled the open suitcase on the floor.

"I thought we'd travel light," he said. "We'll only be there for a day."

Amy drew close and took his hands in hers. Panic flared in her eyes.

"We have to leave, David. For good. It's not safe to stick around any longer."

He'd never seen her like this. "Amy, we're almost there. We have the Prepuce. In a few days, we'll free my friends and leave the Temple behind."

Amy shook her head. "It's not that simple, David. The Temple will hunt us down." He opened his mouth to argue but knew she was right. A tear fell from her eye. "It's my fault. I should never have gotten you involved."

Now she was just beating herself up. "Amy, I got myself into this mess, remember? I started the Trio, and you saved my life a bunch of times. Now, maybe the Temple will let us walk away and maybe they won't. It's a chance we have to take."

She looked away from him, brooding. "Something's changed at the Temple. They don't trust me anymore. We have to leave the country now. I know a guy who does passports. We can get new identities and start new lives far away from here."

"Amy, we talked about this. I can't leave my friends with the Temple."

"This isn't about your friends anymore. It's about saving our own lives. I've seen what they do to traitors. We have to go."

Amy had told him how the Temple had disposed of her mother, and David sensed her pain. Now she studied his eyes, waiting for his answer.

"Amy, I'd do anything for you."

"Then do this. Leave with me as soon as the passports are ready."

David hesitated, frustrated at her cornering him. "If I did that, what would that make me? How would we live with ourselves?"

"We'd live."

"If you want to fly out tonight, that's fine with me. I'll

meet up with you wherever you want. But I have to do this, Amy."

Amy shook her head, disappointed. "I will not let you face them alone."

"Good, 'cause I think I'd crap my pants if you did." He won a weak smile from her and capitalized on it. "The Temple still needs the Prepuce, right? We'll be safe so long as we have it."

"David," she interrupted.

"Hear me out, OK? We'll go to Washington and get my friends. Then, immediately after that, we'll catch the first flight overseas."

Amy frowned at his proposal. "Immediately?" She was not happy with the idea, but would rather compromise than let him get killed.

David wiped the tears from her cheeks. "From the JAPI Convention to the international airport of your choice. Express ride, one-way ticket."

Amy bit her lip. "That won't give us much of a head start."

"But we'll have the eternal gratitude of Jordy and Mitch, and that's worth something, right?"

Amy frowned again, sad but resigned. She was going against her better judgment. Love did that to the human brain.

"At least we've got the eggs," she said. "We can pawn them or sell them to a private collector."

"About the eggs," he said. "I've been thinking. We were going to trade them for the Prepuce to save Jordy and Mitch. But now that we have the Prepuce, we should give them back."

Amy huffed with frustration. "David, when we leave the country with fake identities, we'll be leaving our old lives behind. Our homes, our bank accounts—everything. We'll be fugitives, and a life in exile won't come cheap."

She was right, but not completely. "We'll still have Victory. One golden egg will cover our expenses for a while, right?"

She laughed. "For a while."

"Is that a yes?"

She nodded, and he held her.

Amy pulled away and reached for her phone. "Now for those passports," she said. "I need to call in a few favors."

CHAPTER 44

On a dark street corner in Soho, an unmarked sedan hugged the curb. The man in the driver's seat lowered his handheld antenna and removed the headphones from his ears. He dialed a number on his mobile phone.

"I got something," Officer Damien Brown said.

"Zelig?" said the voice on the phone.

"Yeah. He and the girl have shacked up in Soho. I knew their story didn't smell right."

Didn't smell right was an understatement. Their statement had tormented him like a piece of jerky stuck between his molars.

"And?"

"An exchange is about to go down at the JAPI Convention in Washington this Sunday. Seems the bad guys have got Zelig's friends and they're willing to trade them for a…" He paused, trying to remember the word. "A porpoise?"

"Are you sure that's what they said?"

"I think so."

"What the heck do they want with a porpoise?"

"Beats me."

"Must be code for something. Does he have it with him?"

"Doesn't sound like it. Zelig has some eggs, though."

"You mean 'balls'?"

"No, sir. *Eggs*. They sound valuable." The information conjured a memory. "Wait a minute. Remember that break-in at the Met a few weeks ago?"

"What about it?"

"This is a long shot, but Fabergé eggs were on exhibit at the time. Could the burglars have stolen the Fabergés?"

"But nothing was taken from the Met."

"Not officially. But what if the museum covered that up? As I said, it's a long shot."

The voice on the end of the line chuckled. "Sounds more like a conspiracy theory to me."

"Yeah. Either way, this Zelig guy sure has a lot of secrets. Do you think he's connected to the… what you call it, that other conspiracy thingy… the Jewish one?"

"What conspiracy?"

"You know. The Elders of Zion. That's it."

"Please, Officer Brown, don't be ridiculous. Everybody knows that's a myth. Mention the Elders of Zion and you'll become the laughingstock of the Agency."

"I was just messing with you. So, should I bring them in?"

"Nah. Stay on their tails. Whatever he's up to, Zelig is a pawn. Let him lead us to the big fish. And talking of fish, let me know if that porpoise turns up."

"Will do, boss."

"Oh, and Officer Brown?"

"Yes, sir?"

"Let's keep this just between the two of us for now, OK?"

CHAPTER 45

TOP SECRET
FEDERAL BUREAU OF INVESTIGATION
OFFICE OF PROFESSIONAL RESPONSIBILITY
Transcript of interview with Mr. Hyman Schneider
Also present:
Special Agent A. Maynard
Special Agent in Charge M. Reed

M. REED:
Seriously, Mr. Schneider? Not only has the Temple infiltrated the FBI, now the Elders have infiltrated the CIA?

HYMAN SCHNEIDER:
I warned you. It boggles the mind.

M. REED:
Here's what gets me. Each law enforcement agency had uncovered a part of the puzzle but neglected to share that information. And they let David and Amy move about freely? This shows a major lack of interagency cooperation. And we're talking after Nine/Eleven!

HYMAN SCHNEIDER:

You're onto something, Agent Reed. But I don't want to ruin the end of the story.

M. REED:

OK, Mr. Schneider. I'll hold my questions for later. Please carry on.

HYMAN SCHNEIDER:

With pleasure. Saturday evening, David kept his promise. He brought Amy Anderson, his young lady friend, over to my apartment. My, oh my, was she a looker!

"Welcome," I told them and I shook her hand. I didn't know she could kill me just as easily. Ignorance is bliss.

I sat them down and offered them drinks. David declined the offer, reminding me they had a plane to catch.

"Go ahead and get your things," I told him. "The safe is open. Meanwhile, I'll enjoy the company of this fine young lady."

And a lady she was, all demure and polite. I remember thinking David's father would have liked her.

"That's a beautiful dress," I told her. They had both dressed for a night on the town.

"Thank you," she said. "It's new. We went shopping to-gether."

"David's looking sharp too." In hindsight, he must have bought the clothing to avoid returning to his apartment in case the Elders were watching. He didn't know they were already onto him.

He had only a few days to enjoy what remained of his bank account before setting sail into the great unknown with his lady love. They made good use of their time, eating at the finest restaurants, dancing at the best clubs. They spent every moment together, living as young lovebirds do, as though these were their last days on Earth.

"I've known David since he was a little boy," I told Amy, keeping my voice low. "I was at his bar mitzvah. A Pavarotti he would never be, but he stuck it out. His father, rest his soul, was very proud."

I used this opportunity to talk up David's family.

"They've done well, the Zeligs," I told her. "From the mud villages of Poland to the helm of Hollywood. That's a long distance to travel. Did you know that his great-great-grandfather was a traveling salesman? I kid you not. He sold kitchen pots and *shmatas*. That's Yiddish for kitchen rags. He opened a store in Cracow and expanded into a bunch of smaller towns. But then the pogroms started again. He sold his stores for peanuts, packed up his family, and made the long and arduous journey to the United States. That's been our people's story for centuries. When the haters rise up, it's time to go. You can always replace possessions. Life is what matters. Life is sacred. Don't you agree?"

Now, I thought I was just making conversation, but she fixed me with such an intelligent and appreciative stare, I almost wanted to elope with her myself.

"Thank you, Mr. Schneider," she said. "I believe that with all my heart."

I now know what she was thinking. David's great-great-grandfather had left behind all he had in Poland for the love of his family. Now David was doing the same in his love for her. If she doubted his resolve, that old story was just what she'd needed to hear.

David returned with the metal briefcase and cardboard box. "Hymie knows our family history better than I do," he said.

"Isn't that so," I said, and I laughed.

M. REED:

Mr. Schneider, you still had no idea as to the contents of the briefcase and box?

HYMAN SCHNEIDER:

None whatsoever. I feel a little foolish now, even naïve. At the time, I didn't think about it. I was overjoyed he'd found such a lovely young lady. I've told you that before, haven't I? My apologies, I keep repeating myself. My wife says I'm getting old.

Anyway, David apologized for having to rush off. Amy shook my hand and said she'd enjoyed meeting me. I wished them safe travels and told them I looked forward to seeing them when they got back. Little did I know, I would never see them again.

CHAPTER 46

"The first thing I'll do," Jordan said, pausing between push-ups, "when we get out of here… is take a bath."

"Forty-six," said Mitchell, who was keeping count. Their exercise regimen had become the focus of their daily sanity routine. Their prison offered no exercise yards or dumbbells, so they made do with the cold, hard floor of the dungeon cell.

"A nice, long hot bath."

"Forty-seven. Sounds great."

"Mm-hm. No more washing in a bucket of cold water."

"Yeah, that sucks. Forty-eight. Want to know what I'm going to do?"

"Sure."

"Forty-nine. A steak, man. I'm going to eat a nice, big, juicy steak."

"Oh, God, yeah. We're going out for steaks. On me."

"Thanks, pal. Fifty. And I'll never eat lentil soup again. Like, ever."

Twice a day, their robed, sword-bearing guards unlocked the cell door and slid two bowls of lumpy lentil soup into their cells along with two dry heels of bread. Once a day, they emptied the chamber pot and filled the water bucket.

The prisoners rolled onto their backs for stomach crunches. To avoid soiling their only pair of clothes, the friends stripped to their boxer shorts for their workout.

"We'll think back on this place and laugh," Jordan said. "Like this was a detox retreat."

"One," Mitchell said. "You won't have time to think about this place, man. Two. You're going to be really popular with the ladies."

Jordan chuckled.

"Three. Look at you, man. You're ripped. Girls will line up to be with you. Four."

Mitchell was right about the muscles. Thanks to their low-calorie vegan diet and constant exercise, Jordan had traded his belly flab for a six-pack.

Their routine included squats, skipping without a rope, and a series of kicks and punches they had learned at the FBI training camp. Mitchell had even taught Jordan to backflip off the wall. To Jordan's surprise, he had mastered the trick without cracking his skull.

"And then there's our startup," Jordan said.

"Five. You serious about that?"

"Why not? It's a great idea. Computer games are in, especially mobile."

"Six."

"Sell the game for free," Jordan continued. "Make money from in-app purchases and merchandising."

"Seven."

"It's a proven revenue model."

"Eight. And you're sure about the name? Nine."

"*Templar Run* is the perfect name. I'll cover the seed money."

"Ten. Thanks, Jordy. You're a pal. Eleven. To be honest, I just want to play the damn thing. Twelve. So I can shoot those Templar dicks in the head. Ha! Thirteen."

Jordan chuckled again. Steaks. Girls. Hi-tech exits. They had a lot to look forward to when they got out.

When they got out. They always talked about *when*, never *if*.

The fantasy, like the exercise, kept them going.

There was a good chance their crazy captors would tire of waiting for David to return and execute them. But Jordan pushed that scenario out of his mind. If the Temple decided to behead them, the friends would have little time to stress over it.

A key rattled in the lock, and the door of the cell creaked open. Mitchell and Jordy sprang to their feet. Judging by the weak ambient light, it was noon, and their next bowl and crust were hours away. A tall robe stood in the doorway, the cowl over his head. This was not their regular guard. What was going on?

The visitor sniffed the air, and the cowl tilted sideways, the robed equivalent of wrinkling his nose. The cell smelled of sweat and human excrement, but Jordan's nose was used to the stench.

Two plastic-wrapped bundles of clean folded clothes landed on the floor. "Wash yourselves and put these on. We leave in five minutes."

Jordan glanced at Mitchell, who ran a hand through the stubble on his chin and let his friend do the talking.

"Where are we going?" Jordan asked.

The dark cowl glared at him. "Out. Your friend has something for us."

"David?" Jordan said, excited. "Did he get the... whatever he was supposed to get?"

"We'll see. Now wash up. And make it snappy!"

The friends rushed to the bucket. Slapping water on their bodies, they wiped the grime from their arms and legs and toweled off with their old clothes. Jordan reached for a wrapped bundle of clothes.

"Wait," the visitor said. "These go on first."

Two robed guards entered the cell, each carrying at arm's length what looked like the lovechild of a G-string and a stick of dynamite.

"Keep still," the tall visitor commanded.

Sensing danger, Jordan did as he was told, and the guards

attached the device to Jordan's boxer trunks. The heavy stick of dynamite pressed against his crotch.

"What is this?" Jordan asked.

"Insurance," the visitor said, a smile curdling his deep voice. "In case you do anything stupid. I wouldn't if I were you. Not if you want to keep your balls."

CHAPTER 47

Sunday morning, David eyed 9th Street from the Toyota Camry Hybrid he'd picked up at Washington's Dulles International Airport. The rental car was one of the last purchases he'd make with his credit card. The sedan seated four adults with room to spare. This time, Mitchell would have no cause to complain. He had missed Mitchell. He'd even missed his whining. Today, David would undo all the harm he'd done his friends. One way or another, today the Trio would cease to exist.

The Washington Convention Center's bulk of cement and glass loomed over the street. David and Amy had idled at the street curb for over ten minutes while vehicles streamed into the underground parking entrance.

"Are you sure he's coming?" David asked.

"He'll be here," Amy said. She sat beside him, as cool and collected as the well-trained and super-deadly operative that she was.

She rolled up her window as a man walked by. "That was him," she said.

David hesitated. "But he walked right past us."

"Yep."

"What about the transaction?"

"All done."

He turned to look at her. Lo and behold, she was right. The white envelope of cash had disappeared, and she now held two gun magazines crammed with stubby bullets.

"Wow," David said. "I didn't even see that happen."

"Good. Let's hope nobody else did either." She hitched up the skirt of her business suit and pulled a white polymer handgun from the holster between her legs. Sliding one magazine into the gun's handgrip, she slipped the gun and spare magazine into the straps on her inner thighs and straightened her skirt. The white polymer had eluded the airport's metal detectors.

Amy had sent David to the drop-off at the Israel Day Parade without an armed escort, and she would not repeat that mistake.

"How do I look?"

"Drop-dead beautiful."

She grinned. "Just don't drop dead on me, OK?"

"I'll do my best."

David shifted the stick into Drive and joined the line of cars. Security personnel, rifles slung at their sides, eyed the vehicles. Through the window, David handed the guards his conference registration and driver's license, and they waved him through. He took a parking ticket from the machine at the gate, then selected a spot in the middle of three empty spaces on the second underground level. Amy reviewed their last-minute checklist.

"Prepuce?" she said.

"Lost it, ah, eight days after birth."

"Focus, David."

"Sorry, I joke around when I'm nervous."

"Yep. I noticed that when we first met. Prepuce?"

He tapped the jacket of his tuxedo. "In my breast pocket."

"Victory?"

"In the trunk with our bags." They had packed their travel clothes in two carry-on bags so they could board the next flight without having to check their luggage. David had placed the bubble-wrapped Fabergé egg in one of them.

Their luggage did not include the briefcase with the other nine Fabergé imperial eggs. Saturday evening, David had stopped by the Met, which had reopened to the public. He deposited the steel briefcase in the museum's coat-check facility, knowing that the eggs would find their way back to their rightful owners.

"Passports?" Amy asked.

"In the bag."

"Not anymore. I'll keep them with me." She winked at him. "Just in case."

"Just in case we need to leave in a hurry?"

"Exactly. Ready to go?"

Did a nod of the head count as a lie? He hoped not. "I love you, Amy."

"I love you too, David."

"Is it too late to elope?"

She laughed. "I'll see you inside."

They kissed. Amy got out of the car and walked to the nearest elevator in the parking garage. In her business suit and high heels, she looked trim and professional. How did she store so many items on her person and still look good? She must have learned that skill in the FBI.

David got out of the car and thumbed the remote, locking the doors with a satisfying double beep. Then he straightened the lapels of his tuxedo jacket and marched to the elevator. He followed the signs pointing toward the JAPI "Protect America's Minorities" Convention.

Tuxedos and evening dresses packed the wide lobby, squeezing around the thick pillars and triple escalators. David had stepped onto a glacier overrun by penguins—hungry, noisy penguins. His eyes scanned the attendees as they made small talk and gobbled finger food. None of the faces belonged to Jordan and Mitchell. None present wore dark robes or carried flaming torches either.

A hand clapped him on the shoulder. "David Zelig, in the flesh!" Gerry Cantor had the unique ability to make a man feel cornered in the center of a large room.

"Hi, Gerry," David said, trying to sound upbeat.

"David, I can't tell you how thrilled I was when you called to accept my invitation. I'll thank you on stage, of course." He cleared his throat. "Did you review the talking points for your speech?"

"What talking points?"

"I sent a list to your email along with the lineup. The keynote speech introduces the themes for the entire convention. Did you not get my email?"

"Oh, right. Sorry. I remember now." David had received the email but neglected to read the contents. He had also neglected to write his speech. It didn't matter. By the time Cantor called him to the stage, he'd be on a plane with a one-way ticket to wherever. Cantor would always remember him as the keynote speaker who got away.

"And?"

"And what?"

"What angle are you going to take in your speech?" Was the JAPI chairperson concerned David would offend the other donors and dignitaries?

"Don't worry about it, Gerry. Nobody listens to the speeches, anyway."

Gerry's plastic smile faded to an expression of painful constipation. David's flippant attitude had done nothing to reassure him. An attendant whispered in Gerry's ear, allowing David to return to the troubling task at hand.

He scanned the crowd for the Temple's contact. Would he recognize an operative if he saw one? Except for Luke, the Temple Father's monk-like right-hand man, the Templars had been a blur of cowled robes, motorcycle helmets, and ski masks. He'd have to wait for them to find him.

The foyer emptied fast as the attendees flowed into the main hall. A hand closed around his arm.

"David," Gerry said. "You're up."

"What?"

"It's time for your speech. You hear that?" His raised finger indicated the muffled rumble of an amplified voice from behind the curtains. "That's the MC. He's introducing you."

"Already?"

"You're the keynote speaker, David," he hissed, his constipated face turning purple. "You're on first."

"Oh." Beads of sweat prickled David's forehead, and the world shifted off balance. *Do not faint, David. Your friends depend on you.*

"Follow me." Gerry bustled off, and David tried to keep up. They passed through a side door, weaving their way around dangling curtains until they glimpsed the stage from the wings.

A man stood at a podium in a circle of spotlight and droned into several microphones. David peeked around the curtain at the crowd. Thousands of expectant faces filled the floor and grandstands, and stragglers hurried to their seats.

"Oh crap," David muttered, his mouth as dry as a crypt. His pulse throbbed in his throat, and his palms became clammy. A tear formed in the corner of his eye, and he felt the sudden urge to pee. He should have fainted while he had the chance.

CHAPTER 48

"Amy, is that you?" said a familiar male voice.

Adrenaline burst into Amy's bloodstream, and her body tensed for fight or flight. That voice spelled trouble. Deep trouble.

From the corner of the foyer of the Washington Convention Center, she had watched the suits mingle but failed to locate her contact. Temple operatives were easy to spot, cloaked or not. Their body language gave them away.

Thanks to years of modesty training, their eyes avoided the female form at all costs, a habit they found hard to shake even in the field. The henchmen found it easier to gun down a woman in cold blood than gaze upon her body. Amy added this observation to the many ironies and moral inconsistencies she'd noticed in the religious cult.

David stood at the opposite end of the foyer, his eyes combing the shifting crowd while a thin, gray-haired man chewed his ear off. After today, David wouldn't have to worry about annoying lobbyists. With their new identities, she and David would disappear into blissful anonymity. Or so she had told him.

The dream was irresistible: no more lies or deception; no constant need to prove her loyalty; the freedom to enjoy life with the man she loved. But that romantic vision was a mirage.

David loved her—enough to abandon the life he knew. But he could not turn his back on his friends and family to elope with her. He thought he could earn that dream life without sacrifice. He was wrong.

Amy tried to block David from her mind and suppress her feelings for him. She had answered the question that had tormented her for weeks. Could *she* turn her back on *her* friends and family for David? Standing before the Father's throne last week, she had made her decision. Human emotions like fear—or love—would only prevent her from following through.

The foyer emptied as the attendees filed into the convention hall, and still, the Temple's operatives had not shown themselves. *Where were they?* Amy could no longer ignore her premonitions. Something wasn't right. By the time the familiar voice called her name, she was edgy as hell.

Amy turned to see the honest and astonished face of Special Agent Eddie Worth. "Eddie, what are you doing here?"

"What am *I* doing here?" His left arm hung in a sling, the white edge of a plaster cast jutting from under his suit jacket. "I thought you were dead!"

Play it cool, Amy. Make something up. "I am dead," she said. "As far as you know. I had to go deep undercover, so we faked my death."

"Man, that is messed up. You had a funeral and everything. Wait a minute, who's *we*?"

"You know, the Bureau. Marco, actually. He was the only one who knew."

"Marco?" Eddie seemed more confused than before. "Marco was all torn up over your death. You should have seen him."

"Yeah, he's a good actor, right?"

Eddie frowned. "Well, he sure fooled me." He chuckled at a happy realization. "Did Marco fake his own death too? We found a body in Brooklyn, burned to a crisp. Just like you.

We thought it was him. Ha!"

He tapped his nose, in on the secret. Then he shook his head, mortified. "Man, you should have seen his family at the funeral. They sure thought he'd died for real. Wait a minute. Do you know where the Trio is? They disappeared off the face of the earth since the Israel Day Parade. Jordan's parents filed a missing person report, and the NYPD is leaving no stone unturned."

"Why are you here, Eddie?" Amy asked before he could poke any more holes in her cover story. "Is the Bureau expecting trouble?"

"Oh, yeah." Eddie hushed his voice. "We received new intel. The Elders will attend the convention today. Tactical teams are waiting a few blocks away. I'm supposed to call them in when Elders operatives show up."

A premonition in Amy's gut boiled over. Both Temple and Elders operatives were attending the convention, a combination as explosive as nitrogen and glycerin. This could not be coincidental. Did the Father know? Had Luke lied to her, sending her to the convention not to trade David's friends for the Holy Prepuce, but to destroy them all along with the Elders?

She dismissed the theory. The Temple had tried for years to infiltrate the Elders. Without her in the FBI, they could not have known what the Elders were planning. But if the opposing cults ran into each other here, they'd blow the JAPI Convention sky high. And an FBI tactical team would only add fuel to the flames. She had to make the trade and leave the building before the convention turned into a bloodbath.

A man in the crowd drew her eye, his tuxedo trying and failing to contain the muscular bulk of George "The Razor." The Temple had arrived, and Amy had to lose her old FBI colleague fast.

"Eddie," she said. "I've got the inside. I need you to watch the street."

"But we already have eyes outside."

"Listen to me, Eddie. Remember that undercover mission

I mentioned?"

"The one you died for?"

"The same one. Well, everything depends on me being here alone during the convention. I don't have time to explain. Do you understand? I'll call you back when the time comes."

Eddie nodded solemnly. "Roger that. I wouldn't want to ruin all your hard work." He shook his head like a wet dog. "Man, I'm looking forward to seeing Marco again. His family will be so excited. Mad at him too, I guess, but excited."

"Eddie," she hissed. "You can't say a word of this to anyone."

"Ma'am, my lips are sealed. I'll be out front." He walked off, still shaking his head.

She watched him go. The foyer was almost empty, the waiters unloading the buffet tables. Within the main hall, a voice droned on the loudspeakers.

George "The Razor" crossed the foyer, pretending not to see her but stopping nearby. "Is the Jew here?" his low, gravelly voice murmured. He smelled of Old Spice and spilled blood.

"Yes," she said, as the doors of the great hall closed. To a casual onlooker, they were two strangers loitering in the same corner of the lobby, their attention focused on opposite ends of the room.

"Does he have the package?"

"On him."

"Good. Bring him to the second parking level in five minutes. We'll make the exchange there. Don't make us wait."

"Understood."

He lingered, and a smug grin crept into his voice. "I suppose we should get used to spending more time together."

Amy cringed. "Right," she said. The Temple Father could pressure all he wanted, but the thought of marrying the brute still grossed her out.

"I'm looking forward to getting to know you," he added.

"In the Biblical sense."

The Razor chortled, and his muscular bulk sauntered off. Amy rolled her eyes. That Temple knight needed a course in basic chivalry.

Speaking of chivalry, where was David? They had to meet downstairs in a few minutes. She hadn't seen him enter the main hall.

Applause reverberated from beyond the closed doors. The sonorous voice had stopped droning, and now another voice spoke.

Her body tensed as she recognized the speaker. *Oh, no.* She hurried to the door of the convention hall. The voice belonged to David Zelig.

CHAPTER 49

Two hands pressed against David's back as Gerry Cantor shoved him forward and onto the stage. The man at the podium had spoken David's name twice. But David had stood rooted to the spot, his hazy mind filling with a single sickening thought: *That is a crapload of people.*

Men and women filled the endless rows of seats above and below like countless swarming insects. Immense television screens hovered in the void over their heads like a cube-shaped alien spaceship. The face of the master of ceremonies filled the oversized displays.

David's legs turned to jelly. Did Cantor expect him to go *out there?* Then the jelly froze, marooning him in the liminal space between the wings and the podium, an iceman carved from pure terror.

"Go on," Gerry Cantor hissed behind him. "You're up!"

The man at the podium turned to David and smiled. When David made no move to join him, the MC marched over. He gave David's hand a vigorous shake, clamped his arm around David's shoulders, and frog-marched him to the podium. Ocean waves crashed on the shore. No, not waves—the audience! Myriad hands clapped, and the sound mesmerized him.

His eyes shuttered as they stepped into the spotlight. His hands gripped the podium for support, and he discovered he was alone. The MC had abandoned him, and a new face stared at him from the floating screens, its expression blank and shell-shocked. Who was that? He lifted his hand to shield his eyes, and the face saluted. *His* face! This was all horribly wrong and unreal. *Please, somebody, wake me from this nightmare!*

The applause faded and an expectant silence sucked at his mind. There they all sat, waiting, expecting him to say something entertaining and meaningful. Unfortunately, David had forgotten how to speak. He moved his lips, trying to jump-start his mind, but they could no longer form words. Why hadn't he prepared an effing speech?

"Ladies," said a voice, startling him as it boomed from the giant speakers. The voice sounded strangely familiar. "And gentlemen," the voice continued. Wait a minute! His lips had moved. That was his voice!

A smile broke across his face. What a relief! He could speak again! He'd started off his speech pretty well, too. Now what? What the hell was he supposed to say, and would those faces all please stop staring at him! Cameras flashed. A woman coughed. A man cleared his throat. His dramatic pause became an awkward silence. People whispered in each other's ears, hiding their smiles behind their hands. David Zelig had forgotten his speech. David Zelig was making a fool of himself.

The door opened at the edge of the floor seats, and a shapely young woman stepped into the hall. She turned toward the stage and stared in disbelief.

"Amy," David blurted, his disembodied voice carrying on the speakers like the voice of God.

Amy stood there, a question on her face, the same question that rang in his own terrified mind. What the hell was he doing? In the crowd, the bemused smiles became irritated frowns. Was the keynote speaker drunk or high?

Go on—say something else. What follows "Amy"? David's tongue switched to autopilot. "Winehouse," he said. "Amy

Winehouse."

There—he had spoken a familiar name! The crowd's hard crust of irritation softened. He was starting to make sense. He might even say something interesting. David had something to say, didn't he? A burning purpose. Now was his chance. His tongue loosened.

"She said it best, didn't she?" he continued. "'I died a hundred times.' 'My tears dry on their own.'"

Heads nodded in the sea of faces. He had spoken of loss and isolation. Who couldn't relate to that? Wasn't that what had made him start the Trio—the soul-burning injustice of the world, his desperate need for consolation?

Amy pointed downward urgently and slapped her left wrist. Even David, a failure at Charades, understood her message. They were running late. He had to get off the stage. But he had started something, and he needed to finish.

The silence stretched away again. Then he glanced at Amy, and he knew what he wanted to say.

He turned to his audience. "Looking at you," he said, "I see love. So much love." Smiles blossomed on the faces. They liked that. Hands came together, and the roar of applause surged again. This wasn't so bad. The crowd's embrace was addictive.

Amy gestured at him wildly, pointing to herself and then the exit. *Oh, crap.* He'd forgotten all about the Temple and the Holy Prepuce. Amy had located her contact, and they had to get his friends. David needed to bring his speech to an end— the shortest, most cryptic keynote speech in JAPI history. He should thank the convention's organizers.

He glanced at the wings. Gerry Cantor stared at him, his face as pale as a bedsheet. The JAPI chairperson was not alone. A fist of armed men pressed around him. They wore black uniforms, not tuxedos, and black bandanas emblazoned with white Arabic script. They pointed their heavy-duty rifles at Gerry's chest.

"Guns!" David said, and the audience gasped. The Islamic Elders of Zion had crashed the convention, and they were not there to make speeches.

He spun around, ready to escape out the opposite wing of the stage, but another group of armed jihadis blocked his way. He was trapped.

Gripping the podium, he turned back to the audience. "Guns are not the answer." Someone whistled their approval, and the hands in the crowd came together again.

He found Amy on the floor, pacing. She held up her hands in frustration. He had to warn her but without causing pandemonium or setting off the terrorists.

In the wings, a jihadi prodded Gerry with the barrel of his rifle, and the JAPI chairperson beckoned for David to join him. The Elders wanted him. They wanted the Holy Prepuce.

"Haters are all around us," David said, fear raising his voice an octave. Amy Winehouse sprang back into his mind. "'Some Unholy War.'"

The crowd cheered and applauded their approval of the quotes from the tragic Jewish songwriter.

"Don't let them get to you," he said. The jihadis raised his weapons at him. "'Our Day Will Come!'"

David lunged forward as the crowd applauded. He dashed around the podium, dropped to the floor, and—to the sound of gasps from the audience—slipped feet-first off the stage.

The drop was higher than he had expected. He tumbled, rolled to his feet, and stumbled along the front row of seats. Amy ran down the aisle, their trajectories converging toward the nearest exit. He looked back at the stage. The jihadis had not followed him onto the stage. They would double back and cut him off in the foyer.

David ran. The audience rose to its feet, hands clapping and smiling with amusement at their speaker's unconventional exit. Hands reached out to shake his.

"The Elders are here," David told Amy, breathless, as they pushed through the exit doors together. "They've got guns."

With one fluid movement of her arm, Amy slipped the gun from between her legs. "The Temple too. Follow me."

CHAPTER 50

"We're going to die," Jordan said, his voice matter of fact.

Mitchell said. "I know."

For once, Jordan wished his friend would disagree. The inky black interior of the car trunk was as silent as a coffin. The stuffy air stank of sweat and rubber tires. His shoulder hurt from the hours spent on his side with his hands tied behind his back. His legs had fallen asleep too. As Jordan had feared, his life had turned into a Tarantino movie.

After hours of driving on what seemed to be a highway, the vehicle had stopped, and their captors had left the prisoners to stew alone.

Intense emotions had boiled within Jordan for most of the journey: fear, indignation, frustration, and resentment. Hours later, those feelings had evaporated, leaving him in a state of Zen-like calm and resignation. He would die here, and death had a silver lining. He had nothing left to achieve, nobody to impress. As the story of his life neared its brutal and untimely end, the loose ends no longer mattered.

Jordan didn't want to die. He was young, healthy, and wealthy. Most of his life still lay ahead of him. If David Zelig hadn't talked him into joining the Trio, Jordan would have enjoyed a good if uneventful life. He would have looked forward to a peaceful death at a ripe old age. His loss would devastate his parents, of course. He wished he could have saved them that grief. But he was no longer angry at David or Mitchell. He had let go.

Jordan shifted painfully on the rough lining of the trunk. The so-called chastity belt itched like hell, but he didn't dare to touch it. In the final minutes of his life, he'd prefer not to blow his balls off.

"Mitch," he said. "For what it's worth, I'm glad we made peace with each other."

"Yeah, me too. I wish we could have done that over a cold beer and not in a dungeon, but it is what it is."

"And a steak," Jordan said. "Don't forget that juicy steak."

They laughed, two friends facing death with easy camaraderie. That wasn't a bad way to go. Everybody died. Many people died young. Dying from dementia or in a car wreck wouldn't make his death any more meaningful.

The same morbid thoughts occupied Mitchell. "At least we died doing something spectacular," he said. "Most people die without ever having lived, without even having reached for their dreams."

"Yeah," Jordan said. "We aimed high. Nobody can accuse us of not trying."

Without warning, the trunk popped open and fluorescent light blinded him. Hands closed over his arms and pulled him upward, out of the trunk and onto his wobbly, tingling feet. They were in a crowded parking lot—a fancy one judging by the shiny paint and illuminated signage.

Their captors had identical crew cuts and gray suits. One was tall and brawny. Jordan braced for a summary execution but saw no guns in the operative's hands. What he did see rekindled the hope in his heart.

David Zelig stood before them, looking sharp in a tuxedo. While they'd rotted in a dungeon, he'd gotten a clean shave and gone to a cocktail party. But Jordan didn't begrudge him either of those. It was so darn good to see the bastard. Jordan hazarded a smile.

Then his eyes fell on the woman beside David, and Jordan's jaw dropped open. Special Agent Amy Smith stood beside David, alive and unburned.

"We thought you were dead."

Amy pouted an apology. "I was."

"Enough small talk," Tall Goon said. "Where's the Prepuce?"

"I have it," David said. "Let them go."

"First the Prepuce."

David hesitated, and Jordan's heart skipped a beat. Had David acquired the Holy Prepuce or had the FBI hatched another elaborate deception like the fake Fabergé eggs? If so, the Temple had just called the FBI's bluff.

"No," David said. "My friends first."

Jordan's nether regions itched beneath the explosive belt.

Tall Goon grinned. "Don't push your luck." He lifted his hand, which held a remote. "Or your *friends* will have balls of fire."

"Chastity belts?" Amy asked, appalled. Wait a minute. How did she know about those?

Amy placed a cautionary hand on David's arm. "They've rigged them with explosives."

"Jesus," David said, horrified and subdued.

"Hey, watch your mouth," Short Goon said. Blowing up a man's testicles was OK, but cussing was out.

David reached into his breast pocket and withdrew a vacuum-sealed plastic square. Stepping forward, he handed the foreskin to Tall Goon, then stepped back.

Amy said, "The Holy Prepuce of Calcata."

The thug turned the specimen over. "How do I know it's legit?"

David said, "Zheltkov said people taste it."

Tall Goon glared at him, then slid the Prepuce into the pocket of his suit jacket. "I'll take your word for it."

"OK," David said, putting his hands together. "You've got the Holy Prepuce. Now let them go."

Jordan's entire body trembled. David had done the impossible. He had obtained the Holy Prepuce, and now Jordan and Mitchell would go free. They would not die today. Jordan wanted to kiss David.

Tall Goon grinned again. "Sorry, but I can't do that."

David looked as surprised as Jordan felt. "What do you mean? That was our deal."

Tall Goon cocked his head back, enjoying every moment. "Too many loose ends," he said.

David shot a quick glance at Amy, and so did Jordan. Amy could handle herself in a fight better than the other three combined. And she did not disappoint.

She stepped sideways, a white gun appearing in her hand. But then something went terribly wrong. Instead of pointing the gun at the Temple thugs, she aimed her weapon at David.

CHAPTER 51

David blinked at Amy and at the gun in her hand. "Amy," he said, the ground falling away from under his feet.

The bodybuilder Temple operative chuckled. "You didn't see that coming, did you?"

"I... I don't understand."

He loved Amy; she loved him. She had begged him to elope with her and leave everything behind. Why was she doing this? He searched her eyes for an answer.

"Jesus," Jordan said. "She's with the Temple?"

"I said, watch your mouth," the shorter operative said.

Amy ignored the others. "I'm sorry, David, but things could never work out between us."

Dave's heart sank.

"Wait a minute," Mitchell said. "Are you two going out?"

David ignored him too. "Don't say that, Amy. Things *can* work out and they will. I promise."

She shook her head. "There's no escaping the Temple, David. Father gave me one last chance to redeem my soul. I can't just walk away from him."

David almost choked on the bitter betrayal. How could she sell him out when they were so close to their goal? "Amy, why the hell not?"

"Because he isn't *the* Father to me; he's *my* father. My biological father."

David opened his mouth, then shut it. Amy had begged him to elope, and he should have listened. The Temple would never give up on their leader's daughter and the Jewish boyfriend who had poisoned her mind; the Temple's assassins would hunt them down wherever they went.

"Hold on," Jordan said. "You *knew* she was with the Temple and you still teamed up with her?"

David answered his friend, his eyes still locked on Amy. "I thought she loved me. When Hernandez tried to kill me, she saved my life."

"She didn't save your life," the bodybuilder said, cutting in again. "She protected the Temple's investment. Without you, we would never have laid hands on the Holy Prepuce. Now that we have it, we no longer need you."

"Sorry to interrupt again," Mitchell said, "but my head is exploding. Did you say Hernandez tried to kill you?"

"It's a long story," David said. *Keep them talking*, he thought. Any second, the Elders would pour into the garage, creating a diversion that might allow the Trio to escape. But how was he supposed to defuse the explosive belts?

"And a story you'll never hear," the bodybuilder said. "Amy, finish them."

Amy gripped the gun in both hands, and her eyes hardened. "I will. But we have bigger problems, George. The Elders are here."

"What?" The news seemed to unnerve George. "How many?"

"Dozens. They'll be here any moment."

David scowled at her. She had ruined his plan.

George's face turned red. "This is the Jew's doing!"

"Not this time, George. The Elders are after the Prepuce. The FBI is watching the street too. Change in plans. We need to secure the Prepuce at all costs. I'll terminate the Trio and handle the FBI. You should leave right away before the gunshots draw attention."

George, a man used to taking orders, nodded. He spoke into his shirt sleeve. "Brothers, the Infidel is here. I repeat the Infidel is here. We're moving out but prepare to engage." Lowering his arm, he told Amy, "A knife will be quieter."

"I'm on it. Go ahead, I'll meet up with you later."

George nodded, then lifted the remote again. "If I don't hear from you in five minutes, I'll blow the bastards to hell."

Amy nodded. "Godspeed."

"Godspeed."

George and the other goon closed the trunk of the car and drove off.

Amy kept the gun trained on David's chest, and his strength left him. The woman he loved was about to gun him down in a parking lot.

"Amy, you don't have to do this."

No, not the woman he loved. That woman didn't exist. She was a role Amy had played to serve the Temple.

Amy didn't respond. Deadly efficient as always, she got right to business.

"Drop your trunks."

The men glanced at each other in anxious confusion. Was she going to humiliate them before their execution?

Amy rolled her eyes at their slow uptake. "Jordan, Mitch. Lose the pants so I can disable the explosives. OK? We've got five minutes before George the Razor presses the button and your junk goes kablooey."

Jordan and Mitchell got to work on their trousers.

"So you won't kill us all?" David said.

Amy lowered her gun. "I had to make it look convincing." She stepped up and kissed him.

David wrapped her in an embrace. He wanted to cry with relief.

Jordan cleared his throat. "Um, sorry to spoil the moment and all, but we've still got dynamite strapped to our effing testicles."

"Yeah, guys," Mitchell said. "Please. Get a room."

David released Amy. She dropped to her knees and examined the explosive rig taped to Jordan's nether regions. She swore. "They're booby-trapped. Removing them won't be easy."

"Have you done this before?" Jordan said.

"You're the first." She looked up at David. "Maybe you should… get the car. You know, so we'll get out of here faster." David swallowed hard. She was getting him away from them in case the explosives detonated. "Now," she said with an urgency that did not allow for discussion.

"Guys, I'll be right back." David trotted off toward his rental car. He was of no use looking over her shoulder, anyway. He pulled the car keys from his pocket. Now, where had he parked the Camry? Right, over there!

He made for the car at a brisk pace. No wonder he'd had trouble finding the car. The two empty spots on either side had filled with identical black vans. The car beeped as he thumbed the remote. But as he reached the trunk, a door opened at an exit and men in black uniforms and matching bandanas poured into the garage, their rifles at the ready.

David ducked, hiding behind the car. Had the Elders seen him? The feet of a dozen armed operatives echoed off the cement walls. Their footfalls grew louder. They were heading his way.

A noise behind him made him spin around. More footfalls. Had Amy and his friends followed him? He eased around the edge of the van, then snuck a peek. Gray suits. Close-cropped hair. And more firepower than an NRA convention. *Dear God.* The Templar army had arrived too. *This can't be happening.*

The padding of tactical boots whispered around him, the sound of predators sneaking up on their prey. The Temple and the Elders had surrounded him on either side.

Soon, the fighters would be upon him. Opening the car door now would give away his location, so he dropped to the ground, crawled under the Camry, and waited.

And waited.

The sounds of hushed footsteps petered out. The opposing groups, the Christian Crusaders and the Islamic Jihadis, faced each other, weapons drawn, each side waiting for the other to fire the first shot.

Doors slid open nearby and shock absorbers creaked. Black military boots stepped onto the floor on either side of the Camry, the many legs enclosed in camouflage trousers. The soldiers must have been waiting inside the black vans. Magazine clips clicked into place and metal charging handles shifted, noisily loading cartridges into firing chambers.

David kept still and tried not to breathe. Over a dozen armed men surrounded the Camry. Were they Temple or Elders, FBI or CIA? And did they have any idea they were sandwiched between two heavily armed rival criminal organizations?

A smoking cigarette dropped to the floor, and a black boot stepped on the stub, extinguishing the flame with a grinding twist of the ankle. "OK, boys," a gritty voice said. "Let's go kill us some Jews!"

The fighters answered the statement with cheers of "Yeah!" and "You bet!" David tried not to empty his bladder. If he sneezed, the anti-Semitic thugs would have him. The boots walked away, then halted after a few steps. The voice said, "What in tarnation...?"

And the world around David exploded.

CHAPTER 52

"Got a light?" Eddie asked. The Latino guard outside the parking entrance of the Washington Convention Center wore black Ray-Bans and rested his hand on the butt of the M16 slung over his shoulder. He glanced at Eddie as if waking up, then fished a plastic lighter from his shirt pocket and ignited the end of Eddie's Winston.

"Thanks." He stuck the cigarette between his lips and held out the pack. "Want one?" The guard shook his head. "Suit yourself."

Eddie exhaled a long plume of smoke into the sunny late-morning air. Nicotine calmed him, and right now he needed calming. He had pushed to receive this assignment, his first since his week of sick leave for his wounded arm. The Elders had all but disappeared since the Israel Day Parade disaster. But their lack of activity was misleading, the eerie silence before the thunderstorm. Eddie had jumped at the opportunity to strike the secret society that had killed his team leader and good friend, Special Agent Amy Smith. Then, minutes ago, he had spoken with his dead commander and everything he thought he knew flew out the window.

"I quit smoking five years ago," Eddie told the guard and chuckled. He was glad to have someone to talk to. This was the kind of news he could only share with a stranger, a listener who knew none of the people involved. "Then two of my fellow agents got killed in the line of duty, and I bought a pack of Winstons. But I didn't buy a lighter. That way I could tell myself I hadn't really started smoking again." He laughed at his little self-deception.

"Sorry to hear about your friends," the guard said. "Is that how you got the cast?"

Eddie glanced at his stiff left arm. "Yeah. I got this when we lost the first agent. The other died a few days later in a separate incident."

"Where do you serve?" Eddie extracted his badge and showed him. "FBI? Nice."

"Special task force," Eddie said with pride. "Top secret and all that. The thing is, a few minutes ago, back in there," he pointed to the Convention Center, "I bumped into my old colleague."

"Wait—you mean the dead one?"

"Mm-hm. I thought I was seeing things, losing my mind. But it was her, all right."

"No kidding?"

"To make sure I wasn't hallucinating or whatever, I walked right up to her and said hello."

Somewhere in the distance, firecrackers went off. *Damn kids.* Eddie recovered his train of thought.

"You know what she told me? She said she'd faked her death as part of a deep undercover mission. Can you believe that?"

"That's totally messed up, man. She didn't tell you before that?"

"Not a word. I had no idea. But it gets worse. Turns out my other dead colleague was in the loop."

"Did he fake his death too?"

"Mm-hm."

"Man, that is crazy. You see, that's why I didn't sign up for the FBI. Too much crazy shit going on there."

"You're telling me." Another set of firecrackers exploded,

longer and louder than the first. "I'm Eddie, by the way." He held out his hand, and they shook. "You know, you remind me a little of one of my colleagues, the second one. What's your name?"

"Marco."

"No kidding. He was a Marco too." A suspicion unnerved Eddie. "Would you mind lifting your glasses for a second?"

"What, you think I might be him?" The guard laughed and raised his glasses.

"Nah, you're not him. Maybe I have gone crazy."

They laughed. It was good to laugh. After what he'd been through, Eddie needed a good laugh. The third set of firecrackers went on and on. The louder bursts sounded like grenades.

Eddie stubbed out his cigarette. "What is this, the Fourth of July?"

"What do you mean?"

"The fireworks, man. Don't tell me I'm hearing things too." Was he hearing things? Had he imagined his conversation with Amy too?

The rat-a-tat of muffled explosions continued, multiple bursts overlapping as though an entire fireworks factory had gone up in flames.

Marco the guard frowned. "Not fireworks, man. Sounds to me like gunshots."

They glanced at each other for a silent, dreadful moment, then swore. Marco reached for his radio receiver, as Eddie pulled out his phone. He dialed the number of the SWAT team leader as crowds of well-dressed men and women poured out of the convention center and onto the street. "This is Special Agent Worth at the convention center. You need to get over here right away!"

CHAPTER 53

David lay on the ground beneath the Camry, his palms clamped over his ears, as shards of shattered glass danced on the parking bay floor around him. Above him, the car rocked on its suspension, engine pipes nudging his head as bullets tore holes in the car's body. The battle raged around him in every direction, a man-made earthquake shaking the floor and trapping David at the epicenter.

Black boots changed position around the car. Legs in camouflage fatigues knelt and dodged and shifted. The anti-Semitic militia was the flame that had ignited the tensions between the warring secret societies on either side of the parking garage. They fielded enemy fire from every side and paid the shooters back in kind. Car alarms wailed and the acrid scent of burned gunpowder wafted in the air as the bursts of machine-gun fire became more frequent.

Spent bullet casings pelted the floor. David yelped as a hot casing bounced under the car and singed his hand, but nobody heard him over the ruckus. Suddenly, his ankle felt wet and slimy. Had they shot him? He reached for his leg. Thankfully, no blood returned on his fingers, only a familiar pungent smell that made the hairs on his neck stand erect. Gasoline. The car was leaking fuel all over him. He had to get out of there!

A gunman fell to the floor beside the Camry. His body shuddered, then lay still. His naked arm bore a swastika tattoo. David shifted away from the glazed stare of the corpse. As if the Elders and the Temple weren't enough, fate had tossed trigger-happy neo-Nazis into the conflagration.

David looked around for an escape path not filled with the sounds of firing weapons. He had to abandon the Swiss cheese of a car, but first, he needed to extract his travel bag from the trunk. He and Amy could always get new clothes, but the Fabergé egg was, literally, their nest egg for the rest of their fugitive lives. Without Victory, they'd never stay one step ahead of the Temple's assassins.

An empty magazine clattered to the ground as a gunman loaded another. An explosion erupted, and David turned his face away from the heatwave and tongues of flame that spread beneath the rows of parked vehicles.

Wounded men cried out and groaned, but the machine guns blazed on. Another explosion detonated. The world went silent except for the ringing in David's ears. Something bumped into David's chest—a gloved hand, the fingers scorched and smelling of grilled chicken. David yelped and flicked the detached limb away like a dead cockroach. The stench of burnt hair and flesh almost made him puke.

Screw the egg! David had to get out of there. Bodies littered the ground, around the Camry and further afield. Boots pounded the cement as fighters sprinted to new positions. A small clump of militia gunmen still huddled at the front of the car. David crawled backward away from the booted feet, shifting around to see where he was going. Wherever he looked, cars burned and gunmen charged, sparks leaping from their weapons. If he could crawl out from under the car and sprint to the next row of vehicles, he could run back to Amy and…

Oh, my God. In the conflagration, he had forgotten all about his friends! Had they escaped the battle? Had they been injured in the crossfire? David had heard multiple explosions.

Had Amy defused the chastity belts in time?

His questions scattered when another gunman in camouflage fatigues dropped to the floor. The shaved head stared at David, and the man's brow wrinkled with surprise. *Oh, no. No, no, no!* The armed neo-Nazi had discovered him. David was going to die!

Then, blood trickled from the man's mouth, his head thudded to the floor, and his eyes unfocused. But David's surge of relief was premature. The dead man's hand opened, and an egg rolled toward David. Not a golden Fabergé egg—a hand grenade!

CHAPTER 54

"Get down!" Amy yelled. The air rang with the sound of automatic gunfire.

"What about the bombs?" Mitchell said.

"They won't matter if you lose your head."

"Got it."

He joined Amy and Jordan on the floor of the parking garage beside an old Jeep SUV at the end of a line of cars.

"Lie down," she said, "both of you."

For once, Mitchell did as he was told without arguing. The rapid-fire reports from the other side of the parking bay explained his sudden obedience.

Amy hoped David had reached the car before the firefight had erupted. With all the firepower on the loose, escaping the parking lot would be tricky.

She focused on the task at hand. George the Razor had strapped the chastity belts on tight and passed a suspicious wire from the detonator through their underwear. Any attempt to remove the belt would trigger small packages of dynamite. Not enough to level a building, but sufficient to remove critical body parts. Only the Temple could have invented such a device, an ironic mix of puritanical mores and inhumane cruelty. The cult had honed both specialties over the centuries.

Nope, detaching the devices was not an option. She'd have to defuse them first. Removing a strip of the black insulating tape revealed three thin wires. She wished she'd taken that explosives course at Quantico.

"Pick a color," she said. "Blue, red, or yellow."

"What?" Mitchell said.

"There are three wires here. We need to pull one of them. Or all of them. We've got seconds before George remembers to press the button. Maybe a minute. He's got other problems right now."

Jordan said, "You want *us* to pick the wire?"

"Might as well. It's your package, so to speak. I can't re-move the bomb without triggering an explosion. I'm sorry, but bomb disposal isn't my specialty."

"The red wire," Mitchell said. "In *Armageddon*, they cut the red wire."

"*Armageddon?*" Amy asked.

"The movie. You been living under a rock?"

"Pretty much." Amy took the red wire in her fingers.

"Wait," Jordan said. "The blue wire. They cut the blue one in *Armageddon*, Mitch."

"Are you sure?"

"Yes. First, they chose red, then they cut the blue."

"Jesus! I don't know."

"Mitchell," Amy yelled. "Make up your mind already. Give me your hand." She guided his fingers. "This is red, this is blue. Just give us a few seconds to move out of the way, then pull the wire hard."

"Why do I go first?"

Jordan said, "I'm not going first."

Amy shrugged. "We don't have time for a debate."

"Hold on," Jordan said, spreading his hands. The prospect of losing his testicles had galvanized his brain. "The bombs will explode if we remove them?"

"Correct."

"And they're attached to our underwear?"

"Yes. Your point?"

"What if we just… removed our underwear?"

"What?" Mitchell said. "It can't be that simple."

Amy blinked at Jordan. She hadn't thought of that. As she crouched over them with their trousers at their ankles, removing their underwear had been the thought furthest from her mind. She'd bet the Temple hadn't imagined that their captives would remove their undies in public. Their puritanical mindset would be their downfall.

"You're right," she said. "Do it."

She looked away as the two young men wriggled out of their trousers and underwear like their futures depended on it. In this case, they did.

"What do we do with them?" Jordan asked.

Amy didn't turn around. "Are you dressed?"

"The bombs, Amy! What do we do with them?"

Jordan had outsmarted the Temple, but he had no clue about basic survival.

"Jesus, Amy, we've put on our pants."

"Why didn't you say so?" Amy gripped the booby-trapped boxer shorts between forefinger and thumb and lobbed them over the next row of cars. She waited for the telltale sound of explosions, but none followed. Time to move on.

Amy crouched beside the old Jeep, her gun at the ready, and listened to the continuous exchange of gunfire. She peered through the windows of the Jeep, searching for the Toyota Camry.

"Where's David?"

"He went down there," Mitchell said, pointing toward the raging battle.

He was right again. Hoping to save time, she had sent David into the middle of a battlefield. Fighters cried out. Hand grenades detonated. Armageddon wasn't a movie; it was playing out right here.

She stole another glance through the window. The Temple's suited operatives stood to the right, their assault rifles raised and firing. On the left, an Elder fighter with a black bandana tossed another hand grenade. That made no sense. The groups were too far apart for grenades.

Then she spotted the third group of fighters between two black vans. A dozen skinheads in pseudo-military uniforms spat bullets in all directions, taking on both clandestine militias at once.

All sides were taking heavy losses. Cars burned, the flames licking the ceiling. Alarms wailed like a chorus of yowling alley cats. The situation was out of control.

Wait a minute. She stared at the windowless, hole-peppered Camry between the two vans. That was their car. Was David trapped inside? She saw no sign of him inside the car. *David, where are you?*

Then, before her eyes, the Camry exploded. The car rose into the air on a ball of fire, flipped over, and slammed down with a gut-wrenching groan of collapsing metal. Amy gaped at the wreckage. David wasn't inside the Camry. He couldn't be. She hadn't seen him in the car, had she? The force of the explosion knocked the vans sideways, and flames engulfed them too. Amy stared at the fires of hell, transfixed.

The spurts of gunfire shortened, the gaps of silence lengthened. A fighter in camouflage fatigues limped toward an exit until a spray of bullets downed him. The last men standing moved among the dead and dying and mopped up the survivors.

Overhead, sprinklers whirred to life and rained cold water over the entire garage, waking Amy from her trance. She had to find David. They all had to leave the scene before the FBI SWAT team locked the conference center down.

She turned to David's friends. "Know how to boost a car?"

"You mean, steal a car?" Jordan said, offended. "No."

"Break the back window."

"How?"

"With something hard."

"A brick?" Mitchell asked. He picked a red brick off the ground.

"Perfect."

Amy took the brick and smashed in the rear side window of the Jeep. The alarm sounded, but the chorus of wailing cars drowned it out. Reaching inside, she unlocked the front door, got in the driver's seat, and messed with the wires under the steering column. Years had passed since she'd hotwired a car, but she remembered the basics. This Jeep might just be old enough for that to work. She connected the ignition and battery wires, then sparked them with the starter wire, taking care not to electrocute herself. The engine turned and purred. They were in business. Now to break the steering lock and they were on their way.

"Nice work," Mitchell said, brushing his damp fringe from his face.

The two men clambered into the back seat, when a large hand grabbed Amy's arm, pulling her from the car and throwing her into the air. Amy broke her fall, curling up and rolling on the slick floor. She shot back onto her feet, her arms raised in a fighting stance as water rained down all over.

"Traitor!" George the Razor roared at her. "Heretic!" He took off his torn suit jacket and tossed it on the wet floor. His damp dress shirt was speckled with red, and his ear was a bloody stump. Buckshot pockmarked the side of his head with open wounds that oozed blood. His injuries had done nothing to improve his mood.

"I should have shot you all myself."

He towered over her, dripping water from the sprinklers. Luckily for Amy and the Trio, he seemed to have misplaced his assault rifle.

Amy eyed the idling Jeep behind him. Her polymer handgun lay on the front seat.

"Who the hell are those psychos?" George yelled. "Did you set this up?"

She made eye contact with Jordan through the broken window of the Jeep and shifted her gaze to the gun on the front seat. Would Jordan take the hint? The Razor glanced back at the Jeep and chuckled.

"Say goodbye to your friends. I hope they were worth eternal damnation." He pulled the remote from his pocket and pressed the button. To his surprise, the men in the Jeep did not burst into flame. Instead, two loud cracks sounded twenty feet away. Glass tinkled on the floor, and two plumes of smoke rose behind the next row of cars.

The Razor growled with frustration and launched at her. Amy dived sideways, avoiding his powerful groping hands. Sliding to the floor, she spun her leg around and knocked him off his feet. He collapsed to the ground with a wet splat. Amy dashed for the driver's seat and her hand closed around the polymer gun. Two bullets to the chest would put the Razor out of action for good.

She turned to fire, her finger curling over the trigger, when a large hand clamped over hers, pushing the barrel off target as the pin fired. He squeezed her hand. She winced and, to save her fingers, she dropped the gun, which clattered to the floor. His other hand came down on her head, but she blocked with her forearm and kicked him in the groin for all she was worth.

Razor George released her hand from his iron grip, and she kicked again, this time aiming the sharp heel of her shoe at his solar plexus. The blow would have winded him, maybe even shattered a few ribs, had he not caught her foot and twisted. Amy twirled around to save her knee from breaking. She tumbled to the ground and kicked free, her heel coming away in his hand.

Amy reached for her gun, but his boot came down on the hardened plastic, shattering the casing and rendering the weapon useless. On the floor, her hand throbbing with pain, she didn't see the next blow coming.

Her cheek pounded the damp floor. Hands grabbed her hair and lifted her to her feet. A foot shorter and half his weight, she was a rag doll in his iron grip.

She slammed her remaining heel down on his dress shoe and elbowed him in the ribs, but his hands clenched tighter, pulling at the roots of her hair. Amy flailed her arms, chopping at the hand, hoping to break free.

With a telltale whoosh, he slid his hunting knife from its scabbard and raised the blade in the air for her to see. George would gut her like he'd gutted countless others.

"Prepare for Judgment Day!" he yelled. "Traitor bitch!"

Time slowed down. Amy thought of David. He was dead too. She would see him again once the Razor ended her. With that final consolation, she closed her eyes.

There was a grunt, a loud crack, and a shudder. The Razor released her hair, and Amy slipped to the floor. A hunting knife dug into the concrete floor near her feet. Behind her, the Razor dropped to his knees, then fell onto her. Amy rolled the brute off her body and got to her feet. Mitchell stood over the Razor, the cracked brick still in his hand.

"Good job," she muttered, out of breath, her hand burning, her cheek stinging. "Let's get the hell out of here."

She gathered her other shoe and retrieved the Prepuce from the Razor's jacket pocket. Then she got in the driver's seat and reversed out of the parking spot. Tires squealed as she careened around a corner. The car bounced as she drove over dead gunmen. Halfway to the exit ramp, she slammed on the brakes.

The upturned Camry smoldered between the bullet-riddled and lopsided remains of the two black vans. The cacophony of car sirens had petered out, and only the whispering of the water sprinklers remained.

"Is that your car?" Jordan said.

She nodded.

"Jesus," Mitchell said.

Anyone inside the Camry had been crushed to death and roasted. Amy wiped tears and a strand of wet hair from her face. She said, "He must be here somewhere." Her voice was coarse. "David could have hidden somewhere."

His friends in the back seat said nothing. Their solemn silence said it all. She was sobbing now, her chest trembling with every shallow breath. A hand touched her shoulder. "He'd want us to keep going."

Amy nodded. Jordan was right. *We're not free yet. Pull yourself together.* She pressed her bare foot to the accelerator, and the Jeep sped away.

CHAPTER 55

Water sprinkled on the back of David's head. He lay face-down on a hard surface, soaked from head to toe and his skull aching. His mind constructed a likely narrative. He had fallen asleep in the shower after a night of heavy drinking. *Bad David.*

But the coarse cement that pressed against his cheek was not the tiled floor of his bathroom. He opened his eyes and rolled over. A fluorescent light panel flickered on a gray ceiling. He lay on a white line between two parked cars. And he remembered....

Panicking, he scanned his surroundings but found no black-booted gunmen. The thunder of gunfire and deafening explosions had ceased. He had survived the battle. He was alive and, as far as he could tell, whole.

He struggled to his feet and massaged the tender bump on his forehead. Other than the patter of the sprinkler system, the parking bay was ghostly silent. He limped forward, water squelching in his shoes, shards of broken glass crunching underfoot.

The parking bay of the Washington Convention Center had become a war zone. Flames rose from wrecked cars. Dead bodies littered the floor along with severed limbs, orphaned hubcaps, and mounds of spent bullet casings. The smells of burned gunpowder and grilled chicken hung in the air.

He found what remained of the Toyota Camry. The vehicle lay upside down, charred, and flattened. His corpse might have been under there.

As the hand grenade had rolled toward him, he'd made a decision. Better an uncertain death outside than a guaranteed cremation under the Camry. He'd shimmied out from beneath the car like a caterpillar on ecstasy and sprinted to the nearest car that was not already ablaze.

That was the last David remembered. The blast must have knocked him off his feet, and, hitting his head against a car door, he'd lost consciousness. How long had he been out cold? Not more than a few minutes, he guessed. The police had yet to arrive at the scene. He had to get out of there.

The squeal of car tires shoved him downward. Crouching beside a bullet-riddled car, he watched from a distance. Over the roofs of destroyed cars, an old Jeep SUV took a corner on two wheels. Then the vehicle barreled down the parking bay, slowing only to mount a few low obstacles. David could guess what those obstacles were. The SUV slammed on the brakes opposite the upturned, smoldering Camry. Through the open windows, three faces surveyed the carnage.

"Amy," David mumbled. She was alive! So were Jordan and Mitchell! Oh, thank God!

The Jeep launched down the parking bay.

"Amy!" David yelled. He ran after the Jeep. "Guys! Wait!"

The Jeep turned a corner and climbed the ramp to street level. David sprinted after his escaping friends, waving his hands and leaping over dead gunmen. "Amy!"

They hadn't seen him. They'd left him behind. David chased them on unsteady feet, knowing he'd never catch them, but what else could he do?

He turned the corner onto the ramp and halted. The Jeep idled before him. Then a door opened, and Amy rushed at him. Their bodies collided, embracing and pressing together.

David could die now, in her arms, and he'd die happy.

"I thought you were dead!" she said, choking on tortured emotion.

"I guess we're even now."

More doors opened. "Dave," Jordan said. "You made it. Thank goodness."

Mitchell said, "We thought we'd lost you, man."

Outside, sirens wailed, and their new predicament muddied their moment of relief. They ran to the SUV and climbed in. Amy floored the accelerator and raced up the ramp into daylight. The rising arm at the exit broke clean off as the Jeep rammed through the security gate, the wheels leaving the ground. Then sparks flew as the Jeep's nose brushed the asphalt, and Amy turned into the flow of traffic, missing a bus by inches.

They drove down the street as though nothing had happened. On the sidewalk, a man in a brown suit directed the flow of tuxedos out of the Washington Convention Center and along the sidewalk. Two black vans with the words SWAT painted on the sides sped by in the opposite direction and turned into the center's parking bay.

"Is that Eddie Worth?" David asked.

Amy nodded. "Yeah, I bumped into him in the foyer."

"Wow." David pulled the paper parking stub he'd kept in his back pocket. "You know we could have just paid the ticket?"

"My way was faster. And we don't want the FBI to trace your credit card back to a stolen car that left the convention in a hurry. We'll need that credit card soon."

David considered his soaked and soiled tuxedo. "Yeah, we need new clothes." He shook his head in disappointment. "I liked this tux."

Amy said, "I guess this means we lost the egg."

"Yeah. Victory was in the trunk. By now it's toast."

"Hard-boiled," she said.

David laughed. "And scrambled. So much for our nest egg." It felt so good to be alive, losing a multimillion-dollar golden egg didn't seem too high a price to pay.

"What nest egg?" Jordan said.

"A Fabergé."

"How do you still have an egg? Didn't you trade them for the Prepuce?"

"In the end, we didn't need to. We had all ten imperial Fabergé eggs. It's a long story."

"Nine," Mitchell said. "There were nine eggs in total."

"Yeah," Jordan said.

David and Amy exchanged a knowing look. "Like I said, a long story."

He told them about their ill-fated meeting with Peter Zheltkov, from their crash landing in the jungle to their rescue aboard the USS *Detroit*. The revelation about the Elders' infiltration of the CIA floored his friends.

"So what do we do now?" Jordan said. "The Temple wants us dead more than ever, and the same goes for the Elders. And as for Amy—no offense, Amy—but you'll have to do a lot of explaining at the FBI."

Amy reached into the inner pocket of her jacket and handed David a zip-lock bag containing four dark-blue booklets. He opened them and handed two to his friends in the back.

Jordan leafed through his. "Terry Rawlins?" When Mitchell laughed, he added, "What's your new name, Smart Ass?"

"Lawrence Brown. I kind of like it."

"If it's any consolation," David said, "I'm Harry Carter, and she's Peggy Gould."

Jordan said, "So this is the plan, Harry? We're just going to disappear and start over—leave everyone and everything we know behind?"

"At least we'll have each other," Amy said. "Suck it up, boys. The alternative is a slow, painful death."

Jordan swallowed, and again David felt that pinch of guilt. "Guys, I'm really sorry. This is all my fault. I should never have dragged you into this."

"You kidding me?" Mitchell said. "You should have seen

how I knocked out that Temple guy. That was epic. He was huge! I saved your girlfriend's life, you know. She owes me big time."

Amy rolled her eyes. "Yeah," she admitted. "You saved my life. I'm eternally grateful."

"How grateful?"

"Don't push it, Mitch."

"And Jordy, here, well, his quick thinking saved both our balls, and I mean that literally. He's not the brains of the Trio for nothing."

Despite himself, Jordan smiled, but the jokes didn't change their reality. David, at least, had found Amy, the love of his life. But he'd screwed up his friends' lives, and they had nothing to show for it.

"David," Jordan said. "Those other guys, the ones in camouflage, were they with the Elders or the Temple?"

"Neither," David said. "Neo-Nazis. It sounded like they were about to attack the convention." Again, he sensed the hidden bulk of the iceberg in the murky depths.

Amy took the turnoff for Dulles International Airport, then turned on the radio, switching stations until she found a news update.

"... attempted a large-scale hate crime at the Washington Convention Center today. No civilian casualties are reported, but the incident is still ongoing. In a preliminary statement, the Washington Police Department identified the perpetrators as members of a neo-Nazi organization. The terrorist group is unaffiliated with the Black Hebrew Israelite extremist faction that attacked the Israel Day Parade in New York a week ago."

The broadcast cut to an ad for laundry detergent, and Amy switched to a music channel.

"Black Israelites?" Jordan said, confused. "What are they talking about?"

"It's a cover-up!" Mitchell said.

"Amy?" David asked, his heart still galloping as it had on the battlefield. "Would the FBI do that?"

She shrugged. "Unlikely. The neo-Nazis today were real enough. But who knows? I'm out of the loop now."

A new song began to play on the radio, "Our Day Will Come," by Amy Winehouse, the song David had quoted onstage. What were the chances? For the first time in weeks, he felt they all might put their secret society ordeals behind them and start a new chapter in their lives.

They parked in the airport long-term parking and rang up five thousand dollars in clothing at Burberry. The sales rep, who had welcomed his bedraggled customers with poorly disguised anxiety, seemed surprised when David's credit card cleared. David and Amy stopped by the Air France counter to buy tickets.

"The Ivory Coast?" Jordan said, surprised, as he studied his ticket.

Mitchell said, "Where the hell is that?"

"It's the first flight out," Amy explained, "and the country has no extradition treaty with the United States."

"Oh. Got it. Cool."

This was happening faster than David could digest but still not fast enough. After showering in the Air France–KLM lounge, they ordered burgers and fries at the food court. Then they attacked the pile of food with a ravenous abandon unworthy of their fashionable new clothes. Jordan and Mitchell ordered steaks.

From an ATM, David withdrew two thousand dollars in cash, his daily limit, and divided the money between them. Then he emptied his wallet of credit cards and other identifying details and dumped them in a trash bin.

"Now for the moment of truth," Amy said. "Passport control. We'll split into pairs. If anyone asks, David and I—I mean Harry and Peggy—are a couple. You two are old roommates. We're all on vacation. We don't have time to prepare more complex cover stories. Chances are we won't need them."

Having no luggage to check, they proceeded to the security lines. David eyed the bag scanners and tried to relax. He remembered Victory, the golden egg, and his heart twinged. The loss was for the best. An egg from the missing Imperial Collection would forever link him to the world of covert organizations and religious conspiracies.

David took off his new shoes and belt and placed them on the conveyor belt of the scanner. He handed the uniformed security attendant their plane tickets, stepped through the metal detector, and spread his arms and legs for the pat-down. So far so good.

He dressed and winked at Jordan and Mitchell, who tied their shoelaces in the next line.

"Sir. Ma'am," said a security officer, an African American woman. "Please come with me."

David looked to Amy, who shrugged. "Sure. Is everything OK?"

"Yes, ma'am. Just a random-selection security check."

"OK."

The officer led them to a side room with a table and four chairs. David and Amy sat down and said nothing. David looked for a hidden camera and found none. *A random security check*. David had never been randomly selected for anything good.

"Let me do the talking," Amy whispered. "To avoid any complications."

"No problem."

The door opened, and yet another security officer led two more passengers into the room—Jordan and Mitchell. David pulled at the collar of his new shirt.

The two couples nodded at each other, the polite and silent greeting of strangers. But they were all thinking the same thing. This security check was anything but random. The authorities were onto them.

They waited. They waited some more. Amy glanced at her wristwatch.

"Honey," she said, in a petulant, uncharacteristic voice. "We'll miss our flight." She was playing a role.

"I'm sure everything is fine," he said, for the very well-concealed cameras.

They waited again.

When the door swung open, five officers entered the room. Unlike airport security, who wore the blue uniforms, these men wore navy-colored suits and dark glasses. Their leader gave the four civilians a broad grin. His four clones held rifles at their sides. The leader glanced at each of the detained passengers.

"Jordan Brody," he said. "Mitchell Joffe, David Zelig, and Amy Smith, or should I say Mary Rudolph." He winked at her. "We've been expecting you."

CHAPTER 56

David leaned forward, his elbows on his knees, his head hanging. Once again, he found himself in the back of a van and under armed guard, moving inexorably toward his fate. The numb sensation in his gut told him that this time he had reached the end of the road.

The floor rocked below his new shoes. Amy, Jordan, and Mitchell sat beside him in silence. The Men in Blue had confiscated their fake passports but said nothing about their destination.

It didn't matter. The end result would be the same. David would end up in prison. What charges would they bring against him—conspiracy to commit conspiracy? The FBI had set the Trio up. What did the lawyers call that? Entrapment. He needed to remember that word. That argument should at least reduce their sentences.

But what defense would Amy have? Infiltrating the FBI as a double agent probably amounted to treason. There would be no reduced sentence for her.

He squeezed her hand. These might be their last moments of physical proximity. They didn't deserve this. They deserved a long and happy life together.

On second thought, they wouldn't spend much time in

prison. Wherever they landed, the Temple would find them and settle their debts. Unless the Elders got to them first. Ironically, the Trio would have united the competing secret societies in a common purpose.

"We were close," Mitchell said. "So close."

"Yeah," Jordan said.

The thick stubble on their jaws was the least of the changes his two friends had undergone in the Temple dungeon. They had abandoned their constant bickering and displayed an easy friendship. If their life expectancy had not dropped below a few days, they might have written a book about their experiences and invented a new form of psychological intervention. Want to end a feud? No problem! Simply drop the enemy parties into a dungeon cell for a week and voila, they'll be best friends forever.

The van slowed, reversed, and stopped. The doors at the back opened and the armed guards beckoned for them to exit. They obeyed without question.

"Follow me, please," said the Men in Blue's cheerful leader. Did these guys ever take off their sunglasses? They walked down a long corridor lined with closed office doors.

A scary thought made David's skin crawl. What if this wasn't the FBI or the CIA? What if they'd already fallen into the hands of the Temple or the Elders? Were they on their way to a death chamber? Would the Men in Blue dispose of their remains without leaving a trace?

The leader opened a door. The room was white and contained a single desk chair.

"I'll ask Amy to wait here until we're done."

Amy glanced at David, fear in her eyes. Had the same suspicion entered her mind?

"No," David said. "Either we stay together or you'll have to drag us every inch of the way."

"It's for her own protection. She'll be right here when we're done. Then you'll all be free to leave, I promise."

The man didn't guarantee they'd still be breathing when they left. And why did Amy need protection any more than the rest of them? Amy decided the matter for him.

"It's OK, David," she said. She stepped up to him, took his hands in hers, and kissed him. "I'll wait here for you." She stepped into the room and sat on the chair.

The leader closed the door, flashed them another toothy grin, and they continued on their merry way.

David put his hand in his pocket, releasing the plastic envelope Amy had slipped into his hand. Whatever the Men in Blue were planning for her, she had preferred not to have the Holy Prepuce on her person when it happened.

David followed their mysterious captors down the corridor. This didn't feel right. What was this place? Who were these people? And why had they split them up? The further David fell down the rabbit hole, the more questions he had.

They waited beside a chrome elevator, then stepped inside. The leader waved a white keycard over a sensor and pressed the button for the third floor, the top floor. The building had many more floors below ground level. They were somewhere in Washington or within a twenty-minute drive.

The elevator doors opened onto an open-space office filled with cubicles—the work area of a newspaper or a technology startup. The employees, mostly young adults in casual business suits, engaged in hushed discussions over printed documents and mugs of coffee. A pretty woman with long tawny hair smiled at the Trio as they passed.

The low Washington skyline appeared through large windows. Computers were everywhere. Large mounted screens displayed reams of numbers and codes that changed every half second. None of them made any sense to David.

Mitchell said. "If these guys are Temple, we're dead!"

"This doesn't look like a Temple operation," Jordan said, the master of rationality.

David agreed. Somehow he knew that they would not die just yet. Not in this place. The office was too mundane and familiar to admit thoughts of deadly force and summary executions. Or was that by design? Was the calming facade a Judas goat, creating a false sense of security while the smiling operative led them to the slaughterhouse?

The leader arrived at a corner office and rapped his knuckles on the open glass door. "Sir, they're here."

"Good," said a voice.

The speaker sat behind a large oak desk with his back to the door. From his padded manager's chair, he observed the view outside his window, his bald patch rising like a dome above the crown of salt-and-pepper hair.

"Please, gentlemen, sit." His voice was amiable, the accent redolent of New York.

Three visitor chairs faced the desk, which was empty except for a laptop and a framed photograph of a brown-haired young woman and two smiling kids. The Trio sat in the chairs and waited for their host to reveal himself.

When the chair swiveled around, David's jaw dropped to the floor.

"Welcome," the man said, his eyes glinting. "We meet at last. But some of us have met before, haven't we?"

CHAPTER 57

"I don't understand," David said.

The man behind the desk grinned at him.

"You know this guy?" Jordan said.

"Um, David," Mitchell said. "What's going on?"

David hesitated. "He's Luke—the Temple Father's right-hand man. He's the one who sent me to trade the eggs for the Holy Prepuce."

The monk behind the desk nodded his head in recognition.

"Holy crapola! He's with the Temple?"

David spoke to Luke. "You're not really with the Temple, are you?"

Luke smiled. "You're getting warmer."

"So," Mitchell said, "you're with the Elders?"

"Colder. Anyone else? Jordan, you're supposed to be the brains of this outfit."

David was sick of this game. "Where are we? What is this place?" Unless he had completely misinterpreted the situation, Luke wasn't their enemy. Or at least, not the kind of enemy who would decapitate him for asking questions.

"Gentlemen," Luke said, "welcome to the National Security Agency."

"The NSA?" Jordan said, unconvinced. "This is the NSA?"

"Mm-hm. Washington branch. Head office."

"So the NSA planted you in the Temple?"

"Bingo."

David said, "How long has the NSA known about the Temple?"

Luke glanced at the ceiling while he scanned his memory. "About ten years. I've been undercover for five."

"Five years—and you've done nothing to stop them? They've infiltrated the FBI!"

"Oh, I know."

"Hold on," Jordan said. "The NSA doesn't do undercover operations. The NSA intercepts communications."

"That's true. Most of our work involves signal intelligence. But when the bad guys go offline, like the Temple, we do whatever's necessary to protect American citizens. And I wouldn't say we've done nothing. Our moles in the Temple have gathered most of our intelligence on the Islamic Elders of Zion."

David connected the dots. "You used the Temple to get the FBI to recruit us to infiltrate the Elders?"

"Well, officially, the Temple did that. We just didn't intervene. It served our purpose. We couldn't flush the double agents from the FBI until we'd identified them all. The same goes for the Elders operatives in the CIA."

"You knew about the CIA too?!"

"We had our suspicions. The Elders confirmed those suspicions when they used their CIA contacts to place their operatives on Zheltkov's jet. As you know, those operatives are no longer a concern."

The memory of Nasim and the mustachioed pilot getting sucked out the jet window made David feel sick to his stomach.

"So what were we—bait?"

"No, not bait. That was never our intention. Once you exposed the Elders' inner circle, the NSA would dismantle the

Elders and the Temple. You would return to your civilian lives. But, as you know, the heist didn't go as planned, and the Temple intercepted the eggs."

"But you *are* the Temple. Surely, you knew they'd do that!"

Luke grinned ironically. "The Father doesn't always heed my advice. Things went from bad to worse from there. You can't imagine what hoops we've had to jump through just to keep you three alive. The Israel Day Parade was a *very* close call."

"The Israel Day Parade," Jordy said, having a revelation. "A group of Black Israelite terrorists tried to attack the parade. We heard that on the news. And the neo-Nazis in the parking garage wanted to shoot up the JAPI Conference. Did the NSA use the Templars and the Elders to prevent those attacks?"

Mitchell's eyes widened. "Whoa, that is awesome!"

David had to admit, the intelligence agency's skillful manipulation of events impressed him. Who needed a Jewish Elders of Zion? The NSA already had their backs.

Luke coughed. "Actually, no. The NSA wasn't tracking the Black Israelites. We knew nothing of a neo-Nazi attack at the JAPI Conference either. Those were happy coincidences."

"Happy coincidences?" David said. "C'mon, Luke. The Grandmaster told us he would hit the JAPI Convention. And then the Temple just happened to schedule the drop-off for the same time and place?"

Luke leaned forward on his desk. "Our intelligence indicated that the Grandmaster wouldn't reveal his true intentions. We let the Elders learn about the drop-off through the CIA to lure them to the convention, where a SWAT team was waiting to intercept them. The convention was our trap."

"Let me guess," David said, his tone crusty with cynicism. "That didn't go according to plan either." He was reevaluating his opinion of the NSA's so-called intelligence.

Luke shrugged. "We didn't expect them to bring so much firepower to the conference. It seems they might have planned to attack the conference, after all."

Jordan's reaction was less diplomatic than David's. "The Temple held us in a dungeon for a week, drove us to Washington in the trunk of a car, and booby-trapped our balls. And then you dropped us into the middle of a battlefield? Are you crazy? You could have gotten us killed!"

Luke raised his hands to calm Jordan down. "You're still alive, aren't you?"

"Well, forgive us for not celebrating," Jordan ranted, "because guess what—the Elders and Temple are still out there and both still want us dead!"

"None of you will die," Luke said. "If you cooperate. Here's the deal."

He had the Trio's full attention. Everything until now had been small talk, foreplay. How would the NSA get them out of this mess?

Luke gave David a penetrating look. "First, I need you to hand over the Holy Prepuce." When David opened his mouth to object, Luke cut him off. "The Temple didn't receive it, and law enforcement didn't recover it at the convention center. I know you have it."

David hesitated. The NSA could take the relic from him by force if he didn't comply, but the Prepuce was the Trio's only bargaining chip.

"The Prepuce is the only thing keeping the Temple and Elders from killing us," he said. "If we hand it over, we're dead."

Luke waved their concerns away. "We'll take care of them. The Temple and the Elders. The same goes for the FBI and the CIA. We'll erase you from their files. You'll get your old lives back as if this was all just a bad dream."

The three friends shared looks of desperate hope. This was exactly what they wanted. The offer sounded too good to be true.

"Why should we trust you?"

"We're the good guys, remember? So are you. You stuck your necks out to help each other and returned all nine

Fabergé eggs to the Met."

David glanced at his friends, sending a silent warning not to mention the tenth egg. He had lost Victory, anyway. If Luke knew about the tenth egg, he hid that well.

"Why do you want the Prepuce?" David said. "You don't believe in its magical powers, do you?"

"Of course not. But when this is all over, we'd like to return the Prepuce to its rightful home in Calcata."

David couldn't argue with that.

"What's the catch?" Mitchell said. "There's always a catch."

Luke leaned back in his chair and steepled his fingers. "The Trio ends here and now. No more secret societies, no more reboots of the Elders of Zion."

Mitchell said, "Is that it?"

"That's unfair!" David blurted, louder than he had intended, and startling the others. The NSA's condition had riled his persecution complex. "Muslims have a secret society. Christians have had theirs for centuries. Only the Jews can't have one? That's discrimination!"

"David!" Jordan and Mitchell hissed.

David ignored them. "That's a double standard!"

"There's no double standard," Luke said. "The NSA will dismantle the Temple and the Elders. Nobody gets special treatment. But for the record, your Trio has given us major headaches these past weeks. So what do you say? Do we have a deal?"

Glee reflected in the eyes of David's friends, but David had one last nagging concern. "What about Amy?"

Luke raised his eyebrows. "Amy was a federal agent. She has blood on her hands. We can't let that slide."

"Come on, Luke. Everything she did was for the FBI or to save innocent lives. She's broken with the Temple. You know that. She deserves a fresh start too."

"David, Amy is not on the table."

"That's too bad because without her there's no deal. Amy saved our lives. We won't abandon her."

David folded his arms over his chest. Not long ago, he'd apologized to his friends for ruining their lives. Now he was ruining their lives all over again.

"Yeah," Mitchell said. "Either Amy gets the same package, or the deal is off."

"Agreed," Jordan said, "We're all in this together."

David turned to his friends with infinite gratitude. They had pulled through for Amy.

"You hear that, Luke?" Mitchell said. "The Trio stands united."

"You don't understand," Luke said. "This isn't an offer you can refuse. If the NSA steps aside, the Temple and Elders will dance on your graves."

"Yeah, well, if we gave you a headache while we're alive," Mitchell said, "we'll come back to haunt you when we're dead." David looked at Mitchell with undiluted admiration. Making outrageous claims was his superpower.

"He's right," Jordan said. He seemed to have resigned himself to the fact that they were dead anyway and might as well go out in style. "Ever hear of Zelig Pictures? Well, this story will make one hell of a movie."

"What story?"

"All of it," David said, following their lead. "Before the convention, I recorded everything on video. Everything we know about the Elders, the Temple, the FBI, and the CIA."

"Yeah," Jordan said. "And that recording will go out to every major American newspaper. Unless Dave stops it."

Luke scoffed. "You're bluffing."

"Oh, yeah? Try us."

"Nobody'll believe it."

"Oh, they will. Especially if we turn up dead. You thought Snowden was bad? After this, Congress will shut you down for good!"

Mitchell high-fived Jordan. "That's my man!"

Luke pressed his hands together at his lips in a pleading gesture. Veins pulsed in his forehead and his eyes flicked from side to side, trying to keep pace with his speeding thoughts.

"Fine," he said, eventually. "We'll clear Amy's record too. But she'll have to leave the country for a few months."

"Deal!" David said.

"But the Trio is over. And you never speak a word to anyone about your experiences these past few weeks. Agreed?"

"Agreed!"

"No more snooping, no more vigilante societies."

"We're done."

"Say it!"

David turned to his friends. "Jordy, Mitch, I propose we dissolve the Trio. All those in favor, by a show of hands." Three hands rose in the air. David clapped his hands together. "Then it's settled. The Trio is no more."

Luke rose from his chair and reached over his desk to shake their hands. "Congratulations! Now, if you don't mind, David—the Prepuce?"

"Oh, right." David reached into his pocket and tossed the vacuum-sealed square onto the desk. Luke examined the Prepuce, smoothed the plastic flat, and dropped the relic into a drawer.

"Gentlemen, have a seat. There's one last thing."

Mitchell swore. "I knew it! I knew there was a catch! And don't say we have to do one final mission."

Luke said, "You have to do one final mission."

This time all three members of the former Trio swore. They sat back down. "What kind of mission?" David asked.

Luke told them. Now David understood why the NSA had offered them such a sweet deal.

Mitchell said, "This time we'd better get guns."

Luke's mouth twisted into a wicked smile. "We can arrange for that."

CHAPTER 58

Adrenaline pulsed through David's body. Night vision goggles painted the world in shades of green. Beyond the barrel of the semi-automatic rifle in gloved hands, a low, dark building crouched beside a copse of willows. His fellow soldiers stood at the ready in camouflage gear. He'd entered a virtual reality military video game. But this mission was no game.

An elbow poked him in the ribs.

"Man, this is so cool," Mitchell whispered.

Jordan said, "You're right. It's pretty awesome."

David kept his eyes on their target. The single-floor building on the grassy knoll in New Jersey gave no clue it housed America's most wanted terrorist. But the NSA stood behind their intelligence, gathered from the corpses of Elders operatives at the Washington Convention Center. The terrorist had gone into hiding since the JAPI Conference. But David and his friends would serve him justice. Here and now.

A familiar voice crackled on the communications speaker. "We're in position," said Captain Ripley of the National Guard's Green Berets. David and his friends had joined his Alpha Team only recently. "Awaiting your green light, Mr. President."

"Go ahead, Captain Ripley," said the voice of the President of the United States. "And may God be with you."

Mitchell squealed with delight. A thrill shot through David's body. The Commander-In-Chief had joined the mission by video conference. They'd better do a good job.

"Thank you, sir," Captain Ripley said. "Team, move out!"

The team ran toward the building and fell into formation around the door, backs to the brick walls. A soldier shot out the locking mechanism with his rifle, breaching the door, and stepped away just in time. Automatic gunfire sounded from within. Bullets kicked up dirt and grass. A soldier lobbed a grenade through the opening, prompting anguished cries within, which ended with a deafening detonation. The soldiers waited for the smoke to clear, then rushed inside, the laser sights of their weapons slicing the darkness. Clearing the room and stepping over the downed terrorists, the soldiers located a metal trapdoor beneath a coffee table and a patterned rug.

Descending a ladder, they discovered several interlocking rooms. The rifle barrel switched this way and that, searching for fighters and finding three. The bearded men in dark uniforms raised their arms in surrender and respected the calls for silence.

"Gentlemen?" Captain Ripley asked. "Which of them is the big boss?"

David studied the faces of the subdued terrorists. "None of them," he said. Jordan and Mitchell echoed his assessment. David's stomach tightened. Had their target slipped away?

Captain Ripley stepped up to the terrorist lineup. "Where is he?"

The three captured fighters pointed in unison at the side of the room. When a soldier kicked the door in, the man within the booth looked up in annoyance, then surprise, at the array of rifles aimed at his head. Sitting on a toilet, his trunks at his ankles, their target held a dirty magazine in one hand.

"That's him!" David said. "That's Abdul, the Grandmaster." He would never forget the bald man with the well-trimmed goatee who had ordered the Trio's execution. This bully would get what he deserved.

Abdul hid the magazine behind his back, but the damage was done. The woman on the cover had been naked except for the nun's habit from her shoulders up. Two soldiers pulled the half-naked criminal mastermind from the commode and unceremoniously tied him up.

"Mission accomplished," the President's voice said. "Great job, all around!"

"Thank you, sir," Captain Ripley said. "We'll take things from here."

The screen went dark, and Luke turned on the lights in the Situation Room far below the NSA building in Washington. Jordan and Mitchell blinked their eyes in the bright light. The smiles would stay on their faces for a very long time.

Two seconds later, the President's face grinned at them on the screen. He sat at a conference table and wore a sweatshirt. This was not an official presidential communication but a live feed from the Situation Room.

"I have a special message for our civilian assets," the President said. "This mission will remain top secret for some years, so regrettably, I won't be able to thank you in public. But please accept my gratitude on behalf of our nation. You've done our country a great service and at great personal risk. If you need anything, anything at all, our friends at the NSA will take care of you. God bless America."

The screen went blank. Luke placed the remote control on the conference table, and the projector screen retracted upward.

"Congratulations, friends," he said, and he shook their hands. "You fulfilled your end of the deal. And we're keeping ours. With the Grandmaster in custody, we'll soon capture the rest of his command hierarchy. The Islamic Elders of Zion will cease to operate. Other Special Forces teams are raiding the Temple's bases as we speak. Soon, you'll be free to return to your old lives."

"Thank you, Luke," David said.

"You're welcome. We've arranged a safe house for you to use while we round up the remaining conspirators. Any questions?"

"Yes," David said. "What kind of help can the NSA provide?"

Luke chuckled. "Well, we're in the middle of an anti-terrorism operation, so I guess we could apply the Patriot Act."

David had hoped for that answer. "In that case, we'd like to accept the President's offer."

Luke cleared his throat. "Um, sure. What can we do for you?"

David glanced at his friends. During their long hours at the NSA headquarters, they had discussed how the agency's cutting-edge spying capabilities might solve their problems. The President's offer was just the opening he had needed.

David grinned. "I need a small favor."

CHAPTER 59

TOP SECRET
FEDERAL BUREAU OF INVESTIGATION
OFFICE OF PROFESSIONAL RESPONSIBILITY
Transcript of interview with Mr. Hyman Schneider
Also present:
Special Agent A. Maynard
Special Agent in Charge M. Reed

HYMAN SCHNEIDER:
More whisky, gentlemen? Another cigar?

M. REED:
No, thank you, Mr. Schneider. We've had more than enough.

HYMAN SCHNEIDER:
Please, call me Hymie, for crying out loud. I feel like we're old friends. Don't tell my wife, but I think I spent more time speaking with you this week than I have with her this entire year!

M. REED:

To sum things up, Mr. Sch—Hymie, the NSA infiltrated the Temple, which in turn, infiltrated the FBI. Meanwhile, the Islamic Elders of Zion, the Temple's archenemy, had placed moles in the CIA. Temple operatives in the FBI tried to embed the Trio in the Elders, and all the resulting intelligence bubbled up to the NSA.

During its short lifetime, the Trio unintentionally flushed double agents from both the FBI and CIA. And by identifying the Grandmaster, the Trio enabled the NSA to dismantle both the Elders and the Temple.

Quite accidentally, the fighting between the rival secret societies foiled two large-scale anti-Semitic attacks by unrelated supremacist groups in Manhattan and Washington.

David, his friends, and Amy were flies caught in this very sticky web of conspiracy and deception. In the end, all the flies wriggled free. Is that it?

HYMAN SCHNEIDER:

I couldn't have summed it up better myself.

A. MAYNARD:

Hymie, I have to ask. How did you find this all out?

HYMAN SCHNEIDER:

I'm glad you asked. David dropped by my apartment one last time before he and Amy left the United States for their extended vacation. Remember that the NSA's condition for clearing her record was that she leave the country for some time. David didn't tell me where they were going, and I didn't ask.

David felt bad about having to keep me in the dark, so he told me the entire story from start to finish, just like I've told it to you. Crazy as it sounds, I believed him. The change in David was undeniable. No longer the tortured young man who'd asked me about the Elders of Zion, he radiated the wisdom of hard-won experience.

He'd found love. And he'd learned about hate. Haters might demonize their targets, but it's the haters who suffer the most. Their delusions of victimization devour them inside and prevent them from seeking real solutions to their problems.

The whole episode inspired me to do some research. Do you know when the demonization of Jews began? In the fourth century. St. John Chrysostom, an early church father, was annoyed that his flock still attended the local Jewish synagogue. After all, the first Christians were devout Jews. So John began to preach that the synagogue was "the temple of demons, the cavern of devils, and the abyss of perdition." It was only a matter of time before Jews were accused of demonic deeds too, such as killing Christian children to drink their blood.

By the way, a Jew would never imagine such a crime. Jewish law forbids the eating of blood. The Christians of the time, on the other hand, believed they ate Christ's blood and flesh during the Eucharist sacrament. So you see, the blood libels were a projection of Christian religious ideas onto Jews.

In the same way, *The Protocols of the Learned Elders of Zion* projected Imperial Russia's lust for power onto the unfortunate Jew. The irony would be comical if it wasn't so deadly, for one of *The Protocols'* greatest fans was a failed Austrian artist known as Adolf Hitler.

Oh, I almost forgot. David's friends have started a company together. Jordan and Mitchell are developing a game app for smartphones called Templar Run. They invited me to join their series A funding, but I don't know. I've had bad experiences with technology startups and I'm not eager to get stung again. I'll stick with what I know.

Since that last meeting, I haven't seen or heard from David. Wherever he is, I hope he's happy. His father, Sol Zelig, wherever *he* is, would be proud.

Then, a few weeks later, you fine gentlemen came knocking on my door.

M. REED:

One last thing, Hymie. You said that the Trio took up the President's offer of help from the NSA. What did they ask?

HYMAN SCHNEIDER:

Did I say that?

M. REED:

Um, yes, you did. It sounded like a personal favor for David.

HYMAN SCHNEIDER:

Ha! I think you're right. Let me see... a personal favor. What could that have been? This is embarrassing. Memory is the first thing to go, so they say. And now I can't seem to remember what that favor was!

CHAPTER 60

Special Agent Andrew Maynard of the FBI's Office of Professional Responsibility pressed the button on the Dictaphone to stop the playback. This was the second time he and his boss had listened to the recording of their interviews with Hyman Schneider.

"That's quite a story," Andrew said.

"You mean, a tall tale," said Michael Reed, the Special Agent in Charge. Two decades in the Bureau had turned Andrew's boss into a cynical hard-ass.

"You think he's bullshitting us?"

"Are you serious, Andy? The FBI infiltrated by the Knights Templar, the CIA by Islamic terrorists who call themselves the Elders of Zion? That is beyond ridiculous. Don't even get me started about the NSA. I think this David Zelig likes to spin a good yarn and the old geezer swallowed it whole. That's what I think. David wrote conspiracy theory scripts. Hymie said so himself. This was probably one of them."

Andrew wasn't so sure. Seeming to sense his doubts, his boss continued.

"For starters, his story is full of holes." Michael paged through his copious notes. "Hymie said David visited him the

Saturday evening before the JAPI Convention. He said and I quote, 'Little did I know, I would never see them again.' End quote. But he also said David stopped by days later to say goodbye. That's when David told him the entire story. So, obviously, he *did* see David again."

"Hmm. Maybe he mixed up the sequence of events?"

"Please, Andy. And then there's the question of why David would tell Hymie the whole story in the first place. He'd promised the NSA he'd never say a word. Why would David do that?"

"That's a good point."

Michael tapped his pencil on his notepad. Something was bothering him, but Andrew would need to tease the information out of him.

"The break-in at the Met was real."

"Yeah, well, anybody could have read about that in the papers. And nothing was stolen, by the way. The Met returned the Fabergé eggs to their owners without delay."

This fact didn't contradict Hymie's story, but Andrew decided not to point that out.

"The shootout at the Israel Day Parade also happened."

"Yeah, yeah, and the foiled attack at the JAPI Convention. Same story. Hymie—or David—heard about those in the media like the rest of us. That doesn't prove nothin'."

"What about the girl, Special Agent Amy Smith?"

"I looked her up. Or tried to. There's no such person in the FBI's records. No Amy Smith, no Amy Anderson. I even tried Mary Rudolph." The two officers eyed each other in silence. "I know what you're thinking, Andy, and the answer is no."

"What?"

"C'mon, Andy. You were thinking that doesn't prove anything either. The NSA could have deleted her from the FBI databases. That was part of their deal with the Trio."

"And the island?"

"Tsarlandia? Don't make me laugh. That's the weakest link in the narrative. Even the *National Enquirer* wouldn't print that story."

His boss hesitated, then cleared his throat. "Just to be sure, I checked the service log for the USS *Detroit*. The vessel sailed four missions in the Atlantic over the few days when the ship supposedly rescued Zelig."

"And?"

"None of the reports mention any rescued civilians."

Michael chewed his lip. His boss was holding something back.

"Then I guess that settles it, Mike. If we can account for all the missions…"

Michael sighed. "There's a minor irregularity. Two of the reports are identical—the same route, the same crew, the same incidents, the exact same phraseology—everything except for the dates. It's almost as though…." He trailed off.

Andrew's inner conspiracy theorist completed the sentence in his head. *As though one report was copied and pasted over another.*

Michael sighed. "I'm sure it's nothing."

"What about the collector?"

Michael glanced at his notes. "Peter Zheltkov? Surprisingly, he exists. A British national. He sued his insurance for a private jet that supposedly went missing over the Atlantic during a routine transfer. He was not on board at the time. As far as we can tell, he's alive and well."

"Really?"

"Really."

Michael drummed his pencil on the notepad. "Hymie Schneider dropped out of the JAPI Convention at the last moment by coincidence and not because he knew about the attack. He's a nice old man and all, but he's easily taken in. And he has those memory lapses too. I think all that whisky has pickled his brain."

Andrew chuckled. "Yeah, he sure likes his whisky."

"The cigars were nice, too."

"Yeah, they were. Should we question the others?"

"What others?"

"The friends, Jordan Brody and Mitchell Joffe."

"Nah, don't bother. Why start rumors? Let's close the investigation. In your report, chalk up the Bureau's failure to prevent the Washington attack to human error or something."

"OK, Mike." Andrew picked up the Dictaphone. "I'll file the transcripts in the system."

"Wait," Michael said. His pencil danced on the notepad again while he ground his molars. "In the wrong hands, these tall tales could destroy the Bureau's reputation. You know the Golden Rule."

"'Don't Embarrass the Bureau?'"

"Exactly. Lock everything in my private cabinet for now."

"Yessir. You're the boss."

"Yes, I am, Andy. And don't you forget that."

CHAPTER 61

Preston Clancy did not allow unscheduled visits, but when the attractive young woman entered his corner office late that afternoon, he made an exception.

The girl's silky auburn curls fell to the shoulders of her stylish leather jacket. Her long, toned legs rose to the matching leather miniskirt. She lingered by the door, her hands behind her back. From her good looks and confident posture, he guessed she was an aspiring actress. From the teasing smile on her lips, he understood she was up to no good.

"What do you want?" Preston said, his voice making clear his irritation at the interruption.

People always wanted something from him. Directors wanted a green light for their pet projects, screenwriters wanted residuals, actors wanted that breakout role. As president of Zelig Pictures, Preston could make all their dreams come true. He was an entertainment god.

The wiser supplicants brought sacrifices. Preston had no qualms about devouring their offerings. He'd worked hard to get where he was and he'd gorged himself on the fruits. This girl piqued his curiosity. What was she hiding behind her back?

His tone did not deter the girl in the slightest. "I have

something for you, Mr. Clancy." This girl was a wise suppli-
cant. Her voice was sultry and mesmerizing. She'd make a
good leading lady.

Preston leaned back on the soft upholstery of his manager's chair and steepled his fingers.

"And what might that be?"

The girl locked the door behind her without taking her
eyes off him. Then she sauntered toward him, swinging her
shapely hips like a fashion model on the catwalk. Preston
could guess what she was offering, and his mouth watered in
anticipation. Through the tall windows of his office, the sun
set over the San Fernando Valley. Most studio employees had
gone home for the evening. This meeting would move to the
sofa by the wall.

In his five years at the helm of the studios, Preston had
taken advantage of the casting couch at every opportunity.
But since the recent wave of sexual harassment allegations,
Preston had to be careful. This pretty young thing might be
setting him up, and he did not want to join the rogues' gallery
of the "Me Too" movement.

The girl reached the edge of his desk and, with a flourish,
revealed what she was holding.

Preston sagged with disappointment. Instead of a bottle of
wine, she offered him a sheaf of printed pages. Not an actress, then—a writer. Preston hated writers. They whined all
the time and took rejection so personally.

"You can leave that with my secretary. She'll make sure it
reaches the right people." By the right people, he meant the
recycling bin.

"It's not a script," the girl said, that teasing smile still on
her lips.

Preston sighed and accepted the pile of pages. Playing
along seemed like the fastest way to get rid of her. The pages
were lists of line items and numbers.

"We already have an accountant," he said, his irritation
growing along with his confusion.

"Zelig Pictures turned a very tidy profit this quarter," she said.

"Yes," he said, giving her a perfunctory grin. "Under my leadership, the company changed direction and climbed out of debt."

"But until a few months ago, the studio was hemorrhaging money at an alarming rate. It's all there in the report. Zelig Pictures paid Shadow Industrial Effects a king's ransom for years, producing pictures at a loss. Good thing you weaned the studio off their services."

Preston glanced at the figures again. Wait a minute. These were the financials for Zelig Pictures. How had she gotten hold of these?

"Like I said, we changed direction."

"You've been through five chief financial officers in as many years. That's quite a churn rate, don't you think?"

Preston had fired his CFOs as soon as they started asking the wrong kind of questions about the company's financials. It was the only surefire way to keep his methods under wraps.

Who was this girl—an investigative journalist? Fear wrapped a clawed fist around his intestines. Then he remembered that he'd covered his tracks. He didn't need to panic. There was no way a newshound could have discovered what he'd done. He forced his expression to remain calm.

"Yeah, it's hard to find good employees these days. Listen, this is all very interesting, but it's getting late."

The girl glanced at the pages. "Read on. It gets much better."

Preston turned the pages, and his facade of calm shattered.

"I'll skip to the punch line," she said. "As it happens, Shadow Industrial Effects belongs to you, Mr. Clancy, doesn't it? The shell company in the Virgin Islands was a nice touch. Very hard to trace. Almost as hard as Graf & Keller Holdings, the Swiss hedge fund that bought Zelig Pictures. The hedge fund belongs to you too, Mr. Clancy. What a coincidence."

Preston rifled through the pages. The evidence was all there in black and white. But that was impossible!

"Where did you get these? I encrypted the files on a private computer!"

The girl laughed at him. "Oh, you're good, Mr. Clancy. But not good enough."

Preston dropped the wad of incriminating documents on his desk. His face felt hot and feverish. A ball of pain burned in his chest, and he had trouble breathing. Was he having a heart attack?

The girl tutted. "You've been a bad boy, Mr. Clancy. Stealing from widows and orphans. Not cool. In the right hands, these documents will put you behind bars for a very long time."

"What is this—blackmail?" Preston said, his voice raspy. "Do you want money? I'll give you whatever you want."

She shook her head at him, disappointed. "I want you to turn back the clock and fix your mistakes. Read the last few pages." Preston did. The share transfer deeds had all the details filled in. "Just sign on the dotted line, and Zelig Pictures will revert to its rightful owner, Sol Zelig's widow."

"You've got to be kidding me!"

"Afraid not. But wait—there's more! The last page is your letter of resignation. You'll need to change careers too. How does the saying go? 'You'll never work in this town again?' Yeah, that sounds about right."

Preston curled his fingers into fists. He would not hand over Zelig Pictures, and he sure as hell wasn't going to prison. His body trembled with outrage and pent-up violence. He was taller than her and double her weight. Overpowering the girl would be easy. Strangling her would give him great pleasure.

He kept his voice level when he spoke next.

"You think you can just waltz in here and take everything away?"

She wrinkled her nose. "Can't take away what doesn't belong to you."

"I'm the boss here. I call the shots. Nobody talks to me like that, you little slut."

He lunged forward, springboarding from his chair, stepping onto his desk, and diving on top of her. But when he hit the floor, she was no longer beneath him. He struggled to his feet. Where was she? His hands itched to close around her neck. Then pain exploded in his groin. As he doubled over, his arm twisted behind his back with a mind-numbing sensation that made him forget the trauma to his testicles. A large serrated hunting knife appeared before his eyes.

"Try that again," she growled in his ear, "and I'll take your balls. Believe me, Mr. Clancy, you have more to lose than money and freedom. So much more."

Seconds later, Preston signed on the dotted lines, his fingers trembling uncontrollably, and he handed the documents back to the girl.

"Good boy," she said. "You behave now. We're watching you very closely."

Preston nursed his injured shoulder. "Wh-who are you?" he muttered.

She grinned. "Your worst nightmare."

Papers in hand, she sheathed her knife and sauntered back toward the door.

"Oh, and one last thing." Amy paused on the threshold, remembering the parting words David had asked her to use. They would send shock waves of terror through Preston's addled mind. "The Elders of Zion send their regards."

FROM THE AUTHOR

Hi there!

Thank you for joining David and his friends on their madcap adventures. If you enjoyed this book, you'll love the top-secret Epilogue.

But beware—the Epilogue contains another huge twist. Hymie says it will boggle your mind.

The Epilogue is available exclusively as a free download from my website at:

dansofer.com/elders

But let's keep this just between the two of us. If anyone asks, you didn't hear it from me. We can't be too careful now. You never know who's listening…

Dan

ACKNOWLEDGMENTS

Thanks go to my dedicated beta readers, Janis Funnell, Teresa Collins, and my father-in-law, Gavriel Meron. Their excellent feedback on an early draft of the novel led to a far more satisfying story.

Thank you, Julie Gray! Your many helpful pointers not only improved the last third of the book but also saved me from some embarrassing factual errors!

Thank you, Christine LePorte, for your thorough and insightful editing of all my novels, including this one.

Special thanks go to Amira, my wife and first reader, who made sure family members won't think I based characters on them. I didn't!

ABOUT THE AUTHOR

Dan Sofer writes dark comedy-thrillers filled with history, myth, and legend.

He calls his novels "popcorn for the curious heart." So far, they don't seem to mind.

Dan lives in Israel with a supermodel, a princess, and a mermaid. You can find him on his website—dansofer.com— and social media.

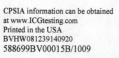

9 781950 139040